HOW TO GET AWAY WITH MURDER

TAM BARNETT

Boldwood

First published in Great Britain in 2025 by Boldwood Books Ltd.

Copyright © Tam Barnett, 2025

Cover Design by Head Design Ltd

Cover Images: Shutterstock

A CIP catalogue record for this book is available from the British Library.

Paperback ISBN 978-1-83633-052-3

Large Print ISBN 978-1-83633-053-0

Hardback ISBN 978-1-83633-051-6

Ebook ISBN 978-1-83633-054-7

Kindle ISBN 978-1-83633-055-4

Audio CD ISBN 978-1-83633-046-2

MP3 CD ISBN 978-1-83633-047-9

Digital audio download ISBN 978-1-83633-050-9

This book is printed on certified sustainable paper. Boldwood Books is dedicated to putting sustainability at the heart of our business. For more information please visit https://www.boldwoodbooks.com/about-us/sustainability/

Boldwood Books Ltd, 23 Bowerdean Street, London, SW6 3TN

www.boldwoodbooks.com

For Hannah, forever and always

PROLOGUE

Blimey! There's no way I'm sleeping after that. A bootleg documentary about American serial killer John Wayne Gacy. Did they really have to show quite so many of the unreleased pictures of the overcrowded crawl space under his house?

Urgh, who am I kidding? The grisly content is the entire reason I streamed it off a dodgy site. No filter, no preoccupation with making it palatable to a broad audience. Just the facts, in all their horrific, unspeakable realness.

How do I shut out those hideous photographs now though, given they feel so monstrously unforgettable? I shuffle into a comfier position on the sofa and check my phone. It's 2 a.m., of course no one's texted me. Next stop... Twitter.

I know Elon wants us to call it X now, but it's still Twitter.

Am I a professional doom-scroller? Probably. Come on algorithm, throw up a distraction. Anything! I refresh the feed for the most meagre, pathetic dopamine hit known to humanity.

A new post lands at the top of my screen:

Are you a clinical psychopath? Take our free test and see...

Oh algorithm, you are *good*. And it's not just some tabloid clickbait bullshit. The link is literally to the British Psychological Society.

Tap.

Let's go.

I've read about the 'Psychopathy Checklist' before – 20 characteristics that hint you might be part of the club. For each trait you get 'one point' if it partially applies or 'two points' if it strongly applies. Out of this potential psychopathy score of 40, the subject must reach 25 to be considered, in scientific terms, a psychopath. For scale, Ted Bundy scored 39/40. Show off.

I thought I'd just rank myself on each characteristic, see if I reach the magic number. But the questions are cleverer, more subtle: How would I react in this situation? What emotion would I feel if someone said such-and-such? Bet I'm not even close to the 25 mark.

Test completed, I enter my email address and hit 'submit'. The results are loading, loading, load... Ping!

You scored 23/40. You're not a psychopath, but show more psychopathic tendencies than 98% of the population.

Huh. That's a relief, I guess. Shame to be so close and miss though. I think back over my answers. Was I a bit reserved? Maybe. I go back to Twitter and tap on the link again.

1

The lamps are dazzling, oppressive like those bulbs that illuminate a corpse in a forensics lab. I'm blinking as I squirm against the brightness. A dead body suddenly floodlit would be far less fussy; eyes locked open, still shackled to the last thing they ever saw – their killer.

I've never done a TV interview before, not a sit-down chat anyway. I was invited on a couple of the local news stations after Dick's sentencing, but nothing like this. A Netflix original. Eight hour-long documentaries, each about a different murderous psychopath. And Dick's made the cut.

He was chuffed to bits by the inclusion, though, as always, he said no to being interviewed himself. He only speaks to me. But after getting his blessing to take part, here I am in a plush hotel room in Liverpool preparing to speak with glamorous celebrity presenter, Annabelle Ludgate.

She oozes confidence in a smart turquoise jacket and matching pencil skirt that shimmer against the lighting, her legs crossed and one of her black stilettos tapping to a silent beat. She's yet to say a word to me sitting opposite her.

I've watched all her true crime shows. They're very mainstream, anything too physically or psychologically harrowing gets airbrushed out. She's an entertainer rather than a real aficionado of the sport.

What seems like a whole rugby team of aides and camera crew mill around us, fiddling with monitors, checking I'm not thirsty, dabbing Annabelle's slim, beautiful face with more blush.

I need to smile, be enthusiastic. This will probably be the only time I ever reach such a wide audience. Or at least it *will* be the only time if I don't impress.

Annabelle shoos the make-up woman away, looks up from the clip-board in her lap – and just like that. Click. I exist to her.

'Kelli Amari, yes?' she says in her soft Scottish burr.

'That's right,' I reply, pushing out a big smile which she misses as she peers back down at her notes.

One of the voices from the scrum shouts that they're ready to start and a hush falls. All lights are off now except the concentrated beams on the two of us.

'Miss Amari, I'm sure in all your research and time studying serial killers, you must have come across many who thought they'd pulled off the ultimate crime, who believed they'd covered all their tracks and got away scot-free.' The presenter makes real eye contact for the first time. 'So my question to you is, if I could guarantee you wouldn't get caught, that you could pull off the perfect murder and no one would ever trace it back to you... would *you* do it?'

I give a little laugh to buy time, but thankfully an answer is forming. This needs to sound playful or I could come across as unhinged. 'I guess rule number one of committing the perfect murder would be convincing everyone you weren't contemplating murder at all.'

Annabelle gives a tiny snort of appreciation. That was a test. I passed.

'We're here to talk about The White Widower, Dick Monroe,' her tone is sober but easy. 'What is the first word that comes to mind when you think of him?'

'Genius.' I let the answer percolate.

'I wasn't expecting you to offer a compliment,' Annabelle returns.

I shrug my shoulders and smile back, trying to ignore the group of geeky tech men hunching over us, concentrating their professional abilities on making *me* look and sound as slick as possible. It hits me that as fake as this 'cosy one-to-one' really is, it will appear very natural on TV, and the more I can enter into the façade, the more engrossing my answers will feel.

'It's not really a compliment. It's a warning,' I correct her. 'Dick was still able to convince his victims to get in his car, despite the mania surrounding him. The whole of Merseyside seemed to be out looking for him by that final autumn, and yet he kept sweet-talking women into trusting him.'

'But he met his match in you.'

'I was in the right place at the right time.'

'And yet you're still on speaking terms with Dick. You'd think he'd hate you more than anyone.'

'I think he respects the fact I... *we* managed to catch him.'

'By "we", you're referring to you and Rob Grayson?' she asks.

'Yeah.'

'Do you and Rob meet up – reminisce about it? Still both junior reporters at the time! It was quite the scoop.'

I remind her I'm not here to talk about Rob.

'What about Dick then, you close with him?' The question holds a whiff of bitchy scepticism, as if she wants to tell me I'm a complete weirdo but knows that won't elicit an engaging comeback.

'Close?' I scoff. 'As close as you can be to a psychopathic serial killer who's throttled at least eight women.'

The conversation is straightforward after that. Annabelle has several events and pieces of evidence she wants to discuss – mainly on how we managed to snare him. And the critical decision I made to go looking for Dick that icy November night.

There is one awkward question she poses – I'd been bracing for it. It's one that had already been raised in scathing terms by a faceless online crime blogger after Dick was jailed.

'The last victim Janice Benson...' the presenter winds up for her devastating uppercut. 'Surely if you'd gone to police immediately – rather than trying to catch the killer yourself – she might have survived? The police could have caught Dick Monroe in time to save her if you hadn't been so desperate to be the hero?'

It's actually a relief to be asked so directly. A silky-cool calm wafts over me as I nod and breeze into an explanation. 'Rob and I had only narrowed down our search to that location that same evening and I went to investigate. Even then the hunch could have been wrong. I had no idea he'd be out that night. It was just supposed to be a scouting trip. But when I got to the timber yard he'd just arrived. And anyway, Mrs Benson was already dead when he pulled her out of the boot. If the police had shown up instead of me, she would have been dead all the same.'

Seemingly happy with my defence, the TV presenter pushes her hand back through her glossy hair – a luscious light brown mane charged with an auburn sheen by the summer's sun. 'So, what's next for Kelli Amari?'

'I'm back on the Wirral, writing a book based on Dick's case.'

'You're a bit of an expert when it comes to cold-blooded killers. Do you think you have a sixth sense for spotting them?'

I've sort of got a response prepared. It's not quite a direct answer but I'm confident it'll make the edit so I ignore her nothingy question and fire my own thought back. 'I don't know about a sixth sense, but people often say you can tell someone's committed murder because their eyes look empty. But it's quite the opposite – their eyes have far more depth than ours will ever have. A bastardized version of a real person.'

I'm relieved not to stutter, but it doesn't move Annabelle at all. She sits robot-like, only re-animating when she sees another opportunity to speak herself. 'Does surrounding yourself with all these vile, dangerous minds not have an effect on you though? Keep you up at night?'

'No, not really.' I'm not prone to pangs of guilt when lying, but this is such a whopper I feel a heaviness sink in my stomach, the kind of paranoid shame you'd feel when you were naughty as a child.

Even so, my answer is delivered with such nonchalance that

Annabelle just moves on to another quick-fire question. 'Have you ever seen somebody die yourself?'

A pause this time, then, 'No.'

* * *

Leaving the musky camera crew behind, the synthetic scent of a lemon air-freshener sweeps me along the hotel corridor. I replay the interview in my mind. It went well – passionate rather than blood-thirsty, hopefully. Even if they only broadcast a tiny snippet of me in the documentary, I'll still be able to use that to market my book.

'Amari cashes in on scandalous friendship!' A call races after me.

I snap round.

Rob Grayson. Of course it is – the man who speaks in headlines – stalking towards me with his usual mixture of slime and indignation.

'Six years and that's all you have to say?' I respond.

He's in front of me now – he must be here for his own interview slot. I flat-out refused the show producers' plan for a joint chat with this international man of misery when they pitched the idea.

'Doing a documentary like this when you're best mates with the killer. Definition of shameful!' he spits.

'I'm sure you got paid the exact same as me, darling.'

'I told them to give it to the victims' charity!' he cries. 'Oh, you visit Dick all right, but when was the last time you visited one of the families? When was the last time you gave a single thought to the women?'

I smile at his grand flounce. 'You only stay in touch with the families to get splash bylines out of the victims' birthdays and deathdays every year. If there's one face they all can't stand more than Dick's, it's probably yours.'

Mute but simmering, he pushes his spectacles back up his nose. Ever since I've known Rob he's been wearing glasses. But more interestingly, the variety of frames he's accumulated are of a theme – a deadly theme. He has ones that are identical to Harold Shipman's, he has his Ed Kemper ones, his John Christie's, and the smartest pair – his Hawley

Crippen's. In all honesty, it's one of the best things about him –
phenomenally twisted yet phenomenally subtle.

'The Doctor Crippen's today, is it?' I say.

He ignores the olive branch. 'You can pretend this is all a joke, but I
know you haven't recovered.'

'You know nothing about me,' I bite back, immediately regretting it.
He needs to go now. That faceless crime blogger spreading rubbish
about me online – I'm pretty sure it's Grayson. And how dare he say I
don't think about the victims?

'Bet you took all the credit for catching Dick just then,' he
whines.

'Get. Over. It.' I plead in a weary, drawn-out groan. 'No one was
stopping you from going over to the timber yard that night. How can
you still be bitter about this?'

'I come up with the theory, you nod along then go straight there as
soon as I leave the office. You knew *exactly* what you were doing.'

'We both deserve credit for catching him, I've always said that,' I
declare.

He glares. 'You're full of shit.'

'Oh, grow up. And if you *dare* hint anything about me on camera, it's
a defamation suit. So go nuts.'

'Hm, bit touchy. What's wrong?' He still isn't smiling, but patronising concern is plastered over his face. 'You weren't even at the police
presser for that body in Allcreek Woods today. It's on your bloody
doorstep and you aren't even interested. That's not you – not the old
you.'

'I *am* up on the body in Allcreek,' I bluff. 'One of the detectives
briefed me on the phone. I've got some doors to knock tomorrow. Keep
your beak out.'

'Mr Grayson?' A disgruntled producer holds her smartphone in one
hand and beckons down the hotel corridor at my former colleague with
her other.

Grayson leans in at my side, his dark curly hair tickling my ear as he
produces one last steady whisper. 'What doesn't come out in the wash
comes out in the rinse, Kel.'

* * *

I pull onto the long drive, navigating the potholes and bumps with which I've become so familiar. 11.50 p.m. – Ben will be asleep. The track opens up to the yard in front of his house. He's left the porchlight on, thankfully. It's a hulking four-storey property; a semi-detached mansion, the other half of which is owned by an unpleasant old neighbour, predictably called Mildred.

The red brick and ivy is charming by day. But by night all it does is heighten the sense of being trapped in my own personal horror film. The rounded bay windows built all the way up at the front corner of the house make it look very much like HH Holmes' Murder Castle.

I park up, half-jog past Ben's white Toyota camper, push a key into the front door and shoulder barge it open. The clack noise the secured bolt makes as I lock the door again is the purest, sweetest sound I know. Circling the gaping hallway, I flick on every light.

Then, finally, I can breathe.

Wandering into the kitchen, I pull out a carton of orange juice from the fridge; I can't bring myself to go over to pick up a glass from the draining board opposite, though. There's a window above the sink and, at night, it's impossible to tell what's on the other side. It's as if there's someone willing me to nudge a step closer to that black glass so they can leap forward and engulf me. I know this ghost – like all the others in the house – isn't real. And yet I stay looking at the duplicitous window for a moment longer, trying to win a staring contest no one has challenged me to.

After a swig from the carton, I put the juice back in the fridge and scurry to the lounge. The conversation with Rob Grayson is still bugging me. I've had three years in London, three back on the Wirral, all without a peep. But that one interaction is enough to remind me exactly why I loathe him. I don't think he'll ever get over the fact I caught Dick. But writing attack pieces online about me and not even having the balls to put his name to them? That's as spineless as it is cruel. I thought he'd got bored of that perverse pastime. But the venom's clearly as potent as ever.

How *have* I managed not to hear about this Allcreek Woods death though? The woods are less than a mile away. I'm still supposed to be a journalist for goodness' sake. More fool Grayson for bringing it up. I pull up his initial story about the body on the *Liverpool Echo* website. There's so little detail, the police can't have released much yet. I'm definitely still in the game. I'll put some calls in tomorrow, see if I can dig up a news line he's missed.

There's nothing more I can do on that tonight. There is, however, an American series about child serial killers that's just been uploaded to YouTube. I've been waiting for a proper chance to watch it all week. I settle into Ben's lovely squishy sofa – blanket on, curtains very much drawn – and plough through all six episodes.

In no time it's 3.30 a.m.

Watching morbid stuff online is addictive – an endless tube of internet Pringles. Once you pop...

And yet I'm afraid of the dark in my own home. Work that one out! Sometimes I reckon a shrink would have a field-day rummaging around in my head – or more likely, they'd lift the lid, howl in disgust and check *themself* onto a secure ward.

There are three old, endless sets of stairs between me and the bedroom. Every night they terrify me. But short of insisting the whole house is floodlit 24/7, or falling asleep in the lounge every night for the rest of my life, it is a painful ascent that must be made.

I've got a system. The ground floor lights are already on, of course. And I can turn on the first-floor lamp from the hall. So I do that, then turn off the lights down here and try not to focus on the wind whistling under the front door as I jog up the stairs.

I reach the first-floor landing and the coffin-like trunk Ben keeps on it. The same process then starts again: turn the second-floor light on before flicking off the first-floor switch, run up the stairs and ignore the tree branches that scrabble at the window, grabbing at me through the curtainless pane.

Then it gets harder. I know in my head that this stretch up to Ben's bedroom takes less than ten seconds. But with no final light to guide my way, these last few steps seem to take longer than the whole rest of the day put together.

I flick the second-floor switch off and charge up the stairs, not daring to peer over the handrail and down through the storeys I've just scaled.

The voice wasn't there before, but I can hear her now – wailing with such guttural dread it makes my ribs shiver. It's the same every night.

She's down there, forever staring up at me, screaming, 'STOP IT! STOP IT! PLEASE!'

2

ONE DAY SINCE THE BODY WAS FOUND. A.M.

Ben's not there when I wake, nothing new about that – it's almost 11 a.m. I pull on my old lavender-coloured dressing gown, worn thin at the cuffs, and pad down the creaky stairs that, now bathed in summer sunshine, possess none of the malice they held last night.

I find the lanky beanpole stretching out across the three-seater sofa in the lounge and give his bare shins a sharp, playful slap to shuffle him up.

'2 July. Battle of Marston Moor,' he chirps.

Ben likes to announce each day with a little factoid – my nerdy little cherub. I give his soft, clean-shaven cheek a brush with my finger as he smiles. Bless him, he's so pure-hearted, he makes Aled Jones look like a raving fascist.

'How was the filming?' he asks.

'Good, did OK, I think. Rob Grayson was there though.'

'I thought you weren't doing your bit togeth—'

'We didn't. He arrived as I was leaving. Twat.'

'Twat,' he agrees. 'Coffee?'

He's already on his feet, wandering back to the kitchen with an empty mug and the dregs from a cereal bowl.

Ben may be an earlier riser than me, but it doesn't make his daytime schedule any more ambitious.

We met at a small local gig he was playing eighteen months ago – about twelve months before that was his car crash. His fiancée Grace in the passenger seat, his mum and dad in the back – he was the only one pulled from the wreckage alive. It's impossible to comprehend what he must have been through.

And it wasn't his fault. The moron coming the other way dragged his van onto the wrong side of the road, going 60 in a 40 zone, looking at his phone. But still Ben blames himself. An only child, he moved back into the family home rather than sell it afterwards. And the seven-figure payout from his parents' life insurance has only served to erase any impetus he previously had for pursuing his music, or any other kind of career, more seriously.

Instead, he spends his days teaching himself to cook, watching box sets and writing songs he refuses to sing for me.

Who can blame him? I know what it's like to lose a parent. My dad killed someone, got jailed, then collapsed and died in his cell all within the space of four and a half months. That was fifteen years ago and I'm still waiting to feel whole again. Ben, by comparison, lost all three of his main people in one split second – and much more recently. It's tough to fathom the chasms of pain that must leave behind.

He was, by all accounts, besotted with his fiancée Grace and is now living in the stony shade of a broken heart. I have a feeling all those songs he plucks at, on his acoustic guitar, are an ode to her.

Him being 'emotionally hesitant' is genuinely a plus, though. Usually that tag comes with a coldness, but Ben is a beautiful, innocent creature who just craves company more than commitment. Meanwhile, if I can't even get my relationship with the dark under control, how the hell am I meant to navigate an adult connection with a fully grown man? So it works between us. I'm a drunken fist-fight at midnight, he's the paracetamol and hot-buttered toast the next morning.

'My saviour,' I say as he arrives back with a steaming mug of black coffee. 'Hey, did you hear about the murder in Allcreek Woods?'

'Oh, is that what you were going on about?' He laughs.

'What?'

'You seriously don't remember again? You were wandering around the bedroom, confused and talking about the woods, as if you were there, but you were lost.'

'I literally don't remember that at all.' My cheeks colour up. It's almost certainly my potent, highly illegal sedative pills making me sleepwalk. But Ben would take a dim view of me importing contraband via a dubious US website, so I like to keep all knowledge of the teeny terracotta tablets to myself.

I move on. 'I'm going to put some calls in, see if I can dig up any dirt on the case.'

'Sounds good.'

'And then I'm out seeing Dick.'

'Dick? Again?' he checks.

'I need to fill him in on the interview! And there's a lot more to ask for the book.'

'Right,' he mutters, unconvinced. 'Well, I'm going out for a walk.'

He's got his white Nike trainers on ready. At least, they *were* white – they're so mucky right now. Mucky as a *Playboy* centrefold.

The long walks are another quirk of Ben's. He'll be gone hours sometimes, leaving everything at home except his old crappy iPod, listening to the indie bands he and his mates used to cover before the crash. These days he performs solo – acoustic covers at the local pub on Thursday nights.

He heads out and I move across to a comfy armchair that faces my desk at the far end of the lounge. The desk is the one piece of furniture I've contributed to the whole house so I feel a responsibility to use it; if I need to think, or write up notes, or make progress with my book, I always sit here.

Dressing gown sleeves rolled up, notepad in front of me, I know the first person I need to call. Allcreek Woods are definitely on his patch; surely he'll be heading up the case.

'Kelli Amari! It's been a while.'

Detective Superintendent Abe Vickers is a plump Yorkshireman who moved west to Merseyside more than twenty years ago. He has the kind of deep booming voice you'd expect every high-ranking police officer to have. I can imagine his spirits rising at this call from an old friend.

'Abe, please tell me you're extremely busy with a body in Allcreek.'

'I am. And you're here to wish me luck and let me get on with it, yes?'

'Ha! No.'

'You still living with Ben Farrer? Up past the library?'

'I am. Anyway. Sorry to rush. But what can you give me?' Putting the phone on loudspeaker, I start scribbling.

'OK. Called to the woods about 7 a.m. on Friday morning, so yesterday. A dog walker came across a body slap bang in the middle of a path about half a mile away from The Irby Mill pub. We identified him pretty quickly. Male, 57. Not had the post-mortem yet but looks like he probably died between 2 and 3 a.m.'

'Creepy. Name?'

'One of the homeless bunch who've been living in the woods. Maurice Williams.' He spells the name out then adds, 'Now ask me how we found him.'

'Go on.'

'A nail in each eye and one through his larynx. Probably done with a nail gun.'

'Shit.'

'I know,' he says. 'When I catch whoever did it, I might get them to put my decking together.'

'Anything to go on motive-wise?'

'Nada. Probably just another tramp who'd stolen a nail gun then decided to use it after a hard day's drinking. Anyway, that's your lot. Not sure you'll get this to fly with any of your newspaper friends in London. It's all a bit scummy and local. And Rob Grayson's usually across everything for the *Echo*. Only about to release the name and cause of death now though. It was hard finding relatives for the bloke, so...'

'If Grayson rings, don't tell him that stuff, at least for an hour or two, just to give me a shot at getting this published,' I beg.

'He's very good, is Rob,' Vickers says. 'I don't want to piss him off.'

'No, no, I get it. Just give me an hour, please! After that, tell him what you like. Rob said there was a big press conference yesterday so I'm sorry if I missed that, but I'll be first to call wanting updates from now on.'

'Press conference?' Vickers checks. 'No, he just phoned me after getting nothing from the media team.'

Grayson. Lying bastard.

Call over, time is of the essence. I write up the two lines of 'new news' – the guy's name and the stuff about the nails – into a full-page lead. Meanwhile, my mind is racing ahead; Vickers is wrong. You don't just kill someone with a nail gun – direct shots to eyes and throat – in a spur of the moment skirmish. This was a ritual, this was a statement, this was the signature of someone carrying out a pinpoint, premeditated execution. And what's another common trait with such organised killers? They don't stop at one.

I've written up 500 words in thirty-five minutes. I'm on fire. It won't trouble the nationals but I ping it over to the *Echo's* news editor who will have no problems remembering me. Hopefully they'll offer me a freelance fee, but even if they don't, at least I'll be officially back in the game – a name irreversibly printed in connection with Maurice Williams' death. I still have the news editor's number too, so I text him to make sure he knows the piece is coming.

His return call five minutes later, however, is about as warm and positive as a nuclear winter.

'Hi Kel,' he says. 'Got your copy. Look, the thing is... Rob's been running on this already, and he's chief crime reporter now, so it will seem weird if we stick an exclusive byline from someone else on the story when he's our local expert as far as the readers are concerned.'

I plead for it.

He says no.

I plead for it again.

He says Grayson will call the police back and confirm what's in my copy, then write it up himself.

I hang up.

Rob fucking Grayson.

I fall face-first onto the sofa, head in hands, scrunching hard at clumps of hair. The adrenalin that carried me through as I was writing turns to rage and I scream into the cushions. My trusty old contacts are about as useful as oven-baked snowballs – all respect having melted away while I was living in London.

A hatred towards Grayson that had lain dormant for so long is well and truly ablaze. He'll have poisoned the *Echo* news desk against me. Of course he will. And we'd been their rising stars when we caught Dick. Together. A kindergarten Woodward and Bernstein. Then, just because I got more attention off the back of it than he did, he turned into a vindictive, malicious arsehole. I hope he knows the only reason he's the chief crime reporter at the *Echo* is because I left for the *Daily Mirror*.

The timing of this afternoon's visit to see Dick could not be better. Not only do I have a fresh, bizarre murder to pick his brains about, but I also need thoroughly cheering up.

3

ONE DAY SINCE THE BODY WAS FOUND. P.M.

The drive to Manchester is about an hour. Sitting in my clapped-out sky-blue Peugeot in a car park opposite the prison, I apply my lippy assisted by the rear-view mirror. One last check that my hair's behaving: it is, surprisingly. I get out and cross the road.

Strangeways. Hotel to the most interesting lodgers in Manchester. Dad was the first person I ever visited here.

The prison's had its fair share of VIPs though. Harold Shipman was held before his trial; Ian Brady did time as a teenager; even perma-tanned knock-off merchant David Dickinson did three years in the 1960s for mail order fraud. And now it's home to The White Widower.

I coined the nickname myself: *white* – because all of the victims were Caucasian, and *widower* because they'd all had husbands. The *Echo* used it as a splash headline after the fourth murder: *The White Widower strikes again*. And it was picked up by all the nationals after that.

Dick Monroe has murdered numerous women, shows no compunction for his crimes, yet is, without doubt, one of my closest confidants.

I'm led to the visitor room. He's waiting – and grinning.

Dick is bald, but you can tell the barber hasn't been in several days as tiny silver pinheads glint behind his ears, catching the sterile lights above. No chance of him being left alone with a wet razor of his own to keep it tidy. To that end, he's also handcuffed to the table.

'So good to see you, Kel.' He's earnest as he half stands to honour my arrival. I clasp those warm hands tight and he gives me a squeeze as we sit down. His fingers are weathered and thick but never clumsy. There's a dexterous swagger to the way they flick and wave as he talks – like they'd be just as comfortable tying a neat bow in a toddler's laces as they were at wringing the life out of middle-aged women.

Dick possesses a very particular magnetism. An aura that reduces jail warder bulldogs to skittish puppies. No one else in the visitor room dares laugh, cough or even breathe too loudly for fear he'll notice.

'Fresh case on the Wirral,' I begin.

I relay everything.

'A nail gun?' he clarifies. 'Would that actually kill you?'

'Apparently.'

The shackles force Dick to rest his hands forward and stoop his shoulders, not allowing him to show off his impressive frame. 'Two in the eyes and one in the throat?' he checks. 'It's so precise. Doesn't feel like a one-off.'

I agree emphatically. 'It's clinical. But Abe Vickers passed it off as if it was nothing. Just a scummy fight between drifters.'

'Are you surprised? Old *Abberline* couldn't spot a killer if they were stabbing him in the gut. Fat fuck.'

Dick hates Vickers. And there's no love lost in the other direction either. Vickers got the nickname Abberline – as in the detective who famously failed to catch Jack The Ripper – when Dick was still on the loose. When Dick was eventually brought in, Vickers did a pretentious press conference gloating at having caught 'the devil himself'. Dick always thought the detective was a charlatan who'd had the biggest case of his career solved for him by a couple of junior reporters.

But I'm much more interested in discussing the body in the woods than adjudicating in a joust between two men's egos.

'The Green River Killer left dozens of girls in forests. Just because it's somewhere secluded, doesn't mean it's a one-off. In fact, surely that's more of a red flag than something domestic.' Dick returns to the crime at hand. His knowledge of murderers is as encyclopaedic as mine. 'Bet there's a lust element too. The nail gun would be a quick, quiet way to shut the victim up so they can do whatever they want with the body.'

Dick never holds back. He left his semen on each of his dead victims like a calling card. Once that kind of information is in the public domain it's difficult to think of anything you might say or do that could sully your reputation further. He knows how a twisted mind might think and he isn't ashamed to harness that – with me at least. And we have the same hunch; this execution sounds like the start of something, not the end.

We go on discussing it for a while, but then I remember what I'd meant to say as soon as I arrived.

'Your documentary... my interview was last night!' I blurt out.

'I was wondering when we'd get to that,' he says, shuffling again, unable to get comfortable. His mouth dominates his face as he produces a huge toothy grin. 'So, what did they want to know?'

'Asked me whether I'd commit a murder if I knew no one would find out.'

'What did you say?'

'Told her the first rule would be not letting on you were planning a murder at all.'

He gives his bound hands a little clap. 'That's my girl!'

Is it bad that this brings me out in a cheesy smile like a five-year-old with a 10-metre swimming badge? Probably.

He asks me to go through the interview line by line, savouring the fact he was the centre of attention even in his absence.

'It got me thinking of a few more questions in terms of the book, if that's OK?' I eventually ask. Prisons are like courtrooms: no mobile phones or dictaphones allowed. So I've left mine in the car and come armed with good, old-fashioned paper and pen instead. I flap my notepad in the air like a long, lost Hemingway manuscript.

'How's the book going?'

'Brilliant, I've basically written it all. Except the only copy's saved up here,' I tap the side of my head. 'And finding out a bit more about Number Nine would be handy.'

Number Nine. A ninth victim. Police found eight bodies. They charged Dick with eight murders. But when he confessed, he told detectives there had been a ninth one, never found. He didn't know her name and says he can't remember where he left the corpse. Yeah right, I don't believe that amnesia for a second. If I can coax that final confession out of him it'll give my book real oomph. It'll be headline news... which equals free publicity. Plus, that would really stick it to Grayson; no way he can call 'foul' when I beat him to that gem.

'Did they ask about Number Nine in the interview?' he checks.

'Yeah. Told them I'm not sure if she's real or not. You've never bothered to give me anything concrete.'

'Oooo feisty, Kel. Feisty!' He chuckles. 'You stick with me, I'll tell you about Number Nine soon enough.' He sounds even more scouse than usual as he says this, knowing my soft spot for the dialect. But it doubles as the first remindful jolt of the visit; I'm interacting with a psychopath. A compulsive liar. A social chameleon. Someone with no moral firewall. He wants to monopolise my attention, that's why he wants me. Not because he cares about *me* but because I'm the only person willing to come in here and dote on him. Just that manipulative thickening of the accent is enough to sober me up. I've read enough about personality disorders to know that however much I may want an authentic rapport with this man, he does not have the capacity for such a thing.

He's tilting his head to one side and leaning his neck forward the exact same way I am too – physical mirroring, another way to subconsciously lower the guard of the person you're speaking with.

I cast out the dispiriting thoughts and refocus on his days as The White Widower, a moniker Dick says he likes. These glimpses into his mind – into what he was thinking and how he came to make the decisions he made during the three years he was 'active' – are priceless.

His killings across Merseyside became more theatrical, more staged, with each passing body. The first one that was officially found, Julie Reynolds, received blunt force trauma, strangulation, ejaculation. Simple. But soon little extras started to appear at the scenes – personal clues. A cricket bail left next to the body of Wendy Forbes simply because he loved the sport; a postcard of Southampton placed near Barbara Fetherington to mark the city in which he lost his virginity.

By the seventh body he'd become extremely confident and was leaving a lot of clues. And that's when Grayson had his lightbulb moment. What if the killer was getting so cocky he was starting to leave mementos hinting at where he was going to strike *next*? It was a hell of a long shot, but the log slice left under the head of the body of Number Seven *might* just mean he was planning to dump the next victim at a timber yard. There is only one on the Wirral. With no plans after work that evening, I decided to just go and scope it out. I struck gold. And Grayson's never forgiven me.

'Why did you turn the crime scenes into little games of Cluedo?' I ask.

'That came later. Wanting to dominate and destroy – they were the main things. The visions I was having were always basic, carnal. But the game-playing...' he pauses for a second, '...that increased the buzz.'

It is when speaking about these women that something changes in him. A look which only descends on the eyes of a killer – the same look I'd spoken about with Annabelle Ludgate. Beautiful blue is devoured by jet-black pupils and a horrible calm washes over him. It can easily be misconstrued as blank apathy for his crimes, but it is the very opposite. We are delving into the defining moments of his life. The sick urges he denied himself for so long, the brutal acts he plotted in secret, and ultimately, the fulfilment of these fantasies which brought him a level of sexual gratification he can access now only through these memories.

No, it is not apathy with which Dick Monroe speaks of his murders, it is quiet, breathtaking ecstasy; and it freezes the air to my skin every time.

I swallow hard to recentre myself. 'So why did the crime scenes start to become more important later on?'

'It's when I first saw one on the national news. I thought I'd love it, but it scared me. Where do you go from there? Had I peaked? So I started to build my brand, fan the flames – that became important. Then I started to obsess. Every handbag, every ripped bra, every strand of hair was exactly where it was because I said it could be. I was the only one with the power to have changed those things and the police, the media, everyone would be falling over themselves to work out why. I started getting artistic, working out what I was trying to say with my canvas.'

I shut my eyes to digest the analogy. Am I disgusted, terrified or in awe? Maybe they're all the same thing.

4

TWO DAYS SINCE THE BODY WAS FOUND.

'Thanks for getting the table ready outside and making all the salads,' I tell Ben as he comes back in with my coffee.

'I tossed some honey in with the stilton and walnut one, it's pretty good,' he says, unaware of how proud he looks. He brushes my thick black hair to one side and kisses me on the cheek before delivering his fact for the day: '3 July. You share your birthday with Tom Cruise and Julian Assange.'

I've anticipated it today however, and done some research of my own. 'And Vancouver child killer Westley Allan Dodd!'

'If you say so,' he concedes, unimpressed. 'Is it alright if I sort out the shed while the girls are here? It won't be too noisy. I need to mow the lawn too, but won't do it until they've gone.'

I tell him that'll be fine. For my birthday, and against my better judgment, I am keeping up a tradition of hosting a lunch with the school pals. I really could do with finding a new lead to pursue on this body in Allcreek Woods. But then again, it is a Sunday... I'll redouble efforts tomorrow, that's what Mondays are there for.

Teeth brushed, dry shampoo in, mascara on, I'm ready when the doorbell goes.

'Anna.'

'Happy birthday Kelli!' She screams, flinging her arms around me in one of her trademark hugs, a real rib-cracker.

I laugh at the effusive welcome. 'Keep it down! You'll wake the kraken next door.'

She hands over a £50 John Lewis voucher in a crisp white envelope. I don't want to say the customary present is the *only* reason I keep celebrating my birthday every year, but the extra lamp I want for the lounge isn't going to buy itself.

'There better be some bubbles,' she says in her joking-not-joking way. I know it's sunny, but her enormous sunglasses suggest she genuinely believes she's a celebrity hiding from the paparazzi. Her shoulder-length dirty blonde hair is pristine, conditioned and straightened within an inch of its shimmery life.

I retrieve the 'bubbles' from the kitchen and we wander through to Ben's lovely verdant garden. He's laid the table out with plates, sparkling cutlery and his decadent salads. I stand in front of two chairs, encourage Anna to take the one opposite then pour us both a glass.

She whips off her leather jacket to reveal a tight vest top, enough bosom for the both of us. Her fake tan's no match for my natural olive skin though; I'll always have that.

Chinking glasses, I run her through the menu. 'We've got a summer coleslaw with broccoli, a classic Caesar salad, a stilton and walnut salad with honey and a spicy green salad with rocket and jalapeños.'

'Delish! Ben, I assume?' She beams, genuinely enthused.

'Of course!'

'I wish Henry did more cooking,' she sighs.

Urgh Henry, Anna's boyf. Together three years but he still refuses to move in with her. Lots of late nights at the office too. I fear that little worker bee is busy trying to screw anyone he can trick the knickers off. No doubt they'll have a kid eventually, but only so they don't fall behind the rest of the Audi-driving, courgette-spiralling, bubbles brigade.

One thing I will say for Anna – she's unashamed. She wants middle-class, Ocado-delivered utopia and has the confidence not to hide it. Let's not forget, this is a woman who goes skiing every year but still books a beginner's lesson on the first day of each trip so she can look like an absolute prodigy next to all the actual novices. That's the kind of sociopath we are dealing with here, and I kind of love her for it.

Ben wanders out in navy football shorts and a moth-eaten Oasis T-shirt, all four limbs as gangly as they are pasty. Too shy to say hello to Anna, he disappears into the shed on the far side of the lawn.

'You heard about the body in Allcreek?' I enquire, unable to hold off another solitary second on the only story in town.

'Urgh yeah. Horrible, horrible!'

'Two nails in his eyes, one in the throat,' I relay, pulling off a tone of insouciance Dick would be proud of.

'It's too disgusting to think about,' she insists, shaking her head and frowning.

No Anna, it's too disgusting to *not* think about.

'Talking of nails, where d'you get *them* done?' I ask instead, giving up on interesting conversation and nodding at her huge lilac acrylics.

'Thanks. Salon in West Kirby, Lexi's. So expensive – £60! A "sorry present" from Henry for missing our brunch date last week.'

Hmmm.

The faint shrill of the doorbell interrupts. Finally!

'Alright, you old hag,' Polly says as I open up.

We go through and she takes up her seat next to me. Despite the heat of the day, she has her customary long-sleeved white shirt on. If Anna's toned from too much Pilates, Polly is just plain skinny. Her nose is all sheer angles – any sharper and it could open a tin can, any pointier and it could pick a lock. Her bright, natural blonde hair suits the warm weather.

'Here you go,' she says, plonking a wrapped-up present on the table.

I pick it up and shake it next to my ear. 'I'm going to guess... hard-back book?'

She nods. 'It's a signed copy of *Mein Kampf*, cost a fortune.'

I rip off the paper to reveal the actual gift. 'Michelle McNamara on the Golden State Killer!'

'Knew you wanted it,' she mumbles, embarrassed by her own thoughtfulness.

'I love it! Thank you!' I declare.

There's a crash behind us as Ben drops one of the power tools he's carrying out of the shed. We all turn to look at him but he doesn't react to us, just puts the device down on the grass next to all his other DIY kit and plods back out of sight again.

'What do you know about the body in Allcreek?' Pol asks.

I could kiss her!

'Nail gun to the eyes and throat,' I repeat.

'There were loads of police round the back of ours the last couple of days,' she explains.

'Yeah, not surprised. I've been digging; not found much yet.'

'I don't like thinking there's another killer on the Wirral,' Anna admits with a shudder. 'Makes me feel icky.'

'This isn't like Dick though,' I reassure.

'Oh!' Anna exclaims. 'Can't believe I forgot to ask... how did the Netflix interview thing go the other night?'

Yes girl, all is forgiven! 'Good, thanks!' I smile. 'Reckon it'll be out in the autumn, should hopefully make it in for a minute or two.'

'That is so flipping cool!' she cries, throwing her hands in the air. 'We *have* to do a watching party when it comes out!' As a rule, I'm thoroughly against theatrical reactions to things, but I will *absolutely* allow it on this occasion, raising my eyebrows at Anna with a smirk of concord.

Polly takes out a cigarette and tips the packet to me. I pinch a Silk Cut to my lips like the end of a straw as she lights it for me, not breathing enough smoke in to inhale before blowing out again. Conversely, she takes an almost impossibly long drag into her tiny chest.

Anna declines to join us. 'Bad for my pores.'

I always have been piggy-in-the-middle between these two, even back in school. This round of birthdays we're thirty-two.

The general vibe is nice enough, but when Anna pops to the loo, Polly doesn't waste the moment we have alone. 'No wonder she's got those mega glasses on, only thing that'll protect her eyes from those fucking talons.'

I give a guilty chuckle. Polly has a wonderful control over her swear-ing, reserved for her wry asides. My approach to profanity is far more scatter-gun.

'Rob Grayson was at the Netflix thing the other night,' I say. 'He was the one who told me about the body in Allcreek. But to be honest the *Echo* haven't given it much oomph.' I try to inhale the cigarette much deeper this time. However as soon as I come to blow out again the cloud combusts in my throat, forcing up a sharp, spluttering cough; my eyes water with the sting of it. 'Shit, sorry.'

Polly ignores my faux pas. 'Todd was basically dancing round the flat when he found out it was one of the homeless people. Hadn't realised quite how much he hated them. Don't understand it myself.' She's still got that full-bodied scouse accent we grew up with; mine's been eroded by the years I spent being misunderstood in the capital. I could listen to her talk all day; it's the sound of home.

'How is the man of the house?' I check, anticipating her trademark reaction every time I bring up Todd.

'Still a wanker.' She takes another long drag then holds the stub-end of her cigarette up close to her mouth, letting her white cotton sleeve ride up her slender forearm.

I'm interrupted while still formulating my follow-up Todd question...

'Nightmare!' Anna says, strutting back towards us, arms flailing in the air again. 'Sister's car's broken down so she can't pick her twins up from some kid's party in Pensby. I've got to shoot and look after them until she can get back.'

She grabs her handbag off the back of her chair and shakes her head. 'So sorry, Kel. It's been lovely. Don't know what I'm going to do with them – can't *abide* another afternoon of Paw Patrol. Maybe I'll put on something classic. Pingu or Postman Pat or something.'

'I've always thought it would be sexually gratifying to sit on Postman Pat's nose,' Polly interjects.

Anna's struck dumb. My knuckles turn white, clinging to the sides of my chair as I try, and fail, to suppress a guffaw of laughter.

* * *

Ben finally decides it's time to mow the lawn so Polly and I move inside and stick on a mediocre Steve Martin comedy on a movie channel. Having already seen off the rest of the bubbly by herself, she snuggles up to me with a gin and tonic while I tuck into the kilograms of pralines Danny – my brother – has sent over from Australia for my birthday. In that sense, Polly's the perfect guest – she doesn't take a single one of my moreish chocolates.

Eventually Alan Titchmarsh comes back in from the garden and Polly leaves us to it.

As a birthday treat, Ben had offered to prepare some of the haute cuisine he's been dabbling in recently. But all I want is spag bol with garlic bread – and cheesecake for pudding. And based on the smells and clattering coming from the kitchen, he is applying the same passion to my comfort food as he usually does to his more highfalutin creations.

He looks dorkily cute in a cream-coloured apron as he pokes a wooden spoon around one of his larger Le Creuset pots. I go up behind him at the Aga, put my arms around his waist and squish myself against him. While he remains lean and seemingly twice my height, I'm putting on pounds at an alarming rate thanks to his gastronomic exploits.

'The key to a good ragu is to treat it with utmost respect,' he explains.

He's always coming out with pretentious guff like that, as if he thinks he's a character in *The Bear*. I tell him as much; he responds by patting a splodge of the sauce on my nose. Really, I'm more than happy for him to play Head Chef for us both. It's not that I can't cook, but I do often end up using the smoke alarm as a timer.

When my birthday dinner is served, it's divine as always.

Stuffed to the rafters, we collapse on the sofa. We've been working our way through *The White Lotus* so stick that on.

'Shall we go upstairs?' he offers after a couple of episodes.

I've mentally prepared for the fact we'll have sex tonight. What self-respecting couple doesn't have sex on birthdays? But in all honesty, there's little spice in our relationship. We'll do it maybe once a month, if that. But Ben is very vanilla: missionary; bang bang boom; roll over; sleep. We don't discuss it. And I think that's because we're both quite content with the dynamic. Ben's heartbroken about Grace and I'm turned on by the kind of things that make it easier to keep my predilections to myself.

Congress concluded, I kiss him goodnight and head back downstairs. I'd already flicked on all the lights on our way up, so the descent isn't all that taxing.

I make a hot chocolate and nestle in the comfy armchair at the far end of the lounge facing my desk and open up my laptop. As I study the Allcreek Woods murder story afresh it's even more clear that this isn't a spur-of-the-moment occurrence. I spend the next couple of hours researching all sorts of other cases, looking for any kind of parallel.

With almost every other killer who has this level of skill and precision, the one thing they aren't going to do is stop killing. But a gruesome body alone isn't enough to tickle any pickles down on Fleet Street... Or is it? I don't know.

Maybe I'll be thinking clearer in the morning.

* * *

Noise seeps in gradually as I'm dragged up from a deep well of sleep.

Ben's wagging a sheet of paper at me as I lie in bed. What time is it? What's he saying? He doesn't look his usual self, he looks frightened. Actually, he looks more than frightened. He's literally quivering.

'...phone the police... on our property... new locks... CCTV.'

His words start to string together as my eyes adjust, the thick curtains keeping out most, but not all, of the daylight.

'What?' I snap.

'This was on your car window!'

I snatch the piece of A4 paper he's wobbling in front of me and stare at the note; capital letters written in a blue biro:

HIT ME ON THE HEAD, I WILL NOT CRACK,

BITE ME EVERY DAY, BUT I'LL GROW BACK.
WHAT AM I?

Squinting up at Ben, I wait for him to enlighten me.

'Nails, Kel!' he cries 'It's a riddle and the answer is *nails*. Like that body they found in the woods!'

My jaw drops open but words won't form. Ben's hysterical stare pins me to the bed, drowning the room in dread.

5

THREE DAYS SINCE THE BODY WAS FOUND.

Ben calls Detective Vickers, who arrives less than an hour later. Examining both sides of the paper, he puffs out his cheeks at me and gives his balding head a little shake. 'If *you've* got a note we'll need to see if anyone else has one too. You haven't even had anything published on Maurice Williams, have you?'

Thanks for reminding me.

Vickers passes the paper to his junior colleague – a pretty, petite woman no older than me. Wearing latex gloves, she takes the A4 sheet and slips it into a marked plastic bag.

'Lauren, get in touch with the journalist Rob Grayson, *Echo's* chief crime man. See if he's had anything. Literally anyone sent anything to do with "nails" has to be seen as a potential target,' Vickers tells her.

She nods. Her straw-coloured hair is tied back in a ponytail and looks like it would be an unruly mess if it ever got out of the bind. She's makeup-free and her skin is beautiful and clear. But her vivid green eyes are stern, as if she wants everyone to notice how hard she is trying.

I wonder if I could have taken the police route, rather than the journalistic one. Would that have been more satisfying? Maybe this young detective's as obsessed with killers as I am.

'I saw it on Kel's car windscreen out of the kitchen window when I was making a coffee just after nine,' Ben explains. 'It wasn't there yesterday.'

'And what's the last time you'd have looked out of the window last night?' asks Vickers.

'About ten-ish.'

It means the message must have been planted sometime in the last twelve hours – not a particularly narrow timeframe.

The detective rubs an open palm across his smooth chin. There are several scarlet dots around his jaw where he's nicked himself shaving.

'I didn't hear anything from down here in the lounge last night,' I admit, not quite sure how to react or what to say. 'Who d'you think did it?'

Vickers refuses to be drawn.

The tumultuous day makes me panicky and nauseous. Police are doing checks around the property until late into the afternoon, scuppering my plans to go out hunting for fresh news regarding the murder. By the time the officers leave, the day's wasted. Ben and I watch several more episodes of *The White Lotus* before he decides it's time for bed. He wants me to come too, saying he'll sleep better if he knows I'm safe, but I insist on staying up. 'Police said they're doubling patrols between here and Allcreek,' I remind him. 'I think we're safe.'

He reluctantly agrees, and toddles off muttering about ordering security cameras for the front and back doors first thing in the morning.

I then proceed to watch video after video on my laptop about killers notorious for leaving notes and clues. Zodiac is a classic one. He left cryptic riddles. There are lots of theories for who he was. Never caught though. Fascinating case.

My eternal search for a satisfying diversion sees me stay up past sunrise. Not a sensible or wholesome use of my evening, I know. But who wants to be sensible or wholesome? When I do succumb to exhaustion, the ink-blue light of dawn makes the journey upstairs far easier.

Tomorrow *must* be more productive. I knock back half of one of my sneaky sleeping pills, set my phone's alarm and promise to obey its 9 a.m. call-to-arms – less than five hours from now.

* * *

It barely feels like I've shut my eyes when the device's polyphonic jingle pierces the lovely warm silence of my Tuesday morning.

I have half a mind to snap the handset in half, roll over and return to my dreams.

But I can't, not today.

Ben's still in bed, messing around on his phone.

'Get you, early bird,' he says.

'I need coffee.'

'And toast?'

I shake my head. It's my brain – not my stomach – that needs a jump-start.

Dressing gown on and down to the lounge, Ben brings through another of his scrumptious freshly ground brews. He's put a drop of cold water in so I can gulp it all in record time.

'So, what's the plan today?' he asks.

'Going to phone Martin at the *Mirror*. Then off into Allcreek Woods to find the other homeless guys who sleep there. See if they heard or saw anything.'

'You aren't going at night, are you?' he checks with touching concern.

'No! But they always hang around the off-licence so I should be able to find them. Might not work but we'll see. What about you?'

'Going to put a new Arctic Monkeys cover in my set so need to get that straight. Then thought I'd try making mousse au chocolat later.'

I'm envious. I want to stay here and read my new book from Polly, then lick the bowl and spoon once Ben's finished in the kitchen. But he has an excuse for indulging in his hobbies on a daily basis, whereas I'm basically fun-employed – residing rent free, living off life insurance money for two parents who are not my own.

The £4,000 fee Netflix gave me for the interview is the first income

I've had since moving in with Ben last autumn. And I haven't even made the progress with my book that could justify earning so little.

No. For my own self-esteem and to demonstrate to him that I'm not here to leech, I need to carpe the diem, at least while there is a decent lead to chase.

Whipped into shape by self-discipline, I call Martin, a senior reporter from my *Daily Mirror* days.

'Amari, to what do I owe this displeasure?' Martin always thought he was funnier than he was.

'The displeasure's all mine, I assure you,' I fire back.

'How are you anyway? Bored stiff on the Wirral? Missing me?'

Martin knows I'm with Ben, but he also knows I had a bit of a crush on him when we were both in London. He's certainly the most beautiful man I've ever seen naked. It was my first Christmas party at the paper, we'd been flirty all evening and by 2 a.m. – bolstered by prosecco and cinnamon vodka shots – I bundled him into my taxi back to Brixton. He hadn't been too hard to convince as far as I can remember. The journey home flew by – time tends to when you're kissing a muscly, stubbly colleague. I shared my flat with four fellow twenty-somethings I barely knew. Martin and I stumbled in, sniggering as we bumped and shushed each other along the hall and into my room. Finally able to ogle the bare chest I'd been sliding my hands all over during the ride home, I'm afraid the sense of achievement went to my head. I pushed him on to my bed, pulled down his Armani jeans and showed him exactly how pleased I was to have him over. But afterwards, maybe inevitably, all interest in returning the favour evaporated. He didn't get in touch over the next few days but was decent enough not to blab about it around the office. We've both been happy to keep things platonic since then.

Anyway, that's Martin. Gorgeous, cocky, owes-me-an-orgasm Martin.

'Don't flatter yourself mate. I need an address,' I say.

'Oh, they're getting tight on us giving out anything from the database. They can trace any address searches we do and query it if they think we're not doing it strictly for our own—'

'I know, I know. They were doing that before I left. But I've got a cunning plan,' I say with pride – because I have indeed got a cunning plan. 'I've got a story here, on the Wirral. A murder. If I were to tip you off about it, you might be interested in digging deeper. But you'd need someone on the ground doing the door knocks. I won't take a freelance fee for now to avoid it getting complicated with the expenses team. But it would be enough to justify giving me any addresses that could be relevant. And if it does come to anything, you'll look sagacious – at which point you can pay me handsomely.'

There's then a delicious moment when he asks what 'sagacious' means and I get to mansplain it back to him.

'Go on, what's the angle?' He half-sighs as if he's disinterested – but the fact he's still on the phone tells me all I need to know.

'Homeless guy found in the woods, a nail in each eye and one through his throat, through his larynx actually.'

'A tramp? Who cares? Probably done by another druggie high on meth.' The pompous way he says 'high on meth' in that affected Home Counties accent hints at the fact that Martin has probably never come within a mile of methamphetamine, or any other drug stronger than Calpol. He goes on, 'Way too scummy to get in the paper.'

'But read the runes. It's so specific. Feels premeditated – and that adds to the intrigue. There could be more bodies if they don't catch him.'

Martin still thinks it's too small-fry for the nationals, as I knew he would. But he concedes that the story is legitimate enough for him to pull up the paper's national database of names and addresses without it looking suspicious.

There are about 8,000 people with the last name Williams on Merseyside, he finds. But not a single Maurice Williams. So that's one potential lead extinguished.

'What d'you expect? He was homeless,' Martin scoffs, making me feel one inch tall. 'His family was probably rough too. I wouldn't bother speaking to relatives to lead a story on.'

I cock my secret weapon and pull the trigger. 'The killer also left me a message.'

'Rubbish!'

I talk him through the note on my car and he finally concedes that the story *might* be worth writing up and pitching to the news desk.

'I can always take it to another paper if you...'

'No, no, no. Kel, come on!'

I'm toying with him now – serves him right for being so patronising.

I hadn't wanted to divulge about the note; it draws me away from being a reporter and makes me a part of the story. It's a cul-de-sac, not a stepping stone. But I couldn't stand by and just let Martin ride roughshod over my pitch. And still, at least it's something to rub in Rob Grayson's face. DS Vickers confirmed earlier – turns out I am the only person left such a note.

6

FIVE DAYS SINCE THE BODY WAS FOUND. A.M.

I pull up outside Polly's. She and Todd live in a council flat above Ladbrokes in the village of Newton. It's Allcreek Woods that separate us. Her place backs onto it. Once in the thick of the forest it's all sycamore generals with holly bush lieutenants, every one of them conspiring to block any hint at an exit. If you do find your way out, on the east side – my side – is Irby. There's a post office, an off-licence, inexplicably three barber shops and The Irby Mill pub where Ben plays his gigs. Our house is about a five-minute drive up from there. I've never tried walking to Polly's but I reckon door-to-door it would take about an hour.

She knows I'm coming and meets me at her front door. She's always up for doing anything that involves exercise – Polly has this weird compulsion to do 25,000 steps a day. Mind you, if we're comparing weird compulsions, excessive walking is far more advisable than my favourite pastimes. No doctor has ever looked at a patient and stated, with unwavering medical authority, 'What you need young lady, is to watch five hours of harrowing footage about the Yorkshire Ripper in one sitting.' Well, no doctor I've met, anyway.

'Let's go straight into the woods,' I insist. I did come on a solo trip yesterday afternoon and failed to locate any vagrants. But I won't be deterred.

'The creepy murder woods?' she asks. 'I wish I didn't live so close to them now. There was police tape all around here and all the cars parked up there,' she points as we walk away from the back of her flat and cross the road towards the trees.

'If we see any homeless people we need to talk to them about Maurice.'

'They usually hang out on the far side, your side,' she says. 'I don't think we will though. Todd's been going on and on about how this is the best thing that could have happened because it's scared them all off.'

'Why does he hate them so much?' I probe.

'The fight. You remember, ages ago?'

'Vaguely,' I reply. 'When I was down in London, wasn't it?'

'Yeah. One of them put a brick through his car window to nick his bag while it was parked up at the back here. But he saw them, ran after them, then like four of them ambushed him and beat him up.'

'Rings a bell,' I admit.

'Yeah. I mean they didn't really rough him up bad. The main thing they bruised was his ego but he can't get over it.'

'Well hopefully they haven't been scared off completely because I need to speak to them,' I assert.

'What are you hoping to find in all this? The murderer? I know you caught that other bloke back in the day, but that was like a once in a lifetime hit, wasn't it?'

Her point is astute – and is something that has worried me for a long, long time. I've been interested in killers ever since Dad was jailed. He wasn't a murderer, he was fighting off a pervert who was trying to rape my brother. Long story short, he ended up killing the predator and got done for manslaughter. But ever since, within me there's been a fascination with learning about individuals capable of taking life. So I went into journalism desperate to report on murderers, with the dream of maybe one day even helping to catch one. But then I *did* catch one –

spectacularly – at the age of twenty-six. And the career path I then laid out for myself involved a steady stream of cracked-cases, convictions and commendations, a book deal maybe, my own TV show. But three and a half years in London brought me down to Earth with a skull-shattering crash: I wasn't special, I didn't deserve the inflated salary or the prestigious 'executive crime reporter' title; I was a junior who peaked too early. The *Daily Mirror* let me go. That's what actually happened.

I wasn't getting any big scoops or agenda-setting exposés, my shorthand could barely keep up in the court cases I was sent to. And then those infernal blog posts started popping up. The one suggesting I should have gone to the police instead of the timber yard the night I caught Dick came first. But there were others too, just absolute nonsense. One suggested I'd offended lots of victims' families that I'd doorstepped. Another said I'd made up quotes for several of my stories. It was all categorically untrue, and in most instances I was able to provide evidence to the *Mirror*'s managing editor to rebuff the accusations. But it contributed to the growing cloud above me, definitely. And that's why I *know* that anonymous blogger was Grayson. He despised the fact I got the big break, so chose his own cowardly way to ruin it. Don't get me wrong, things weren't going to plan anyway, but he played his part in the eventual decision to terminate my contract.

If I'm honest, at heart I'm not a reporter at all. I don't want to *report*, I want to *detect* – but without the protocols and red tape involved with joining the police.

As I look at Polly lighting a cigarette I realise she's right – that *is* why I'm so energised about this case. Part of me still thinks that I, Kelli Amari, have got a chance of catching this killer.

I try to be honest, aware it's taken me a few seconds to summon an answer. 'I know it was a one-off with Dick, but this feels like something I can at least get my teeth into. If I could just beat Rob Grayson to one juicy line, I'd feel much better.'

We wander deep into the woods, the swaying branches obscuring the perfect blue sky above. The earth is dry and powdery, but still clings to my mucky boots. Each footstep crunches on brittle twigs.

I tell Polly about the note on my car and she says the same as Ben – we need to get some CCTV cameras for extra security.

'Has there ever been a murder in these woods before?' she asks.

'No, don't think so.'

'Growing up, Grandad would chase me round here, play hide and seek, then once I got too old we'd just come and wander around talking...'

Pol is so guarded as a rule, I feel a slit in the armour for a moment and try to peek inside. 'Do you miss him?'

'Of course I do. Do you miss your dad?' Her tone is wounded and harsh. I chicken out of pushing any further.

Polly's parents were heroin addicts. She was put into care at nine years old. Her grandad agreed to be her legal guardian after that. They were thick as thieves. As far as I can remember, he was always quite impatient with guests and would use the N-word like it was going out of style, which I suppose it was.

But to Polly, he was the messiah.

She took it so hard when he died. He had a fall and never regained consciousness. It was just before I moved to London and was almost enough to stop me going – just so I could look after her. She didn't hide the fact that was desperately what she wanted either. But my contract with the *Mirror* was already signed. And anyway, within two months of the funeral she'd shacked up with Todd – which leads me on to my next question on our walk, sensing the need to lighten the mood. 'How's the man of the house?'

'Todd? Still a wanker. He's always working and if he is *in*, he's actually out at the pub,' she curses. 'Then he'll come back home all annoying and aggressive so I just pretend to be asleep. *And* he's snoring now.'

Todd's a taxi driver. It's clear Polly latched on to him out of desperation after her grandad died, rather than him having any particular redeeming feature. He's obsessed with his car, drinking and not much else. Romantically disabled, I don't think he's ever treated Polly to anything: jewellery, a meal out, even flowers. But then, he lets her live with him rent free and they've been together six years, so who am I to judge? Polly sometimes calls Todd and Ben our sugar daddies. 'We'll trade them in soon for a couple of bankers with huge dongs,' she's predicted on more than one occasion.

She's on her third cigarette as we approach the eastern edge of the forest. I feel an odd electricity thrumming through me at being back in the same woods that this nail gun maniac has frequented. Where did it happen exactly? Have I stepped on the same soil as the perpetrator? It baffles me that no one else seems to get that same rush from walking in a killer's footsteps.

Today, like yesterday, the thrill is mixed with frustration though. We've seen two or three dog walkers. We've seen a couple of chavvy teenage boys chucking sticks at a high-up branch, trying to convince it to drop a shoe that's somehow got stuck up there. What we have not seen is one single homeless person. Right in the far north-easterly corner of the woods we at least find their den – a small pit of days-old ash encircled by crisp packets, empty glass bottles and a charming stench of piss; but there is no one in sight. I suppose if the discovery of the body didn't scare them off, they were probably turfed out when the police came to search the scene afterwards.

I'll have to keep an eye out; surely it won't be too long before they pluck up the courage to return. I turn to Polly just as she puts her fourth Silk Cut to her mouth. Her shirt arm tightens with the movement, pulling her cuff up towards her elbow, and I see it – a dark purple bruise about the size of a plum on her wrist. It definitely wasn't there at my birthday lunch.

'Was Todd working last night, Pol?'

'No, why?'

I think on my feet. 'Oh, just I forgot to say, Ben thought he saw him in The Mill.'

'Yeah, probably. He was there – came back in a foul mood. Wanker.'

I'm staring at the bruise with no subtlety whatsoever. Polly notices. Snapping her arm to her side, she tugs her sleeve back down and grabs my hand in hers. 'Kel, promise me you'll be careful with all this stuff in the woods. If something happened to you, I'd kill myself.'

7

FIVE DAYS SINCE THE BODY WAS FOUND. P.M.

Mum lives about half an hour away in Ellesmere Port these days. She's on her own in a twee, detached bungalow she bought after selling the family home on the outskirts of Irby about a decade ago.

But don't be fooled by her stint on the Wirral, Mum's Scouse to her bones. Born just off the Scottie Road, she worked as a clerk in Lime Street station until she married.

Dad was pure Woolly Back, a Birkenhead native. He was working at a pub in Moreton when Mum came in with some pals and by all accounts it was love at first pint. He was thirty-six, she was twenty-four. They married in 1989 and Danny was born three months later. I followed a year after that.

'Happy birthday Kelli Belly!' Mum bursts as she opens the door. We share a quick squeeze and she presents me with a large bouquet of pretty tulips, which I then carry back inside and put down on the kitchen table as I pull up a seat.

'Can't stay long Mum, Ben's doing tea.'

'OK, OK, just a cuppa.' She pulls two flowery mugs off the drying rack and drops three Twinings tea bags into the teapot. 'I do wish I could have seen you on your actual birthday.'

Fractious, that's the word I'd use to describe Mum's and my relationship. She coped incredibly badly after Dad's death, relying on a spiteful streak and a penchant for sharp putdowns to keep me in check as a teenager. The ice has thawed a little since then, but we're still no Lorelai and Rory Gilmore.

'How's your day been?' I check.

'Urm, OK. One of the shelves has broken in the lounge.' She insists on taking me through to show me. 'It just fell down in the night. Huge crash scared me half to death,' she adds, pointing at the plank of birch wood lying on the carpet splintered at one end with books strewn all over the carpet. There are small, uneven holes in the wall where the shelf had sat.

'Shit!' I blurt without thinking.

'Oh, Kelli. The language! There's no need whatsoever to be...'

'Sorry. Sorry!' Mum hates swearing. Like, really hates it. Hates it more than famines in Africa or Nazis. Hates it so much that if she had one wish in the whole world, it would be to never hear another expletive ever again. I forget sometimes, leading to the ludicrous pledge I'm making now. 'I won't do it again. Promise.'

'Do you think it's fixable – the shelf?' She probes.

'I have no idea,' I confess. 'But Ben's dad used to keep loads of tools – a drill, a nail gun. They're all in the shed still. Ben can bring them over, he'll definitely be able to help.'

Placated by my exaggerated confidence in Ben's mediocre DIY skills, Mum allows us to return to our unmade cups of tea. Neither of us is tall, but we used to be about the same – 5 foot, 3 inches. Recently, however, she's begun to recede – I can see the top of her head in front of me now as we potter. Her hair is still jet black though, even at the roots. Hopefully, bodes well for me in my dotage.

'Talking of nail guns,' I start up once back at my kitchen perch, very much a dog with a bone. 'Did you hear about the body in Allcreek?'

She doesn't seem to know about Maurice Williams but as I begin to enlighten her it's clear she's as reluctant as Anna had been to hear any of the details. Their loss. No need to tell her about the note on my car. I haven't got the energy for the drama she'd make it into. 'Anyway, bookshelf aside, how are you?' I ask instead.

'Oh, y'know, good days and bad days.' That's her new catchphrase. 'Did I tell you I'm down to two shifts a week at Asda now?' she checks.

'Yeah, you said – that was a couple of weeks ago, wasn't it?'

'That's been great, means I can get to aqua aerobics on Tuesdays.' Mum's milling around the pine-clad kitchen in an excited muddle. Packet of biscuits out but no plate; milk out; little jug out; plate for the biscuits; milk back in the fridge; milk back out to actually pour some into the jug; water from kettle to teapot; quick stir; mugs brought over; biscuits brought over; milk jug brought over; tea poured.

I try not to giggle as she continues chattering but eventually I can't contain it any longer.

'Mum!' My shriek of laughter startles her.

'What?'

'You haven't boiled the kettle,' I poke a finger in and out of my mug of tepid water then tap the side of the teapot. 'It's cold.'

Mum howls too. 'What am I like? I'll sort it, I'll sort it.'

We have our cup of tea, which I drink quickly – even once it is piping hot – and then make my excuses, trying not to sound too desperate for an escape. 'I'll take the flowers though, so thank you very much. You know I said "no presents"!'

'I know, but Ben's place is so dark, it needs some colour.'

I grunt and get up from the table.

'Do come over properly soon,' she says. 'Now I'm working less it'll give us more time to catch up. It's not long until the anniversary of the day your dad—'

'I know when it is.'

8

SIX DAYS SINCE THE BODY WAS FOUND. A.M.

I rise painfully early and my hunch pays off – the vagrants have finally returned to Allcreek Woods. I knew they wouldn't be able to stay away from Irby's cheap plonk shop – with its surprisingly witty name of Vino'clock – for long. It's outside there that I find them.

They had indeed temporarily been moved on by police but are back now and are smart enough to insinuate they'll be forthcoming with information about the death in return for 700 ml of Red Square vodka. But £15 later and all I get is a silly idiot saying it wasn't a human that committed the murder at all – it was karma because Maurice owed him some money. The man looks familiar but I can't quite place his blotchy, pockmarked face. I point out to him that a money dispute is a plausible motive for killing someone.

He tells me exactly where I can stick my plausible motive.

I've been down dead ends – for want of a better phrase – many times before. But at the *Mirror*, if a story wasn't stacking up, I'd just be thrown a more pressing lead to chase instead, whereas since moving back up north, I now have as much time as I want for digging. There have been other tales that have piqued my interest since coming home, but impatience usually usurps novelty after a while and I give up on them.

This murder feels different, though. The alacrity that comes with feeling sharp and driven by something is so nourishing. I'm not giving up.

Part of it is an intense desire to crush Rob Grayson. He's had the audacity to message me with pictures of two of his *Echo* page leads regarding Maurice Williams this week. He knows I've been pestering Vickers – the detective must have blabbed. Grayson's message reads:

> Someone's trying a bit harder than they're letting on ;)

What a fool. I message back telling him to check page 18 of yesterday morning's *Daily Mirror* – and the small article Martin squirreled in there about Maurice and the note on my car. Grayson doesn't reply. I hope it really irks him that a letter was left on my car and not his.

I've also been using this gust of energy to make some inroads into writing up Dick's book in the evenings too. I already had his childhood and background, but this was the first meaty chapter. 3,000 words – taking the reader through the first killing and on to the eve of the second. I'm proud of my handiwork – the prose grips as swiftly as it chills, evil meets acumen. It captures him perfectly.

By day, however, I'm focussed on the nail gun killer. Martin says that while the initial story didn't get much space in the paper, the *Mirror*'s deputy editor wants updates if 'anything else happens'. I do wonder whether 'anything else happens' literally means me coming to harm. But still, it's given me fresh impetus to keep pushing Detective Vickers for information. In that spirit, the senior officer is expecting Maurice's post-mortem report back today and has promised to give me the lowdown as soon as he has it.

Back early from the off-licence, I stay in the rest of the morning anticipating the call.

First, while I wait for him to respond, I watch a new documentary on Amazon Prime about Ian Brady and Myra Hindley. What else is one to do on a beautiful summer's day? The programme isn't bad, one photograph in particular of a little girl being tied up and gagged is harrowing. There isn't much else I didn't know already though.

The programme finishes and there's still no response from Vickers, so I turn my attention to the book Polly gave me. It's written by journalist Michelle McNamara about her hunt for the Golden State Killer – thirteen murders, fifty rapes. Tragically the author died before he was caught, but what is so striking about the way she writes is her compassion for the victims. She knows what they ate, what they drove, where they holidayed. She humanises them in a way that makes me feel guilty and callous. Why do I never think about those questions? Why do I always research the killer first?

It's 1.45 p.m. and still no call from Vickers. He will ring back, he always does. But I'm going out to see Dick this afternoon so he better not call while I'm sat phoneless in the Strangeways visitors' room. Plus, whatever extra information the detective has for me I'll want to share with Dick, so it'll be a waste if it comes through later on this evening.

Ben comes into the lounge with some homemade bread and a warm gooey camembert to dip it in.

'Luncheon,' my culinary enabler announces. I wonder if he knows, as he grins, that I'm in danger of actually turning into a dumpling – ready to pop on one of his stews – if I don't stop eating so much. But the cheese is so creamy and rich. And the warm springy loaf is so moreish, with its hints of mustard and fennel making best friends with my mouth. I'm devouring my third hunk of cheesy, doughy nirvana when my phone blares out. Finally!

'So sorry Kel, been mad today but you said you wanted an update.'

'Did you get the PM?'

'Yep, yep. We're pretty sure Maurice Williams was unconscious before the nails were fired, hence no signs of a struggle. No strangulation or blunt trauma either. So theory is he was knocked out chemically, then laid on his back before being shot. Not had toxicology back yet to confirm, but we don't think he was just passed out drunk.'

'Drugged? So whoever did this had a nail gun *and* some kind of tranquilizer? This was *so* planned, this murder. Don't you think?'

'I'm not going to speculate on that,' he says, dull as dishwater.

'And have you got a suspect or anything?'

'Can't comment at the mo.'

'That's a no then,' I conclude. 'What about motive – sexual surely?'

'Pathologist said there were no indications Maurice had been molested or interfered with in that way, and no DNA at the scene.'

For DNA read semen.

'What? So they just knocked out a homeless man, fired a bunch of nails into him, then ran off?'

'We're still working on the "why" of all this. But that's your lot for now. Oh yeah, and we've traced the trainer prints from the scene. Pair of size 10 Nike trainers,' Vickers says.

* * *

Dick's in good spirits. With all the sun recently, he's been using his activity hour each day to sit outside and it's brought some much-needed colour to his cheeks. The top of his head even looks a tad rosy and tender.

I provide the new details from Vickers and Dick agrees that it only strengthens our theory that this is not a one-off. Then I mention the note that was left on my car.

'I can't believe that! They could have been caught so easily.' He's shaking his head.

'No more risky than killing someone in the woods though.'

'No, but that's obviously the fantasy. They go out and do that *despite* the risks to get their kicks. But going to the house of a reporter to scare them? There could be a kind of thrill in it, I suppose.' He laughs, as if savouring the fact a fellow killer has done something that's caught him off guard.

'I'd bet my life it wasn't one of the homeless gang,' he says.

'Why?'

'Do any of them know where you live? I doubt it. Whoever did this either knows you or knows how to find the addresses of journalists.'

Damn, he's good.

'Still a ballsy move though, whoever did it,' he reiterates.

'Yeah?' I'm happy to let him talk. His input on any aspect of the death is precious.

'Definitely. Me personally, I never did anything incriminating in the weeks or months *between* the events.' 'Events' – his special word for murdering women. 'But I did start to get a real kick out of thinking I was scaring people.'

I'm scribbling down so quickly the sparks could set the whole prison alight. I mutter for him to continue.

'I wanted people thinking I was omnipresent. I was everywhere. I was outside your window and I wasn't outside your window – like Schrödinger's Cat. I wasn't just in control of my own mind, I was in control of everyone's. That's why I did one in Liverpool – the larger the hunting ground, the more people I have a hold over.'

'Is the note a power thing then? Ratchet up the fear?'

He doesn't reply so I look up and clock his nicotine-stained grin aiming back at me.

'What?' I ask, narrowing my eyes.

'You love it, don't you?' he chuckles, as if he's been hand-delivered an epiphany.

'No!' I protest.

'You *love* that you were singled out.'

'No, it's creepy and I hope they catch whoever did it.'

'Yeah, but only so you can be part of someone being caught again.'

Stuck for a comeback, I look away and he takes my silence as a victory, laughing harder and giving his shackled hands a clap. Peering back up, his deep blue eyes are locked on mine.

'We're more alike than either of us realise.' It's him who says it, though it might as well have been me. 'Sometimes I think about what we could get up to if I wasn't in here,' he adds.

'You could take me to find Victim Number Nine.'

He smirks and gives a little shake of the head. 'You'd get your answer then ditch me. Can't have that. I need you, Kel.'

I stop for a second, eye contact unwavering, my pulse stampeding ahead of me, and then I whisper, 'I need you too.'

Dick leans in and speaks softly, reeling me in with every word. 'You've got a hold on me, you know that?'

Neither of us is smiling now. I squeeze his thick, warm palms ever so tight and breathe back. 'Do you think about me... back in your cell?'

And then, with his light breath so close it's brushing my cheek, he tells me exactly what he thinks about.

My heart is still pounding when our session ends; I dash back to the car.

Driving like a maniac, I keep the moment alive, replaying what we'd said over and over again: the look in his eyes, the strength of his grasp. Another bolt of adrenalin strikes me.

Pulling up outside home, I arrow my key into the front door and bundle in. Ben's at the kitchen counter, cutting something up. Grabbing him by the waist I haul him round and pull his face into mine. He drops the knife behind him and thankfully catches on to my not-so-subtle plan. We charge upstairs in a way we never have before, clothes strewn in our wake across all four floors.

9

SIX DAYS SINCE THE BODY WAS FOUND. EVENING.

Ben lies on his side of the bed, facing the ceiling.

'That was so good,' I tell him, out of breath.

'I've never seen you like that,' he professes.

'Yeah,' I laugh. 'I don't know what came over me.'

'You asked me to hit you? ...You pinched me!' His tone is confused rather than annoyed, but it's not helping me bask in the afterglow of what's almost certainly the best sex I've ever had.

'We don't have to do that if you don't want.'

'I'd never hit you,' he says, turning to look at me. Bless his innocent cotton socks.

He leaves for his gig soon after. Our little frolic has made him late but he's still out of the door by 7.20 p.m. Ben likes to drive down to The Irby Mill with all his equipment, have a few beers during his set, then sleep the alcohol off in the back of his van before trundling back up to the house in the early morning. That leaves me with nine or ten hours alone in this cavernous and increasingly dark house. I really need to buy that extra lamp with my John Lewis voucher.

I stick on a true crime podcast while running a bath. The episodes are a perfect way to fill all those little gaps you get during a day. I've listened to thousands of shows over the years. Literally thousands.

Serial, obviously. *Man at the Window*. *Who Killed Daphne? The Teacher's Pet*. *My Favourite Murder*. *Someone Knows Something*. *Casefile*. *Up and Vanished*. *Sweet Bobby*. *Atlanta Monster*. And on and on and on. Tonight I'm listening to *Murder They Wrote* and very much enjoying it.

Thursday evenings are just for me. Ben goes out for his gig. I stay in with my hot bath.

Despite us having sex earlier, this will be the last guaranteed chance to have my own fun for another seven days, so the opportunity must be taken. Even more so this week as I missed my me-time slot last Thursday – Anna had called me in floods, Henry being a dick as usual, so I went round to console her. I'm *such* a nice person.

Anyway, I'm here now and I'm ready.

Bath run and podcast finished, I lean my laptop next to the taps facing me at the opposite end of the tub. Pain and torture, that's my go-to porn genre. I've never actually maimed myself, but the videos are a good proxy.

I daren't tell Ben for fear of hurting his feelings; but then again, he's probably up in bed every night looking at photos of women with ridiculous fake boobs on his phone and having the time of his life.

I press play on a video and lose myself among the suds.

* * *

Hair dried and pyjamas on, I don't want to be awake any more. The Brady and Hindley documentary I was so keen to watch earlier is starting to haunt me – yet another example of my duplicitous mind drawing me in, then spitting me out.

Time for two of my sleeping tablets. Roxion pills, that's the trade name – a form of triazolam. Polly introduced me to them. Pharmacist prescriptions were banned in the UK back in the nineties but online forums say they are the most potent sedatives you can reliably order from abroad. They are also my only friend on nights when Ben's not here.

I wash them down with some water in the kitchen, then do my next-light-on-last-one-off routine as I scurry upstairs. That awful voice screeches from the ground floor as the last switch is hit. But once in bed, I let my shoulders slump and soon feel my head sliding into a lovely, warm dream – all angst evaporating as the pills fasten my eyelids shut.

* * *

There is no good way to rouse me in the morning. Even waking up naturally feels like a horrible accident. But an over-excited ringtone is definitely one of the worst ways. Unsure of what's going on, my first instinct is to turn away from the noise. Rolling into the middle of the bed, I collide with Ben. When did he get home? He's pretending to be asleep until I quell the attention-seeking phone. His breath stinks of last night's beer.

Turning back to the offending device I tilt the screen towards me. Why's she phoning this early? I hang up but know I'm going to have to call back.

10

SEVEN DAYS SINCE THE FIRST BODY WAS FOUND.

Fumbling around in the semi-darkness, I pull on my dressing gown and a pair of dirty socks. On the landing – which is bathed in early-morning sunlight – Ben's mucky trainers lie discarded by the bedroom door. Why does he *never* just kick them off in the hall? Phone in hand and eyes still half-closed, I pad down to the second floor and collapse onto a huge leather armchair which doesn't get anywhere near as much love as it deserves most of the time.

'Sorry, didn't mean to wake you,' Polly says after picking up.

I chunter inaudibly about her being right to think I would be asleep at 8 a.m. and that she should be apologising.

'Thought you'd want to know. Police are back. More than last time, I reckon.'

My doziness dissipates instantly, like a gale tearing through fog.

I'm on my feet, pacing the second floor and asking every question under the sun. Polly isn't able to offer much more than she already has; the commotion of officers swarming into the woods woke her up, then she called me. Have a forensic team gone in? She doesn't know. Is Vickers there? She doesn't know. Have they wheeled out a body? She doesn't think so.

I need to get over there. If this is a second killing then this is massive.

Excitement, fear, disbelief, confidence. They're all spinning and blending as I go back upstairs, pull on some skinny jeans with a curry stain on the thigh and tell Ben I'll be back by lunch. I'll just wear my pyjama T-shirt with a thick jumper until it warms up then grab a bra when I come back. Rushing downstairs, I push on a pair of tatty black Vans trainers and head outside.

It's a bad habit, but I tend to leave my car unlocked most of the time and stash the keys in the glove box for convenience. No one's going to nick this old rust bucket.

Getting in, I lean over and open the drawer to retrieve the keys.

My exhilaration slams into a concrete wall, congealing into something much more akin to terror. There, in the glove compartment, is a rag, or maybe it's a handkerchief. I can't be sure exactly. But there are two things I can be sure of: one, it wasn't there when I pulled up at home yesterday evening; and two, it's saturated in blood.

11

THE DAY OF THE SECOND DISCOVERY. A.M.

Grasping the cold, sodden rag, a shiver rips across my shoulders.

It's as if I'm not alone outside the house, like whoever put this here has waited to see what my reaction will be when I find it.

My hands – one stained red now – are shaking. My car keys *are* in the glove box too, but I drop them in my haste to start the engine and get off the drive. I need to get to the scene, I need to get away from the house. But what if the perpetrator's still on the premises? What about Ben? He won't be safe. I'm petrified by every possible connotation of this crimson cloth.

I get back out of the car and feel bolder, strangely. As if the car would have muffled my screams and blocked any attempt to flee if the killer had been in there with me. But now I'm out in the yard I can run or hide if need be and any noise will echo across the neighbourhood. I stalk around the building.

There's no one in the gap between the bushes and the wooden fence that separates our garden from Moody Mildred's.

I peer behind the trees, at the bottom of the lawn, past the flower beds and into the farmers' fields, then to Allcreek Woods in the distance, tumbling away over the hills. Did the killer come straight here from the scene?

Striding back to our cars, I get onto my knees to peer under Ben's campervan, I can't see anyone. The shrubs that separate the driveway from the garden? Nothing. The thick laurel bushes that flank the yard from the property in front of ours? Nothing.

'I'm not scared! I'M NOT SCARED!' I scream, desperate for them to hear me, to believe me. My T-shirt's drenched underneath the thick jumper.

I'm coming back out of the laurels when I see her. A blurry figure peering over at me from next door's front garden. 'Everything all right?' Mildred asks, looking all the way down her long, wrinkly nose at me.

'Yes, fine. Sorry. Just shooing a fox...'

Despite the early hour she looks like she has been up for a long time, her make-up immaculate, her mauve cardigan freshly ironed. 'Just a fox?' she challenges.

'Yeah. Sorry if I disturbed you.'

'Oh, you didn't,' she says haughtily. It's as if she knows I'm lying. 'I can phone 999 if there's something wrong.'

'No. Just a fox.'

Mildred's suggestion of calling the police fills me with revulsion – because a fresh thought has hit me: maybe the bloody rag isn't there to scare me, maybe it's there to frame me.

* * *

That cloth was definitely not in the car when I got home last night. It couldn't have been because I'd clearly opened the glove box to leave the keys in there. And yet it was there this morning – still wet.

I pluck several tissues out of a packet kept in the driver's side door and scour the scarlet stain off my hand, then drive off, leaving Mildred looking puzzled. I phone Polly en route to Allcreek, promising to pop in once I've spoken to people at the scene.

Parking in the alley next to the parade of shops she lives above in Newton, I ditch my jumper and scamper round the back of the premises, now facing the woods.

There certainly are a lot of police cars. Blue capital letters stretch away in both directions on white tape: POLICE LINE DO NOT CROSS – POLICE LINE DO NOT CROSS – POLICE LINE DO NOT CROSS.

Half a dozen uniformed officers are patrolling the perimeter, and that's just on this east side of the forest. A cluster of nosy locals have gathered near a police car and are keeping another officer amused as they try in vain to wheedle a grain of gossip out of him.

'Is it another body?' one elderly woman working in the opticians asks.

'I can't answer that, sorry Miss,' the copper replies.

'There's a free sausage roll if you give us a clue,' says another old lady I don't recognise.

'Sounds good but I can't take bribes, sorry,' he chuckles under his black custodian cap.

''Ere, let's do it as charades. You act it out and we'll guess what you're all doing 'ere,' a man near the back of the pack calls out, to titters from the others.

I shuffle over to the officer from stage right with my empty notepad as if it's a passport and he's the guard at border control.

'I'm a journalist,' I murmur so the rest of the audience can't hear.

It strikes me too late that holding up an empty A6 pad literally proves nothing to anyone. The PC says I'll have to speak to DS Vickers or DI May.

'Are they in the woods?' I check.

'Dunno,' the constable says as he turns away, clearly keen to get back to his assembly of silver-surfing sleuths.

I walk off along the pavement parallel with the woods. My feet are flirting with the forbidden land, one on the pavement side of the police tape, the other firmly planted on the dusty ground of the woods.

It doesn't take long for an officer on patrol to spot me lurking; she closes in calling out for me to step away from the tape.

'Sorry, Kelli Amari...' I stick out a hand that she shakes out of habit.

She reiterates the need to move away from the trees.

'I'm a reporter,' I explain. 'I'm just having a look around waiting for Abe to come out and fill me in.' It feels impressive to be able to know and refer to DS Vickers by his first name.

'DS Vickers has been and gone,' the officer states in a belittling didn't-you-already-know-that? tone. 'A bloke from the *Echo* showed up, the boss had a word with him. But yeah, he's gone now.'

Urgh! Vickers has already spoken to Grayson – a crime infinitely worse than anything that can have occurred in those woods.

'I suppose you can ask Lauren,' the female officer goes on.

'Lauren?'

'DI May,' she adds, nodding at the smartly dressed woman stalking out of the woods behind me.

I've never moved so quickly.

'Urm, DI May... DI May?' I call out. She stops just short of the police tape as I reach her slightly out of breath. There's a glint of recognition on her face but it's clear she doesn't have an immediate response. I take the moment's hesitation to make the symbolic move of swinging under the tape and presenting her with the same hand I offered the uniformed officer.

'Kelli Amari. We met at my house last week.'

'I remember,' she says.

'I'm a journalist... just wondering what there is to report so far.'

'Detective Superintendent Vickers is going to make a statement this afternoon,' she replies, not displaying any kind of affection or familiarity despite our previous encounter.

'Yeah, but I know he's spoken to Rob Grayson at the *Echo* so information is already out there.'

'Grayson's local, Grayson's reliable.'

The fact she's saying positive nonsense about such a buffoon is mitigated in part by that lovely thick scouse accent. She wears the dialect like a badge of honour; it's sexy as hell. But nevertheless, she's talking rubbish about the biggest arsehole known to man so I throw some shade back.

'*I'm* local. I was probably reporting here before you'd even joined the force. Vickers trusts me too. He must have filled you in on our background before you came round to the house last week.'

'He said about Dick Monroe, yeah. So what?'

'Look, I just want the latest. I don't have to quote you. How about you tell me what Vickers told Grayson, and then I promise not to put it out anywhere until I've got Vickers' say-so. Honestly Lauren' – it is Lauren isn't it? – 'I *am* reliable too.'

Maybe it's the pathetic desperation in my eyes, or maybe she's just sobered up and realised that Rob Grayson really is a moron. Either way she ushers me over to an unmarked car and leans against the closed boot.

'Write this down.'

I place my pad on the back windscreen and push my left hand against the paper to keep it steady as I write. I thought I'd got all the blood off my hand, but to my sudden horror, there's still obvious traces in the crack around the cuticle of my index finger. I need to tell her about the rag as soon as she's given me the update. Then it'll be her turn to ask questions. But I need the latest *here* first, so for now I fold the stained finger down against my palm.

'There's another body, isn't there?' I predict.

'No,' she responds flatly.

'No?!' I flash her a look of disbelief.

She doesn't give anything away as she stares back. Good poker face. But then she spills. 'There're two new bodies. Both are—'

'Two?!'

'Keep your voice down,' she orders. 'Two bodies. Both with nails in the eyes and throat. One looks like they were done last night. The other's been there at least a week, probably longer.'

'How could it have been there and no one see it?' I ask in a hushed tone, hoping that my discretion will be rewarded with a decent answer, which it is.

'Found face down in a bog. It was completely hidden, green muddy jacket and legs trapped under fallen branches. An officer disturbed the branches this morning looking for evidence to do with the other body, and the second one floated up.'

'That's disgusting,' I put my pen-holding right hand to my mouth. 'Are they both men?'

'Nope. One in the bog is a woman we think, though identification is harder after that long in the water. The second one is male, ID in his wallet and the clothes he was wearing suggest he wasn't homeless either, but I can't confirm that yet.'

The detective looks ready to shoo me away so I summon up another question before she can get the words out. 'Who discovered the fresh body?'

'Another dog walker. Body was just slap bang in the middle of the path again.'

'Any suspects?'

'Not by name.'

'Have any footprints been found again this time?'

'Grayson wasn't told that.'

'What else *was* he told?'

'Nothing was taken from the victims. That's more understandable with Maurice Williams, but this bloke they've just found, he had seventy quid in his wallet and a Breitling watch on. That's the bit that doesn't make sense. That and the note they left you. We haven't fitted those into the puzzle yet.'

'Any more?' I probe.

'That's it,' she states, taking her maroon suit jacket off as the sun beats down. She moves towards the side of the unmarked car and unlocks it. I need to tell her about the rag.

'Lauren, there's—'

'London dropout arrives second to murder in her own back yard.'

Talking in headlines – I know who that is.

I turn around; Rob Grayson is marching towards us, pit marks already festering under the arms of his tight grey shirt.

He leans his back on the side of DI May's car as I straighten up. Different specs on today – his Harold Shipman's.

'I've got everything Vickers gave you so enjoy sticking it in the *Echo* while I file to the nationals.'

'It's already up on the *Echo* website. So *my* scoop,' he bleats back.

DI May opens the door to the car. 'I'm going to leave you both to it,' she says. 'Check with Vickers before publishing, yeah?' she tells me before disappearing into the driving seat.

I need to tell her! But not with Grayson here. He'd have a field day.

Ask to speak to her privately? No but Grayson will get it out of Vickers before the end of the day if he knows there's something afoot. He's relentless. Tell her anyway? Use it to wind Grayson up like with the note? No, but this is different. This is probably key evidence – a massive clue that points at me if you want to read it that way. He'd publish it. He'd make me sound like a suspect.

Pinned by indecision, I watch in passive paralysis as DI May starts the car and drives away, leaving me alone with the world's worst man.

'Looking a bit strung out, Kel. All OK?' he patronises.

I don't reply and start walking back to my car. He follows.

'Y'know, the Samaritans have an app now, if that helps,' he joshes.

'The very fact you know that tells me everything, Rob.'

He changes tack. 'Two new bodies then. Nothing taken. Killing them quick. It's unusual but not unheard of.' For a split second I remember us as a team, as two peas in a pod, and I want to call a truce so we can solve this mystery just like in the old days.

'Son of Sam was a bit similar. Kinda,' I offer.

'Yeah, I was thinking Sam. What's the motive though? Maurice's wasn't sexual so I'm betting he won't have touched these two either.'

'I really don't get it,' I agree, reaching my car to unlock it. Some respite from the constant bickering is welcome. But the ceasefire doesn't last long.

'I've got a suspect in mind,' he brags.

'Who?' I jolt round to look at him – he's staring straight back at me.

'Ahh, that would be telling.' A small smile curls across one side of his mouth. I remember that cheeky look from our days as juniors. I used to like it. He'd pull it out when he'd thought of something dark and unexpected. However much I despise him now, he's still the only non-criminal I've ever met who shares the same morbid fascination in serial killers as me. Our friendship was always competitive, driving us both to uncover truly heinous and chilling things in cases, just so we could shock or impress the other one.

But the longer this slippery smirk lasts, the more I can feel it's coming at my expense today.

'What?' I snap.

'You can't cope with this new killer on the loose, after last time. You're falling apart.'

'If I'm falling apart and I've still got as much from the scene as you then you probably need to give up journalism.'

He ignores the jibe, smirk intact. 'I've been thinking a lot...'

'Doesn't sound like you.'

'I've been thinking a lot since you did your interview with Annabelle Ludgate. I've been thinking how you've not been the same since the night Monroe was caught.'

'Oh right, so what, that makes me a murderer too?'

'I don't know what you are Kelli. But you're not the same person who went into that timber yard.'

I want to tell him the reason I'm so strung out is because someone's planted a bloody rag in my car. I want to get the rag out and shove it so far down his throat he chokes to death on his grovelling apology. But I can't say anything. He's already full of conspiracies, this is the last thing he needs to know.

'You just shut me out, completely shut me out after we got him. And then within six weeks you were off to London. Accomplice flees the scene.'

'Argh Rob, yeah I found him! Get over it,' I walk round to the driver's side and open the door. I had wanted to pop in and see Polly but I need to get out of here now.

'Have I ever told you what first made me suspicious about Janice Benson's death?' he probes.

'I never asked.'

'It's your 999 call.' His little smile spreads broader, making his nostrils flare.

I wait. I think I know what he's going to say. I think I know because a few weeks after we caught Dick, this same specific detail came to me while I was in bed. It fell suddenly like a beam from the ceiling, crushing me and making my eyes bulge. I remember lying there, a lonely, frightened heap of nerves, unable to sleep, unable to think of anything else except the fact I couldn't have been the only person to notice my mistake.

I say nothing though and stand with my hand on the open car door – staring at him.

'Your voice,' he repeats. 'You phone the police to say you're hiding in the bushes and you think you've found The White Widower, and yet you are speaking normally, as if you're not worried at all about Monroe hearing you. Not even an attempt to whisper. You know what that says to me, Kel? That says you weren't hiding from him at all. That says he already knew you were there. And if you were lying about that, it begs the question: what *were* you doing when you called in? And why have you stayed friends with Monroe ever since? Are you scared he might tell on you?' The last question is doused in mock sympathy.

'Small ideas please small minds, Rob. Next time you think about coming over to speak to me, how about you just fuck off instead, or I'll get a restraining order.'

'If you go to a judge to get a restraining order, I'd be able to tell a court exactly why I'm so interested in you, and we could get it all reported under absolute privilege. Sound good? Because you are lying, Kel. Lying with a capital "L".'

'And you're a runt with a capital "C".' I get in the car and speed off, aiming a ferocious, prolonged scream at the road ahead.

He does know. My one mistake. Why has he never told anyone? Or maybe he has. Thank goodness he didn't post it on his stupid blog. But why?

The morning has been such a kaleidoscope of nightmares that every question I pose seems both inherently stupid and earth-shatteringly important. I feel like I've been spun around ten times and pushed onto a tight rope.

Rocketing along, I have to swerve to avoid a cyclist. My sudden swing into the middle of the road draws an angry horn-blare from a Land Rover coming the other way. What am I doing?

Slow down. Slow everything down. My driving, my breathing, my thinking. One problem at a time. What do I do with the bloody cloth? That's the most pressing issue. OK, a plan. What's the plan? Call Vickers? Tell him about the rag? But then they'll want to know why I didn't tell DI May. It looks like I'm playing games. It'll make them suspicious.

Plus, my DNA is all over it now. Have I missed my chance? I wish it didn't exist.

A modicum of sense drips back into my mind and with it comes an idea. I'll stash it for now. Out of sight, out of mind. I drive deep into the countryside away from Newton, somewhere no one will find the rag. Somewhere I've had to hide something before.

12

THE DAY OF THE SECOND DISCOVERY. P.M.

Rag dealt with, I get home and type up the story of the two new bodies. As expected, Martin from the *Mirror* calls soon after. He wants me to report on the murders exclusively for the paper. In fact, he would 'absolutely kill' to have me onboard. Funny man. My byline, £600 fee per day's reporting plus £3,000 up front if I agree to turn down approaches from other publications.

I can't accept fast enough.

My copy comes together with satisfying ease. I've seen Rob's *Liverpool Echo* version of the story online. It's alright, but it's still only had about 130 shares on the paper's website. Small fry.

Ben comes downstairs, a cute ringlet in his fair hair flopping down over his forehead. He's been on his guitar, I think. If he wasn't so shy he could be an indie band pin-up.

I explain what's happened in the woods; he stiffens up.

'Right,' he says. 'I'm ordering that home surveillance stuff. I'd already Googled it all. There was a Korean brand that looked best. Don't know why I was putting it off.'

The assertiveness is uncharacteristic.

'Front, back, driveway,' he goes on. 'No one's getting onto or off the property without us seeing them. No more notes on the car. No more anything.'

For now, I decline to mention that the perpetrator left something far worse in my glovebox this morning. He lost the plot when he found the note on the car – I haven't got the headspace today to circumnavigate another meltdown.

'I don't think it's safe you sleeping in your van after your gigs at the moment either,' I respond. 'At least two of these murders happened on Thursday nights. And it sounds like they're not just targeting homeless people.'

He nods in disappointed agreement.

The Irby Mill is right on the edge of Allcreek Woods, there's no way he should be alone near there.

'You didn't hear anything while you were in the van last night, did you?' I enquire.

'Just passed out, didn't hear a thing,' he tells me.

Article written, I call Vickers as promised. He picks up and says it's fine for me to use the information. He's surprised I bothered to ask. He won't be giving names out until tomorrow. They now think the first murder took place roughly a week before Maurice Williams', meaning there have probably been seven-day gaps between all three killings. No more to share for now. Too busy.

I read through my copy again. It reads well, already subbed into the paper's style since I know the *Mirror*'s house rules, and written in the past tense since it will be published in tomorrow morning's edition.

I send it to Martin. It starts:

Police were hunting for a serial killer last night following the discovery of three bodies in a single area of woodland in just seven days.

The victims – two men and a woman – are all suspected to have died after being shot in the head with a nail gun.

The first body to be found in Allcreek Woods, Newton, Wirral was 57-year-old Maurice Williams last week.

Officers had already launched a murder investigation over the homeless man's death but were not linking it to any other crimes.

However, yesterday morning a dog walker came across the body of an unnamed man, thought to have been killed the previous night.

And during Merseyside Police's subsequent searches, a female victim was discovered in a bog in the same woods, with pathologists suggesting her body may have lain undiscovered for a fortnight.

The full copy runs to 600 words. Martin suggests it's being earmarked for page 5 – a good showing if it happens.

* * *

Feeling calmer now the story has been filed, I have a shower and change.

Rob Grayson will surely have left Newton so I should be safe to pop in to see Polly. Really, it's an excuse to go back and spy on the police blockade from a perfect vantage point – but I had said I'd call in to see her, and she can get seriously arsey if I promise to meet up and then renege.

I pull up outside – no sign of Creepy Grayson – and wander up the characterless, concrete steps at the side of the parade of shops then turn left on to the passageway, replete with metal railings and graffiti. To the right is the forest; to the left are a row of wooden front doors painted burgundy, each with a small rectangular window made of unfriendly wired glass.

I pass the first flat, then the second, the scent of weed wafting up from under the door. It smells good. Past the third entrance and on to Flat 4: Polly and Todd's. I scan the scene below. Most of the police cars have gone but there's still a couple and several officers patrolling the perimeter. I take a moment to assimilate the fact that three murders have occurred in my village in the last few weeks. It's ghoulish, but I almost feel lucky in a weird, must-never-say-it-out-loud kind of way.

I knock for Polly but get no reply. I'd messaged ahead, she'd said it was fine to come over. I bang twice more at the rickety door. It feels so flimsy that even I, possessing the strength and coordination of a drunk centenarian, could probably kick it down if I really wanted to.

Finally, I see blurred movement rushing towards me from behind the textured glass. Polly opens the door only enough for her tiny skull to squeeze into the gap. The stare she gives me traps my tongue.

'Not now,' she pleads under her breath. She's shaking. 'He's already mad, been in a really weird mood all morning...'

'Who is it?' I hear a male voice, Todd's voice, call from inside.

'N... n... no one,' she answers over her shoulder before returning to face me. 'Please, he'll calm down eventually. Get off the porch in case he comes out.'

The door slams shut again and I do as I'm told, hurrying back down the steps and into the warmth of the sun. What on earth was that? I've never seen Polly so scared. Should I go back up and test just how fragile that door is? Should I go and tell the patrolling officers? I get back into my car and stay silent until my hands have stopped jittering. This day has packed enough punch to floor Muhammad Ali.

I look out of my car at the police van less than ten metres away. I could just ask a constable to go and check everything is OK at Flat 4? It wouldn't take them two minutes, and my conscience would be clear. But Polly hates not being in control of a situation. Despises it, in fact.

A particularly ugly memory careers into my mind. Polly and I had spoken for years about moving into a flat together and had finally settled on somewhere nearby in Heswall. We'd agreed terms with the landlord but hadn't signed yet. And then I got my job offer from the *Mirror*. There wasn't a question – I was going to take the post. Fleet Street is Fleet Street. But breaking the news to Pol was the one roadblock.

I sat her down and explained as sensitively as I could that this opportunity in London was one that wouldn't come around twice. She said nothing except that she understood, and left soon after. For a few hours I thought my tactful handling of the situation had succeeded.

Her grandad found her bleeding out, unconscious in the bath later that evening. Eight nights on a psychiatric ward followed. Whether she intended to commit suicide or not – her surgeon said the wounds were definitely deep enough to have killed her – it was my punishment for making a unilateral decision and enforcing it upon her.

Anyway, all that matters right now is that Polly will not cope well if police barge in and arrest her next of kin at my behest – which would make me, once again, the architect of her solitude. She could flip out. Or more likely, she'd close down, pretend everything was fine, then take it out on herself later.

I message her:

> What was that? Police are down by the woods. Want me to get them to knock on you? Want to stay with us tonight?

She replies instantly:

> All fine. Think he's falling asleep so will just stay quiet. Nothing to worry about. Talk soon xx

What more can I do? She claims she's fine; my immediate options are limited. I need time to process everything, to come up with a plan. So, at least for now, I choose to leave.

I should use the sudden bonus free time wisely. Now the Allcreek Woods killer has struck again, the note left on my car has become a part of a far bigger story, so word may very well reach Mum sooner rather than later. I'd rather tell her in person. She isn't going to like it, but trying to keep Mum happy is more difficult than dodging raindrops in a storm, so I might as well be honest and hope that mitigates whatever disapproval she has to dish out.

Taking my usual perch at the kitchen table, the whiff of the egg she boiled for her lunch hangs unappetising in the air. I explain the developments calmly and it takes her a while to absorb the seriousness of the incident. The information vies for her attention alongside the tea-making and biscuit-offering. At least she's boiled the water this time.

It's as she sits down that the full magnitude of it strikes… 'You need to stop reporting on it then, don't you?'

'No. I'm obviously getting too close for comfort. I can't let him off now. What if he keeps getting away with it because I give in?'

She dismisses the argument like cigarette ash flicked at the wind. Getting up again, she potters about, agitated. Blimey. Imagine how she'd have reacted if I'd mentioned the bloody rag in the glovebox, not just the note on the windscreen.

Barely taller than me even though I'm sitting down, she still somehow manages to exude that intimidating authority only your own parent can; a delicate twist of tone, a lengthy glare and I'm being yanked back to the tellings-off of yesteryear. 'It's the police's job to catch people like that, Kelli. You're being very foolish.'

I want to tell her I'm aware it's the police's job but that's the kind of attitude that would see Dick Monroe still roaming the streets. However, her eyes tell me she's still got a lot to say; and the sooner I let her finish, the sooner I can leave.

'Catching that horrible man was the worst thing that could have happened to you.' She's never said that before. 'Because now you think that's normal. That was a one-off Kelli. That isn't how the world works 99 per cent of the time. You're very enthusiastic and knowledgeable, but you need to drop this now... right now.'

'But I can help find who did it. I've proven—'

'Kel, I'm telling you this because I love you, but that kind of luck is never going to happen again.'

I can feel myself starting to shake, like a kettle with the on-switch taped down. 'Luck' she calls it. Not *extremely impressive detective work*. Not *a career-defining achievement*. Just dumb 'luck'! Fists tight, squeezing my knees together under the table, I need to keep the rage in. 'Agree to disagree,' I say, hardly able to see my surroundings as I fixate on escaping without saying anything I'll regret. Back in the hall I force my feet into my trainers, leaving the undone laces to drag underneath.

'Oh Kelli, please,' she sounds apologetic. 'Tell me what's wrong. You don't seem happy any more.'

'And what would you know about my happiness? If you want to see me, get on a bus, rather than guilt-tripping me into coming round when I'm fucking busy.'

'Don't use that language in my house!' She's less menacing now she's lost her composure. The shout slips towards a wobbly cry but she perseveres. 'I used to think you'd grow out of all this horrible stuff but it's going the other way. Ever since your father went to jail – that's when you started reading about psychopaths and bodies and crimes. You think I didn't notice. It's like you've decided that if you spend enough time studying murderers, you'll be able to work out if your father was one. Well, I can tell you without all your nasty books that your father was a good man. What he did was *not* murder!'

'I'm not talking about this.' I slam the front door and Mum doesn't open it again to chase me.

Of course it wasn't murder. Even the jury decided it wasn't. It's an insult to his memory that she'd even dare make the point out loud.

13

THE DAY OF THE SECOND DISCOVERY. EVENING.

I'm not usually much of a drinker, but today has been an emotional hurricane in a hellscape. Mum putting me through the judgmental mangle is the last straw. I raid Ben's drinks cupboard, stocked with all sorts of colourful and potent potions. Red wine will do. It's one he only uses for cooking, but I screw off the top and pour a small glass.

Straight down the hatch.

It goes to my head immediately. This is why I never drink at home; with nothing to focus on except a television or a book, alcohol makes me queasy. And I haven't eaten anything all day – that can't be helping. But if the room has to spin a little for some relief to take hold, then so be it. In fact, the room can swirl like a Waltzer if it helps me forget about today.

I pour a second, larger glass, carry the bottle into the lounge and join Ben watching TV.

* * *

Waking alone in the lounge is as disorientating as it is scary. Mercifully, Ben's left the light on in here but he's turned all the others off – the hall, the kitchen, the landing. My head is throbbing. Why did I get the wine out? It's 12.20 a.m. When did I fall asleep?

The evening was a blur, basking in the fickle security of pinot noir and my boyfriend's warm embrace. Both those crutches are gone now.

The TV's turned off too, so I put it back on and keep the volume low. I don't like how dark it is in the doorway to the hall, because just beyond it is the spot she's always calling from when I'm walking upstairs to bed. I know it's not real, that she can't be there. That Dick throttled all life out of her. But when her choked yelps, bulbous eyes and mottled face return to me every night, suspending me in abject terror, what's the difference between reality and imagination?

There's a small U-shaped bone in the throat called the hyoid that fractures in about one third of strangulations – when the attack is particularly savage. Pathologists found the hyoid had been broken in all eight of The White Widower victims. These were brutal ends for these women. Brutal to endure. Brutal to witness.

Maybe that's why the thought of her flailing and scrabbling at the brushed oak floorboards in my hallway will not recede until I go out there and turn the hall light on. But right now, I can't bring myself to move any closer for fear she'll bolt forward and subsume me.

Poor, poor Janice Benson. Could I have saved her? That's the thought that smacks me in the jaw every single day. That's the deepest thing cleaving at my conscience when I go to see Dick in jail. Should I loathe him out of respect for her? I don't feel the same debt to the other victims, I never met them. But I heard the last words she ever said, as Dick's grip tightened.

'STOP IT! STOP IT! PLEASE!'

It didn't happen exactly how I told police, how I told Annabelle Ludgate. Janice wasn't dead when I got there, I didn't phone the police from the shadows. I heard her scream from the other side of the timber yard and rushed towards the noise. That's where I found them, illuminated by a car's main beams: a huge bald man hulking over a terrified, helpless woman. But I didn't run in to fight him off, I hid behind a stack of wooden pallets, frozen in fear and shock. She screamed and she screamed.

I peered at them, plotting what I'd tell police. I'd give them a clear description of the killer, I'd give them his number plate, I'd claim I turned up just as he was leaving. Already making my excuses while an innocent woman lay dying. What kind of vile human does that?! The screaming shrank to choking which shrank to nothing. Janice stopped thrashing. I retreated behind my cover. Minutes passed as I pleaded silently for him to leave.

But instead...

'You can come out now.' Those are the first words The White Widower ever spoke to me. The fright struck like thunder. He'd seen me! I was done for – the next victim. I steeled myself to scream until my lungs bled. I stayed hiding, praying I'd misheard.

'Are you police?' he asked louder, but not sounding any closer. He wasn't coming for me, he was just talking, still out of breath from his exertions.

'Yes,' I'd lied.

Then he'd laughed. 'No you're not.' I remember liking his accent already, despite adrenalin coursing through me so intensely I felt dizzy. I'd just witnessed a murder, I'd just found The White Widower. I'd just talked to him. It felt like a dream – not a straight-forward nice one, but something too sudden and abrupt to be real. 'A copper wouldn't have let me finish the job,' he'd added. Even in that moment, he was so alert, so smart.

For some reason, the way he talked made me not scared any more. I moved into the clear. He looked at me, reassured me he wouldn't come any closer, then told me I should phone the police. He's told me since that he knew there and then his reign was over. He'd been found. He could try to escape, but realistically, if he was being tracked right up to the scene of the crime, his time was up. I made the call, the call Rob Grayson knows I didn't make the way I made out. Dick slumped against the front of his car as I did it, staring mostly at Janice.

But critically, I'd frozen as she'd died. Could I have saved her? Maybe if I had tried to interrupt him half-way through, he *would* have killed me too; I could've met the same fate as the rest; then he could have got away to kill again and again. I brought Dick in, that's what I need to focus on – I made the killing stop. So why doesn't it feel like any kind of achievement?

Mum of three, fifty-four years old. Her eldest, Tanya, was expecting at the time, Janice was going to be a grandmother. Her husband, Peter, a paramedic, was sixty-one and thinking of retiring. A perfect family – destroyed by Dick Monroe, and possibly by me.

I hear a low thud from upstairs, not an imaginary thud, a real one. I mute the TV. I'm begging my heart to stop pounding so I can zero in on any other noise, but it keeps booming regardless. There's a long silence from upstairs, and I'm just about to forget the commotion when I hear our bedroom door open way above me and footsteps creak down the steps. It'll be Ben going down to the second floor to use the loo, I tell myself. But the footsteps don't stop there, they come down another flight.

There's a trunk on the landing on the first floor, the click of it opening echoes into the lounge. We keep all sorts of tat in that trunk: old boardgames, gadgets, comics, some of Ben's blunted old chef's knives – we really should just chuck everything in there away.

'Ben?' I call from beneath my blanket – mummified in torment under Egyptian cotton.

Shouting into the blackness of the hall is excruciating when all I want to do is stay silent, but as long as he replies I can relax. I might ask him to come downstairs under the pretence of wanting a drink, but then get him to put the hall light on.

He doesn't reply.

'Ben?' I try a little louder. Still nothing. This is strange, what could he possibly need from that trunk in the middle of the night? And what was that thud?

The steps shrink away up the stairs again, slow and plodding. I can just about make out the sound of our bedroom door brushing over the thick cut pile carpet as it closes again.

I don't like it; Ben would never ignore me, and if I can hear the click of our bedroom door shutting three floors away, whoever it was on the landing definitely will have heard me calling from half that distance. My pulse is racing away with my darkest thoughts.

I keep picturing those old knives in that stupid trunk. And the thud from upstairs. Ben told me earlier not to leave any windows open until his surveillance kit arrives, but I left the first floor one open at lunchtime – it was so hot and stuffy. What if someone climbing in through that window is what woke me up? What if they've gone upstairs and Ben is lying there bleeding to death? What if, like with Janice, I am simply standing by, doing nothing to help, using trepidation as a cheap excuse for inaction?

The bedroom door opens again to more creaking footsteps. They stop at the bathroom on the second floor this time, then the rush of a water tap, the hum of it always squeals through the pipes, announcing to the whole house that someone's up there. But it's only a tap, no toilet flush.

I'm freaking out. A scuffle in the bedroom, a knife retrieved from the trunk, back to the bedroom to finish the job, and then to the sink to clean up.

'BEN? BEN?' I scream, still clinging to the hope that he will answer and everything will be OK. But there is still no response.

I rush through the black hall and into the kitchen as I hear the bedroom door shut once more. Ben's newer knife block sits next to the sink, I pluck out the largest blade in the set.

There's no time to turn the lights on as I go, so I rush past my demons, emboldened by the weapon in my hand and my urgency to reach the top of the house. The murderer, they've got to Ben. The rag *was* a warning.

In the blackness I stumble up to the final staircase. I need to be ready as soon as I open the door, they'll have heard me approaching. Be decisive – duck if they come straight for me, then plunge the knife in between their ribs.

There's the glow of the main light coming from under the door. I'll turn it off as soon as I burst in, that should catch them off-guard.

I'm on the landing now; no time for a deep breath or a fortifying pep talk. Carving knife pointing up in my right hand, I twist open the knob with my left and then slap my palm against the switch on the wall.

14

THE DAY OF THE SECOND DISCOVERY. NIGHT.

There's a split-second before the light cuts out, giving me just enough time to see Ben's petrified face staring at me from the bed, his headphones in, his Game Boy out. He's totally alone.

As I lose his eyes in the sudden darkness, their shock is replaced by his cry. I drop the knife and fall to my knees.

* * *

I'm in the lounge, all the lights are on. Ben's pacing back and forth, still quivering. My head's in my hands and I'm crying with every ounce of energy I have. I am upset, mortified even, but my loud sobbing has as much to do with extracting sympathy as with genuine turmoil. Ben is well within his rights to kick me out; the pity card's all I have left.

'I'm sorry, I'm sorry!' I wail. 'Why didn't you answer me? I called out!'

'I had my headphones in!'

'But what was that thud?'

'I'd knocked over my water. Then I thought I wouldn't get straight back to sleep so went to get my Game Boy out for a bit!'

This has got him rattled good and proper. Fair play for limiting his anxiety to pacing; if *he'd* come up to bed and switched off the light while wielding an eight-inch carving knife, I'd be washing soiled sheets and ordering him a straitjacket off Amazon. Same-day delivery.

'Things aren't right,' he says after an eternity. 'You're hallucinating or something. This case is frying your brain.'

So far, so accurate.

He goes on. 'I wasn't going to say anything, but when I came home after Thursday night and came to bed, you got up again. You were chuntering about something, I couldn't make it out. But then you walked off downstairs and didn't come back up for ages. Like an hour. It was like you were sleepwalking again.'

'Shit,' I reply. I don't remember any of this. 'That might be the pills.'

'Pills?' Ben cries. As horrendous as my day was yesterday with the bloody rag, Rob Grayson and Mum, Ben's *night* has arguably been worse.

'They're to help me sleep, especially when you're not here.'

'Why?'

'Because I can't sleep in an empty house.'

'But you never said.'

'What am I supposed to say?' I feel a glimmer of injustice, as if I'm at fault for not wanting to burden him with my stupid phobias, and for not wanting him to feel guilty about going out to play music which he obviously loves doing.

'How am I supposed to help you if you don't tell me?' he says, exasperation muscling into his voice.

'I can't tell you!'

'TELL ME! TELL ME!' he screams, louder than I've ever heard him speak before.

'You want me to tell you?' I spit, marching over and opening the front door. 'Your car,' I say, striding towards the vehicle barefoot and pointing a righteous finger towards it. 'Before I even park up, I'm faced with the exact same model of Toyota van that the World's End killer, Angus Sinclair, used to rape and murder at least four girls in Scotland.'

I walk back to the front steps and face the house, my hands outstretched. I speak loudly, not caring if Mildred hears me. 'Then the corner of the house has the same weird circular windows as HH Holmes' Murder Castle in Chicago. He killed more than 200. And I'm still not even inside.'

The light does go on upstairs over the fence as I stomp back up the steps and slam the front door shut again. Ben's static in the hall but he can't take his eyes off me.

'The first thing I expect to see when I get inside is the BTK killer, primed with rope and a knife, waiting for me at the kitchen table. If I do venture into there then I can see Jack The Ripper victim Mary Jane Kelly's mutilated, faceless carcass in the window, as if I'm staring out into her room in Whitechapel.'

Back into the hall where Ben still hasn't moved.

'Right where you're standing, staring up through the whole house, screaming for help is Janice Benson.'

'Kel don't do this...'

'The fun continues upstairs,' I butt in. If he wants to know what I'm going through he's going to have to stay for the whole tour. We reach the first landing and I kick that disgusting old trunk. 'Tony Mancini used one very similar to hide his girlfriend's body in Brighton in 1934. There's a picture of her battered corpse squashed into the trunk which I find hard to shake whenever I see this thing.'

I kick it again, less in anger than to symbolically chalk it off my list of demons, then carry on up the stairs. Ben is walking behind, looking nervous. I'm unravelling and he doesn't know how to stop it.

Up to the third floor. 'I have no idea why, but whenever I reach here, I have the overwhelming feeling that Ted Bundy is about to abduct me, rape me and then decapitate me. But we persevere. And the whole time I can hear Janice from the ground floor, always... fucking... screaming.' I don't care any more if he works out that I saw Janice alive, I'm past caring about anything. 'I reach the bedroom door, open it, and a sleeve from your dressing gown on the back of the door wafts into my way as if an intruder's trying to push me back down the stairs.'

I'm in hysterics now. 'Then, even once I'm in our room I have to walk around your extra pillow next to the bed which looks a lot like the white bag JonBenét Ramsey was found stuffed into in her parents' basement aged six in Boulder, Colorado.'

Ben's exhausted frame finally joins me in the bedroom. We're both crying.

'And last of all...' I whimper while pointing out of the bedroom window, '...that little pond by the trees in Mildred's garden – it's just like the one Dad used to drown a paedophile after catching him trying to molest my brother. He beat the man unconscious, then held his head underwater for a full eleven minutes, just to make sure he could never hurt Danny again. It's the anniversary of that day in a couple of weeks.'

I'm panting for breath. Ben stands, eyes streaming, but speechless.

I clear my throat. '*That's* why I can't sleep. You happy? That's why I bought some pills so I can at least knock myself out – give myself a few hours off from the horrors lurking behind every corner in this house.'

'It's not this house Kel. It's you! You think if you moved, you'd feel safer? No chance! You bring all that evil in by consuming it twenty-four hours a day. It's poisoned reality, and yet you keep going back. You're injecting that shit into every vein, and then you wonder why it all comes oozing back out.'

'Oh right, thanks for the support. I told you so you'd understand but all you've got is judgmental potshots.'

'I'm not judging, Kel. But you need to take some responsibility. Either you want to get better, or you want to keep forcing this dark stuff in – you can't do both.'

I crumble in a heap on the bed. The tears are genuine this time. I know he's right. He's told me, Mum's told me. The people I love most, they aren't here to ruin my life, they want to save it. Increasingly I've been wondering if it's even worth saving. Why should I be here when Janice isn't? But after all that's happened this evening, the fact Ben still comes over and is now letting me weep into his shoulder makes me feel closer to him than I ever have before.

'Please don't leave me,' I say, half cringing at the cliché, half desperate for the reassurance.

'I won't,' he replies, squeezing me closer and kissing my head. 'I won't.'

* * *

We stay up, discussing how I got to the point I'm at now – a woman so scared in her own home that she almost mortally wounded her boyfriend as he sat in bed playing Pokémon. I tell Ben about what my mum said about the killer obsession starting when Dad went to jail. Ben thinks that makes sense. He says that of all the ways daughters could react to their father being found guilty of killing someone, becoming interested in serial killers is one of the least selfish or emotionally crippling things I could have done. 'You didn't turn into a bully, or start taking drugs, you just distracted yourself with something that became a fascination... a passion.'

As a rule, I hate the idea of looking to anyone else for affirmation, but as I sit on the bed, his acceptance feels vital.

We have an adult discussion, me on one side explaining that if I cut out every single book, TV programme, podcast, potential story that has an element of death, I'll have nothing left. Ben is measured – the more I can cut out, at least for the moment, the clearer my head will be to plot something realistic and achievable for the coming months and years, rather than making short-term after short-term destructive choices forever.

We compromise. I'll keep going on the Allcreek Woods story but in the evenings I won't read or listen to or watch any true crime content. He wants me to stop visiting Dick too but that's a sacrifice too far. I am still fiercely determined to get an answer on Victim Number Nine for my book.

I do tell him the truth about Janice Benson though – she was still alive when I found her, but Dick was in the process of throttling her and I'd frozen. Knowing this would sound weaker, I'd lied to the officers and told them she was already dead when I found her and Dick. Ben says he understands totally.

It's about 4 a.m. by the time we get under the covers, lying down but still cradling each other, conversation slowing and slowing, until our mouths fall shut; our eyes follow soon after.

15

ONE DAY SINCE THE SECOND DISCOVERY. A.M.

Cranking open an eyelid, my bedside clock reads 11 a.m. I've got two missed calls from Martin at the *Mirror*; he can wait.

Ben's not in bed. I pull on my dressing gown and clomp downstairs to the kitchen.

'Coffee?' he asks as I pull up a seat at the table.

I nod, too dozy to manage words.

Ben pulls a newspaper off Mary Jane Kelly's windowsill and slaps it down next to me. 'Saturday 9 July. The day Kelli Amari got her byline back in the *Daily Mirror!*'

My story! Eager fingers fumble as I flick open the paper, and there it is – page 5 as promised.

The headline is in huge bold sans serif letters across the whole page:

Three killed in woods as police hunt…
THE NAILER

My heart leaps. That's his nickname! Short, catchy, chilling. It's even hashtag-able. Perfect. The hunt will catch fire today – I saw the same thing happen dozens of times on big stories in London. One paper breaks a creepy story, a day later every crime hack worth their salt is scrambling to catch up, desperate to be seen as the authority on the case.

A large photo of Allcreek Woods teeming with police dominates the middle of the page. The main text hugs a column to the left of the photo then runs across the bottom two inches of the paper. My byline sits above the copy, completed by a little box with my face in, the same headshot of me they used when I worked there.

Seeing my byline in print is a thrill I'd truly missed, and everything else about this little achievement seems even more special for having happened organically on the Wirral, rather than being handed to me on a plate by the news desk.

OK, the bodies might be piling up right on my doorstep, that's obviously fortuitous. But *I've* made it into headline news.

I look back at my phone. Anna's seen my story and sent me a photo of herself with the paper and three fire emojis. What a babe.

I'm still replying to her when Martin tries to ring again. I take the call.

'You're back in the game!' he cheers.

'Thank you,' I say, that frisson of desire I still hold for him bubbles up in my chest.

'I mean, it wouldn't have got in without me, but you played a minor role,' he taunts, before laughing at his own joke. 'Anyway, Amari. Now you've signed off on the retainer, the boss wants blood. What's your Day 2?'

'I think we need to dip into your database again. If I can get a name for these two new bodies, I might finally get some family quotes, that's what the Maurice Williams stuff lacked. No collect pics, no background.'

'Sounds ideal. If not, just pump the police for as much info as possible, and try to get stuff off the record they aren't feeding out in the press releases so we can stay ahead.'

'I have done journalism before.' Prick.

'Ha! OK, OK. Oh, just so you know, I've pitched a comment piece to go along with the news lead too for tomorrow's edition.'

'Really? Will that work?'

'Went down a treat in conference apparently.'

'Which columnist?'

'Well, funny you ask...'

I can hear that smug tone he's so fond of and can very well picture the grin slapped across his gorgeous face. 'You're not being let loose on a column!'

'My idea is to let readers know how you called me during the week, adamant Maurice Williams wasn't a one off, that it was the start of something bigger. And how your instincts were bang on. And how extraordinary it is that you outsmarted Dick Monroe, who had the police chasing their tails, and now you're doing the same weird 'psycho whisperer' schtick again with The Nailer.'

'One step at a time,' I say.

'That's enough smoke up your arse, though. Get the names of the victims and we'll take it from there.'

When I call Detective Superintendent Vickers it transpires he's planning to release the names live on TV to coincide with the one o'clock bulletins – if there's one thing Vickers is good at detecting, it's opportunities to keep himself in the public eye. Nevertheless, it does mean he's happy to pass the victims' names on to me 'as long as they aren't on Twitter before one'. As if I'd do that! I only have about seven followers anyway, and at least six of them are Russian bots.

Donna Smyth and Harry Bancroft. Donna is the body that's been rotting for a fortnight, part of the same homeless horde as Maurice – but Harry Bancroft is very much not from that cohort.

'Lad was twenty-two, had a posh grey coat on and skinny jeans when he was found by the walker. As for Donna Smyth, let's just say she was known to police. But you can gauge how much family she has around by the fact she went missing for two weeks and no one missed her,' Vickers gabbles at machine gun pace.

'So this other lad, the one who was killed on Thursday night, he was what? Middle class?'

'Given the size of his dad's house in Caldy, I'd say he was from wealthy stock, yeah. Think he wandered into the woods wrecked, several people saw him staggering out of The Mill pissed around last orders. And just between you and me, we found some cannabis on him. Don't report that though, the family don't need that in the papers.'

Vickers penchant for oversharing really is astonishing given his line of work.

'Nah, don't worry,' I promise. 'He's the victim, wouldn't fit the narrative anyway. But shit, a middle-class boy being killed...'

'He was twenty-two, not a boy.'

'Still, you know what I mean, that gives the story a boost.'

'If that's how you want to phrase it,' he says. 'I hear you were at the crime scene pretty pronto yesterday morning.'

'Not as quick as Grayson.'

'Yes, he is very sharp. He rings the press office five times a day to check he isn't missing anything apparently.'

'Has he been given the names yet?'

'No.'

'Let him find out at 1 p.m. with everyone else then. Pretty please!'

'Amari at her tricks again... OK, as it's you! But this is the last favour. Grayson is a good guy.'

I could kiss him!

'So anyway, Kel,' he goes on. 'Have *you* got an alibi for Thursday night?'

There's a pause. *No.* That's the word that comes to mind: *No.* But as I don't want to say that, the silence draws out a little too long. 'I'm only pulling your leg!' Vickers roars down the phone.

'I know, you cheeky so and so...' I recover to force a chuckle. 'You need to catch them though, I don't want any more notes on my car please.'

'Let's see what we can do.'

The news that one of the victims is a 'normal person' gets Martin even more excited. And sure enough, there's a single hit for a family living in Caldy with the last name of Bancroft. I'm actually going to have to do this.

* * *

Caldy is a 15-minute drive away, and it really is posh. Houses the size of aircraft hangers. Ben's four-bedroom, four-storey semi would be dismissed as a beggar's hovel here.

I turn onto the cul-de-sac. Each monolith has its own ostentatious metal gate and the six-foot-tall garden walls that line the pavement are all red sandstone, a local signature. Harry Bancroft's dad lives at number 8. I pull up outside in my old Peugeot – the definition of riff-raff – and reach into the glove box. That monstrous glove box – another location which will now forever be cursed by evil thoughts. I really need to find a quiet moment to bleach the life out of it, to annihilate any traces of blood. But that will have to wait.

For now, I retrieve from the drawer a tiny plastic container, about the size of a hotel shampoo bottle. I give it a shake then unscrew the pipette lid and lift the tube up, letting three fat drops of the homemade liquid fall into my right eye. It smarts, like *really* smarts. Three parts water to one part lemon juice. A grunt seeps out as I try to blink the pain away before cocking my neck again and repeating the trick in my left eye. I give myself a second for the streaming to stop then dab my face with the loose shoulder of my dress.

It's a trick a veteran agency reporter taught me in London. If you show up to a death knock and it looks like you've been crying, the chance of the homeowner taking pity and letting you in goes up exponentially. They never tend to ask *why* you've been crying, but the fact you're there about their loved one and almost all of their mind is being taken up by that person's death usually leads them subconsciously to thinking you've been weeping about the same thing. It's not a technique male reporters can use though – if a man turns up at a death knock with bleary, tear-soaked eyes it looks like he's there to confess.

I've gone mascara-less to limit the mess, but my tin-box car is baking me alive, and sweat is starting to swell behind my foundation so I get out. There's a buzzer at the gates. I need to get to the front door of the actual house, if possible, the lemon juice tears aren't going to work over a microphone. I move towards the gates and give them a rattle, one hand on each side of the divide, but no luck. There are three cars on the driveway – two 4x4s and a bottle-green sporty one – all sparkling clean in the punishing sunshine. But more importantly, a congested driveway suggests someone's home.

I go back to the buzzer and take a deep breath. This will be my first death knock since leaving the *Mirror*, partly because the opportunity hasn't arisen, but mainly because I avoid them like the plague.

Imagine the darkest, most painful, confusing, sudden end someone could possibly meet: a stabbing, a shooting, found hanged, ecstasy overdose, car crash, drowning abroad. Then imagine that's happened to the person you love more than anyone else in the world, the person you'd planned to spend the rest of your days with, or had sacrificed your life to bring up. Imagine the bouts of despair, anger and grief all smothering you. Imagine as all that's happening, as the fabric of your world is still collapsing, that you receive a knock at the door from a stranger. Imagine that stranger is demanding every grubby detail about the death, wanting every last secret about your relationship and asking for copies of photographs from your loved-one's school days, wedding day, holidays – not because they care, but because they want to plaster it all over a newspaper or website or TV bulletin so you can be tomorrow's tittle-tattle. That's the abominable corner of journalism that death knocks occupy.

I take a deep breath, push the buzzer and wait. Maybe he won't answer. Please don't answer. I plead with the intercom to remain mute.

But then the speaker coughs out a burst of static and a strained, groggy voice mutters, 'Hello?'

I stay silent.

16

ONE DAY SINCE THE SECOND DISCOVERY. P.M.

'Hello?' the voice pushes.

I hold my nerve.

'Hello? I can see you out there.'

I try the buzzer once more and hear it echo back at me from the speaker.

The static drops again and I wait. Moment of truth, this either works or it doesn't. I'm still praying it doesn't.

But then the rattle of a key in a door draws my eyes over to the porch and a grey-faced man, stooped and confused, comes plodding towards me, stare fixed on this intruder at his gate.

'Hello?' He says afresh as he reaches the threshold, little more than a metre between us now.

'Hello, so sorry to bother you. Are you Colin Bancroft?' My voice is weaker, more reverent than usual. Anything to bring his guard down. I didn't want this interview to happen, but now it's in motion there's a whole tool box of tricks to use.

'I am,' he says, as if his countenance doesn't give it away. Desolation personified.

'Hello, Mr Bancroft. I'll be very brief as I'm sure you have far more important things to do. I'm here on behalf of the *Daily Mirror*, and just wondered if you'd like to give a tribute to your son.' I'm right up at the gate now.

'I don't think I'm up to speaking to anyone at the moment, sorry. Maybe leave your number and I'll get back to you. Harry used to pick up the *Mirror* occasion...' The father tails off and squeezes his chin up towards his lips, making an exaggerated frown as he tries and succeeds in keeping the grief inside.

But leaving a number isn't good enough when Rob Grayson could have his dirty tentacles all over the family by teatime.

'Oh, Mr Bancroft, I'm so sorry. Look, could I just check a couple of things then. Harry was twenty-two, yes?' Police have already confirmed it but I need to keep him talking if I'm going to slither between the bars of this cast iron gate.

'Twenty-two, yeah,' Mr Bancroft nods, swallowing hard.

'And was he staying with a friend in Newton on Thursday, or was he due to be coming back here?'

'Urm...' His eyes meet mine. That tiny glimmer of consciousness that's not paralysed by his son's death isn't sure how to compute the manufactured tears I've been crying. 'I dunno. He's here mostly but stays at mates' places sometimes.'

'I see, I see. One last thing Mr Bancroft. I'm afraid there is going to be a story about the deaths in Allcreek Woods going in the paper tomorrow. And at the moment the picture of Harry that's going to be used is off his Instagram.' I have no idea if Harry Bancroft had an Instagram account, but surely he did. Or at least his father can't be sure his son didn't. 'If there is a picture you'd prefer us to use, then that may be one thing I could do to make the tiniest bit of difference at this horrible time for you and the family.'

His mop of silver hair flops as he shakes his head. He runs a hand over the stubble he's amassed over two days of not shaving. It's crunch time, am I in or out?

'Yeah, OK. I know the picture I want. Found it last night.'

He taps in a code on the keypad on his side of the gate; it swings into life.

The next five minutes are easy. Once you're inside, social convention dictates the host can't force you out too eagerly, and small talk must be maintained in the meantime. Small talk, which very often gets published in national newspapers afterwards. That's the skill of the best reporters – leading a conversation in the exact direction you want, without the interviewee even aware they're being interviewed.

I get three gorgeous photos of Harry Bancroft. One of him at school, one of him with both parents before his mother died and one with his twin brother at their joint 21st last year.

Quotes aplenty, Mr Bancroft walks me back to the gate to let me out.

'I really appreciate this, Mr Bancroft. But it must be such an ordeal having people coming and distracting you so I do apologise.'

'Don't worry, thanks for understanding,' he says – still probably under the impression he's not said anything worth printing in tomorrow's paper. To avoid arousing suspicion I've left my notepad in the car but as soon as I'm out of view I'm going to have to scribble down every last thing the father's said while it's still fresh in my head.

'One thing to do if it gets too much would be to stick a Post-it note over your intercom, buzzer thingy,' I say, playing ditzy as a pitiful substitute for innocence. 'You could write "no unsolicited callers at this time". I know as a journalist, I always respect the family's wishes if they do ask to be left in peace.'

'Yes, good idea. Thanks,' he mutters, head bent forward counting his feet.

'Thank you, Mr Bancroft.' I pack a final smile full of solace and he meets my eyes for a split second. Then he turns on his haunches as the gate closes between us.

Back in the car and notes all frantically scribbled, my phone call to Martin comes as soon as I've started the engine.

'Pictures, good quotes, Mum's dead, twin brother. Full package.'

'Really?' Martin squeals with joy. 'This will be page 5 again, no doubt at all. Maybe even the front.'

* * *

I've filed my copy by 2 p.m. and then another hour bleeds away as I watch my previous story roll round again and again on the news channel. I'm not mentioned by name but the BBC bulletins do at least refer to the story 'that appeared in this morning's *Daily Mirror*'. Not in the *Echo*, Rob. The *Mirror*. I hope he spots that.

And then the rest of my day is my own. I'm freelance now. No pesky news desk request trying to eke another couple of hours out of me because I'm on the books. I've provided my story for the day, therefore they'll pay me. I can spend the rest of the time as I please.

Ben's upstairs on his guitar. It's too late to go and see Dick this afternoon though, that's what the warders explain when I call trying to book a last-minute visit. I text Polly and Anna instead to see if they fancy meeting up. Anna's snowed under with work but Polly's up for it.

She suggests going for a walk somewhere, but I'm in no mood for unnecessary exercise so insist on Keen Beans café in the heart of the village. She agrees but asks if we can meet in an hour.

That leaves me time to give the glovebox that deep-clean. Toilet bleach, J cloth and rubber gloves. I also take a bin bag out with me. And on closer inspection my hunch is proved right – everything in the drawer has brown-red streaks on. All tarnished, all need to go: the Wirral A to Z atlas, the torch, the Snickers bar and the little lemon juice bottle. The tissues I wiped my hand on to get rid of the stain are already in the bin bag too. Even the spare set of car keys I'd put in there. I'll have to make do with just one set now, can't risk any trace being left behind.

It's so muggy the air's sweating. A smell like swimming pool chlorine fills the car as I squirt the bleach liberally – I cannot leave an atom of blood on the inside of this vehicle. After what feels like an inordinate amount of time scrubbing, I shut the empty glove box and give the outside of the compartment the same treatment.

The Peugeot sucks in more and more summer heat; countless wet beads abseil down my back as all attempts to mop my brow are dashed by the marigolds clinging to my forearms, and the fact the crook of my elbow is just as oily as my forehead.

Out of the car, I tug off the gloves and throw them in the bin bag along with the J cloth. My eyes are shut as I sit down and rest my back against the rear passenger door, enjoying the feeling of a wispy breeze running between my fingers.

I slump there, recuperating for a while. However, no sooner have I reopened my eyes, then I'm snapping back to my feet, ramrod straight like a meerkat. Moody Mildred is staring at me from her upstairs window, her glare containing the usual ingredients of sourness and suspicion. I produce the fakest of smiles and offer a little wave, at which point she flounces away again, her blow-dried coiffure bobbing after her. Off to chant an incantation about me over a cauldron, no doubt. Old crone.

* * *

I don't dump the bag of bloody, bleachy crap in with our own rubbish. Instead, I drive off out of Irby and on to the old estate Polly's Grandad used to live on, about a mile down the road. It's an unwelcoming cluster of council houses, with much of the street twinkling with a frosting of broken glass. But it's also a place where bulging bin bags are discarded on the pavement just as readily as cigarette butts. An extra one carefully left *in* a wheelie bin isn't going to trouble anyone. I find a suitable culprit at the edge of one front garden, lean over the wall and pop my little sack of goodies in.

Back in Newton I park up outside Polly's, walk around the back of her flat and take a good look at the woods. Police are still circling but all villagers and news presence has evaporated.

I make it to Keen Beans before her; the weather is too warm for a cappuccino so I select a can of San Pellegrino Lemon. It's ice-cool to the touch and I roll it across my forehead, enjoying a moment's peace, free of distractions and angst. There's not much else to look forward to for the rest of today. I'm not allowed to read any true crime books or watch any fascinating documentaries when I get home this evening. Ben's new rules. I can read his complete works of Sherlock Holmes – a compromise I had to fight for – or I can read 'normal thrillers' and watch 'normal TV'. What tedium!

Polly slinks in a couple of minutes later and sits down without ordering and without saying anything. Nothing new there, she can be a mardy cow when she wants to be. But my metal stool scrapes against the polished floor as I look up at her and flinch.

'What the fuck?'

Her left eye is purple. I already know why. I don't want to know, but I do.

'Urgh, stupid really. I was walking early this morning, got out about seven. And I was halfway up Frankby Road when I tripped. Bashed my face on a car's wing mirror.'

I stare back. She can tell me – maybe not out loud – but with a look. She needs to tell me, so I know. So I can help. Todd must check her phone. That's why she wouldn't say anything over text yesterday after she shooed me away. She must know it's better to tell me though, or to hint. Has he just started doing this, or has it been going on longer?

Thoughts are coming and going, stopping and speeding around my head like cars at spaghetti junction. But I'm holding her gaze.

Then, eventually, horribly, her non-bruised eye begins to reflect the room a little more. She blinks and brushes the sleeve of her baggy white cotton top tenderly over the tear to stop it falling.

I try to intimate that I know, that I've understood, but without betraying her by blurting the words out.

'What's Todd doing today?' I finally ask, hoping that's subtle enough.

She pulls a tissue from her pocket, blows her nose and then smiles at me as if to say thank you for sticking to the rules of her silence. 'Had to run some people to the airport in the night so he's still in bed.'

It looks awful. He must have struck the top of her cheek bone as the lump is all underneath the lower lid, squashing the eye shut. The puce, rough swelling makes me wince. The colour suggests it was done yesterday rather than this morning, otherwise it would still be red. I've heard enough pathologists talking about bruising to fill a ten-hour lecture. This is a 'yesterday bruise'.

It's hard to manufacture any conversation but Polly just about keeps us talking about other things. 'I saw that policeman Vickers on the news. I'd never heard of any of the victims,' she says.

'Have you picked up a *Daily Mirror* today?' I can't help but reply.

She hasn't so I fish my copy out of my shoulder bag and do the honours of opening it to page 5.

'The Nailer?' she ponders. 'I suppose so.'

'And tomorrow it's going to be a spread with a news story from me and a feature from Martin about my nose for psychopaths.'

Polly laughs. 'You and your nose, eh? So have you got an alibi sorted for all these murders yet?' she asks, finding some mischief.

'I...' That same awkward feeling I had when Vickers asked chokes me again. 'I don't really – haven't really thought about it.'

'Well that was about as convincing as Hollyoaks.' She flicks her hair away from her face for the first time. Her long blonde tresses had been worn down with a central parting, curving round both sides of her face – most likely to cover a lot of her black eye.

We force ourselves to chat a little longer but I can't keep the charade up.

'Polly, come back to ours tonight. You can't go back there.'

The shutters come down, the same ones that slam into the ground every time I mention her lack of work or her grandad or anything of consequence. 'I don't know what you mean,' she states.

'Pol, you can't just pretend—'

She stands up and interrupts, 'I better go.'

A ball of rage bulges in my throat. I want to scream at her to get real, that the abuse isn't going to stop unless she takes it seriously, unless she lets me help her. But, as always, she's up and gone before I can begin to form any kind of cogent argument.

* * *

Back at the ranch I tell Ben about Polly's eye. He's sensible about it.

'You should message her again, tell her she can call anytime. Something vague in case he *is* checking her phone,' Ben says. 'And maybe try to meet up with her every couple of days to make sure nothing else has happened. But you'd have to be really sure before interfering. Because imagine she *did* hit her eye by accident and you go tellin—'

'And the bruise I saw on her arm the other day?' I point out.

'All I'm saying is, try to keep her safe from afar for now. Don't go charging to her rescue before she's ready.'

Having someone set the boundaries is far more welcome than I'll ever admit. Ben's measured advice on both Polly and my preoccupation with degeneracy is all too easy to take.

With that in mind I sit down on the sofa and haul open his *Complete Works of Sherlock Holmes*. Ben pulled the book out of that horrible Brighton trunk on the first-floor landing and brought it down while I was out, which is kind of him since it weighs as much as a breeze block.

I'm begrudgingly content to settle for Baker Street's finest because there's something inspiring about him. A consulting detective – I'd love to be that. An oracle who the police come to for case-cracking insights. Or would it be more fun to have that extraordinary ability, but then use it to get away with murders rather than solve them? What a feeling that would be. What's the ultimate achievement – outsmarting the world or improving it? Maybe I'm Moriarty, not Holmes.

Either way, after what I've put Ben through, the idea of being transported back to Victorian London for a few evenings doesn't sound too bad as a punishment. And if I get bored, I'll just knock back a couple of my Roxion sleeping pills and end the evening there and...

I stop.

A bullet rips through me. A clean shot of nausea-inducing, reality-obliterating, feral panic.

No.

No, no, no.

I'm suddenly hot, cold and numb all at the same time.

Retrieving my phone from my pocket, I Google 'Sleepwalk side effects triazolam'.

The top search result – from a medical encyclopaedia – drags me further into the abyss:

Triazolam may cause you to do things while you are still asleep that you may not remember the next morning. It is possible you could drive a car, have sex, make phone calls, go shopping, or prepare and eat food while you are asleep or not fully awake.

No. Three bodies. I'd remember *something*. Wouldn't I?

I sit in silence for a long time, utterly still, straining every cell inside me to summon a recollection. But it's like opening your eyes in a pitch-black room – it's not just that I can't make out precise images, there's not even a silhouette of a memory that emerges.

I can't be involved.

And yet I have no alibi. Ben does have his dad's nail gun. He's seen me sleepwalking a lot after taking my pills. If anyone's subconscious is capable of lurching to such grim fantasies while dreaming, it's going to be mine.

And the bloody rag. That bloody, grisly rag. Who else would know my car was open? I'm the only person who ever stores anything in there.

I stand up but feel woozy. Ben appears at the door and tries to say something; I can't make out the words as everything goes dark and I accelerate down a helter-skelter to oblivion.

17

ONE DAY SINCE THE SECOND DISCOVERY. EVENING.

Ben's stroking my head when I come to, lying on the sofa.

'Oh, thank goodness!' he cries as my eyes blink open.

'What happened?'

'You just fainted. I think it's the heat.'

I wish it was the heat. Sitting up I grasp his hand and give an unconvincing I'm-feeling-better smile.

'Scared me half to death,' Ben goes on, handing me a glass of water he must have brought in. 'Has that ever happened before?'

'Don't think so,' I croak, feeling myself becoming more and more present again. 'How long was I...'

'Only about a minute. I reached you before you keeled over.'

'Good catch.'

The reality of why I fainted is back in plain view now.

'You back with us?' he asks.

I can't be The Nailer. Keeping such folly locked up in my mental-asylum mind is what is giving it life. Plus, opening up to Ben about things does seem to help if recent history is to be heeded. 'I'm worried I'm involved in the murders.'

He says nothing.

I go on, 'I don't have a proper alibi for the two deaths they have a firm date on; we could walk to and from the woods over the fields from here – you said I'd been sleepwalking. Apparently, those sleeping pills can make you do stuff you don't remember. Police also think a sedative was used to knock out Donna and Maurice. And we've got a nail gun.'

'Do you have any recollection of being in the woods?' His question is plainly posed. Maybe *he's* in shock.

'No.'

'And what about that message on the car?'

Do I tell him about the cloth? The most damning piece of evidence I have. He needs to know, to understand why I'm thinking like this. My mouth is desert-dry, I take a huge gulp of water. 'I found a bloody cloth in the car. That morning they found Harry and Donna, I was looking for the spare keys and there was a rag covered in blood in the glove box, still wet.'

He's flummoxed and silent again.

'I'm wondering if I've been going into some kind of fugue state. Doing these things and then coming back, going back to sleep.'

'What about the first one? The one they found in the bog weeks later? Surely we were both home that night.'

'They don't know exactly how long Donna had been there, but if it was another week before Maurice then that would be the Thursday I stayed at Anna's. When she was upset about Henry.' I can tell he thinks this is good news but there is a mitigating factor: 'I'd taken one of the sleeping pills that night too, because I was worried I wouldn't sleep in a room on my own. And Anna says she found me wandering around downstairs in the middle of the night. What if I'd gone out, done it, then she caught me as I came back?'

My heart is a bass drum beating.

When is it going to click? When is he going to put the pieces together and recoil in fear?

He stares at me, and stares at me, and stares.

'Say something!'

A grin spreads over his mouth, crow's feet stamping at the sides of his eyes. Then comes a guffaw of laughter, a foundation-shaking howl that sees him collapse over my shoulder as he hugs me.

'It's not funny, Ben! I'm not joking. It's really stressful.'

I'm slipping into indignation but he holds me tight to stop me squirming as he says, 'I'm sorry, I'm sorry. It must be horrible. But you are the only person who would bend logic and facts to imply they *did* commit murder.'

The observation steals an involuntary chuckle out of me and it's impossible to criticise him after that. 'I know things are messed up at the moment,' he adds. 'But this is just another of these tricks your mind's playing on you. Like you were convinced someone had broken in the other night when it was just me getting my Game Boy, now you're convinced you must be linked to something you couldn't possibly have done. You keep short-circuiting to worst-case scenarios.'

'But what about the bloody cloth?'

He sobers up sharpish and blows out his cheeks. 'Yeah that's... If that stupid surveillance stuff I ordered hadn't got delayed we could have had it up by now. We need to go to the police with that.'

'We can't.'

'Why?'

'I chucked it.'

'Where?'

'It doesn't matter. Best you don't know. Off the property.'

'OK,' he mutters, grappling with the bombardment of revelations far better than I would. 'Well, this stuff is due to arrive in the next forty-eight hours now. They emailed to apologise for the delay. So if anyone dares come on the property after that they'll be caught on camera. And if it makes you feel any better, it will catch you if you do try to leave the house during the night too. But think about it Kel, do you even know how to use the nail gun? I don't think you'd know how to flick the safety catch off, never mind load it and fire three nails into the exact same spots on three different people. You have to be damn careful when aiming that thing. And where would you have picked one up when staying at Anna's too?'

This is the kind of talk I need, some much-needed common sense. I sigh and rest back into him. He's right. And his initial reaction, while a tad insensitive, was also very telling. The idea I've been involved is literally laughable.

18

TWO DAYS SINCE THE SECOND DISCOVERY.

'Mum, it's all in the public domain already. How do you think Martin pulled it together? I didn't tell him...'

'I don't care! All my friends, all the people at the shops, talking about me, whispering about my private life.'

Here I am, at Mum's house before 10 a.m. the following morning, turning down calls from the *Mirror* about today's reporting assignment, because she got a tip-off from some loud-mouth at the newsagents that a sizeable chunk of Martin's profile about me was relating to Dad's crime, trial and death. The column is careful not to mention the fact that Dad was protecting his own son during the incident since every sexual abuse victim has lifetime anonymity and identifying the victim as Dad's son would effectively identify Danny. But as far as Mum's concerned, the lack of specifics has only made things worse.

'It makes it look like he just set upon that wretched man for no reason. If they knew what really happened, they'd understand. Anyone would do the same,' she seethes.

I'm sitting in my familiar chair in the kitchen as she vents away. She's been so volatile lately – but this fury is more understandable. If I'd known Martin was going to dig that deep I'd have asked him to tone it down.

'Think how annoyed *I* am,' I interject. 'It was supposed to be all about *me*, not my dad!' The joke lands like a paratrooper without a chute.

Mum can fume all she likes – there isn't much that can be done when the words are already out in the wild. My own unease at the double-page spread stems from a very different source. I'm more confident than yesterday that I'm not The Nailer. Not totally confident, just more confident. But is that a relief or disappointment? The idea of having a personal connection to the crimes was terrifying, but it also lit me ablaze. All this attention, all this newspaper acclaim. If I was killing right underneath everyone's noses, I'd be extraordinary.

But the amount of time I'd have to have been sleepwalking with no recollection of anything at all defies sense. I remember reading about a man in America – John Greer – who drove along a freeway to his mother-in-law's, stabbed her to death, but was then acquitted at trial on the grounds he had been sleepwalking. 'His incomplete arousal from sleep was exacerbated by stress and exhaustion.' I can relate. But the precision, and repetitive nature of the crimes in Allcreek, and the fact the killer seems to be leaving very few clues, surely points to a far more calculating and meticulous individual – not me in a zombified stupor.

Mum's still ranting as I zone back in. 'It's so humiliating. You don't understand, I don't think you even care if—'

'Of course I care. I'm here, aren't I?' As I say this my phone vibrates again in my pocket. It's Martin – I can only fob him off for so long.

Thankfully she's running out of puff. 'At least I'm winding down at Asda. Did I tell you I'm down to two days a week now?'

'You've told me like five times. I really am sorry about this getting in the paper, Mum. But I need to start work. I'll speak to the *Mirror*. I'm back on a retainer so they won't put anything else in about Dad OK, or you or Dan.'

Mum nods but doesn't reply so I get up and give her a big hug, swaying her from side to side, which she can't help but reciprocate.

'I don't like them making out you're some kind of psychic for psychopaths,' she states as we break hold.

'They're exaggerating! But it will look good when I finally get the book done. Great for publicity.'

'You need to look after this though Kelli Belly,' Mum says, tapping her temple with an index finger. 'God only gave you one, don't waste it.'

There is literally a 700-word piece in a national newspaper today extolling the unique qualities of my 'brilliant mind' as Martin refers to it. But obviously, to Mum, that's a *waste*. I haven't got time to be indignant. I edge back to the front door, happening to glance into the lounge as I go.

'Oh, you fixed the shelf already!' I remark, thankful for the change of topic.

'Yes, all sorted thank you,' she says.

'Who did that?'

'Your old friend Rob.'

My hand lets go of the latch on the front door and I push it closed again. 'What?!'

'Rob. Rob Grayson, your old friend at the *Echo*. He had come round and said he could...'

'Rob Grayson was here?'

'He used to come round with you all the time before you left the *Echo*. I was more than happy to see him actually. Very polite boy. Always was.'

'Mum, he's a prick.' No sooner is the word out of my mouth than I'm trying to reach and pull it back in.

'KELLI!'

'Sorry, sorry, sorry!! But he's been nothing but horrid to me for years. Why was he here?'

'He certainly didn't say anything uncouth. You really are using so much bad language these days. I can't abide—'

'Mum. Sorry. Last time. Promise. But what was Grayson doing here?'

The question seems to perplex her, as if she genuinely thinks he and I are still friends.

'He wanted to see if you were alright, if you'd said anything to me about how you're coping.'

My phone buzzes again.

'Mum, I've got to go. But if he rings or calls round again just ignore him. He's twisted. He does my head in. I don't know why he'd be here but it will have been to wind me up somehow.'

'He was very sympathetic to the fact I'm here on my own,' Mum announces, pushing her shoulders back in defiant ignorance of everything I'm saying. 'Said he would pop round more regularly to see me. He was very polite. Put the shelf back up in a jiffy and wouldn't take any money.'

'I don't have time for this. Just please don't talk to him again. For me.' My hand is back on the latch and I swing the door open.

'Are you driving or getting the bus back?' Mum asks as I pace down the path, fumbling for my keys.

'When have I ever got the bus to Ellesmere Port?'

'Oh yes,' she agrees with a shake of her head.

I'd planned on calling Martin straight back from the car but there's suddenly something more urgent.

Grayson picks up straight away.

'What the fuck are you doing? My mum, Rob?!'

'She's worried about you, Kel,' he says with all the charm of a serpent.

'You've gone too far. This is all too far. Just leave her alone – and me.'

'How did you get those quotes from Harry Bancroft's Dad?' he asks. 'He's refusing to talk to anyone.'

'Just because I beat you to a death knock doesn't give you the right to pester my family.'

'Oh, this has nothing to do with that. I went to see your mum before yesterday. And I wouldn't call it "pestering", she seems lonely, neglected actually. Glad I could help out a bit. We both agree there's something not right about you these days, Kel.'

'You don't give a shit about me, or my mum. Leave her alone or I'll get a restraining order!' I'm screaming now, my right foot tense and hard on the accelerator.

'You keep saying that, but you know you won't. Anyway, if your mum wants me to stop going round all she has to do is say. If anything, I think she's desperate for the company, poor thing.'

I hang up.

Martin's umpteenth attempt to reach me is a blessing of sorts, rescuing me from the mire.

'Kelli, I've been trying to get you all morning.'

'I'm here now.'

'The desk are only interested in the Bancrofts.'

'Obviously,' I tut.

'We've found his brother up in Durham so I've got agency out getting quotes. The story will still go out with your name, but it's probably a case of just gleaning anything you can from tributes left at the scene. If we can find a tasty backstory on Donna Smyth – how she's from a nice respectable family but something ruined her life – then all well and good. But it's probably just going to be scummy stuff, isn't it? So don't sweat it too much. Harry's the main man.'

'Right,' I grunt. Of course the female victim is the one that's dismissed without a second thought. I am going right off the patriarchy. Right off!

'500 words, get some colour from the scene. Police still there? Lots of flowers? Whatever. But lead it on the brother's quotes which I'll forward you later.'

'If you say so. Oh, thanks for the puff piece.'

'Pleasure.'

'But please leave my family out in future. Mum went mental about you dredging up all the stuff about Dad.'

'OK, point taken.'

There are several bouquets of petrol station flowers laid around a designated tree on the edge of the woods that police have arbitrarily chosen as the focal point for tributes – cellophane flapping in the breeze and tiny cards with pre-printed messages of sorrow. A couple of mourners have decided to nail their messages to the trunk of said tree. Am I the only one who finds that Alanis Morissette-levels of ironic? All the cards and flowers are for Harry though; nothing for poor Donna.

I text Polly under the auspices of popping in for a quick catch-up, but really it's so I can check up on her, maybe prove to Todd she's not as isolated as he wishes she was.

She replies in a flash:

> Had the police round questioning again today. Todd's a bit stressed. Could we do tomorrow?

How do I message back to check she is safe without him realising that's what I'm asking? I spend a couple of minutes rephrasing and editing my reply before sending:

> If you're OK to wait until then, so am I. Tomorrow?

Her only response is:

> Tomorrow xx

The quotes come through from Durham. Harry Bancroft's brother is 'heartbroken', 'distraught', 'not coping'. Standard family-in-mourning fare. I file my 500 words from Keen Beans cafe, quoting the brother and a few of the insipid condolence cards.

It's still only mid-afternoon so I drive round the woods back to Irby in the hope of finding the homeless gang who must surely have known Donna. If she does have an interesting backstory that would give me a head-start on chasing tomorrow's lead. However, the distinct lack of vagrants in their usual hovel on my side of the woods is less welcome to me than it probably is to the rest of the village.

I have one more port of call while on my side of the forest. I pull up outside the Vino'clock off-licence. The shop boasts a grotty interior and a musty stench of mildew.

Vino has been blamed by a lot of the posher people around Newton and Irby for luring all the homeless people to reside in the woods. For the middle-class residents, the most important detail about this area is that it was name-checked in the Domesday Book, and any attempts to update or modernise since then have been regarded as sacrilege. In fact, a petition – set up by Polly's Todd, no less – was signed by a lot of locals last year calling for the council to do something about the home-less gang's continued presence. Nothing was done though. Because while the suburbanites whinge about west Wirral's dwindling kerb appeal, the thirsty working-class folk care just as much about getting their alcohol at rock bottom prices – and nowhere sells booze as cheap as Vino'clock.

The owner, Jay, knows his clientele. One wall is dedicated solely to two-litre bottles of strong cider – a sign written on a florescent orange card above the shelves reads:

All under £6.00p

The back half of the shop is out of bounds to customers – behind Jay and his cash-only till – lie the spirits; bottles would vanish all too regularly if they weren't kept at arm's length.

I know Jay vaguely, not enough to recall his last name, but he's been running Vino since forever. I was in just last week buying a superfluous bottle of Red Square in return for zero intel. 'Where are all the usual patrons?' I enquire.

He tells me they've scarpered – again.

I ask him where they've gone.

He says he doesn't know.

Thanks Jay, and no I'm alright for warm cans of Polish lager.

Vino is by far the cheapest enabling centre in town. Surely they'll return within a few days – whether the murderer's been caught or not – like they skulked back last time. But that doesn't help me today.

I'll have to come back tomorrow after I've seen Polly. I might knock on all her neighbours' flats facing out into the woods too, see if anyone spotted anything that could be spun into a decent lead. As long as police still haven't got anyone in stocks, the public will lap up stories about who this faceless killer might be.

But that's for tomorrow, and with the afternoon now creeping towards evening, I hang up my notepad for the day.

* * *

Clearer headed once home, I settle on the sofa again with the world's biggest book, determined to make a proper start on it this time. Me, Sherlock and a huge bag of Maltesers to see me through to bed at a reasonable hour.

A Study In Scarlet. I do love Holmes' implied omniscience. Whether it's an unparalleled ability to read human motives, or a pristine recall for chemical interactions, he is just so wonderfully, enviably well-armed to solve any mystery. An early passage sums up the infinity of his knowledge well:

> I gathered up some scattered ash from the floor. It was dark in colour and flakey — such an ash as is only made by a Trichinopoly. I have made a special study of cigar ashes — in fact, I have written a monograph upon the subject. I flatter myself that I can distinguish at a glance the ash of any known brand, either of cigar or of tobacco. It is just in such details that the skilled detective differs from the Gregson and Lestrade type.

Just one brilliant block of expertise that combines with a million others to build his mind palace.

Ben comes in with my requested hot chocolate and then disappears back into the kitchen where he's preparing an Asian-inspired beef stew to leave in the slow cooker overnight.

'There's no point buying beef shank if you don't have a slow cooker,' he explains, typically assured when I go to check on him. 'The same way there's no point buying solar panels if you live in Scotland.'

I tell him to stick to chef-ing rather than stand-up before returning to the lounge and my reading.

The hot weather we've been enjoying is forecast to break tonight and while it's not started raining yet, the gloomy dusk is fading fast when I hear a car door slam from the front garden. I get off the sofa to see who is visiting but before I've reached the window I've changed direction and am running into the kitchen as glossy blue light begins rolling into and out of the lounge.

Ben has his hands in a sink of bubbles and pans. I join him and we stare out, our eyes frozen on the police cars coming up the driveway. This isn't just going to be a friendly chat, not with half a dozen vans and 4x4s in tow.

They think I did it. They must have found something. The bloody cloth. Have they found the bloody cloth?

'Ben, I swear I didn't. I swear. You were right. I couldn't have,' I splutter.

'Don't worry,' he says, wiping his hands dry. 'I'll answer it.'

I stay hidden behind the front door as I swivel round to see Ben open up.

'Can I help you?' he asks, calm but unimpressed. The car lights in turn swamp the hall and then slap it with black shadows – erasing and revealing, exposing and concealing.

I can't leave Ben to answer alone. He might lie and pretend I'm not here, then he'd get into trouble too. I emerge next to him in the door-way; it's Vickers standing opposite us. I link arms with Ben and lock my elbow to hold us tight. They're going to search the house, that's the next thing that hits me. You don't bring the cavalry unless you plan to be here for a long time.

Vickers is already speaking. 'Are you Ben Farrer?'

'Yes.'

'Abe,' I plead. 'Whatever you think I...'

'Don't make this any harder, Kelli,' he snaps before shifting back to Ben. 'Mr Farrer, I'm arresting you on suspicion of the murders of Donna Smyth, Maurice Williams...'

'What? NO!' I shriek.

Vickers blinks hard, then continues, '...and Harry Bancroft. You do not have to say anything. But, it may harm your defence if...'

It takes three officers to wrestle me off Ben. I'm held on the floor in the hall as he's bundled into the back of a marked car.

Ben is not The Nailer. He is not!

Now it's me, not Janice Benson, who is pinned down and howling up through the house. And just like her, my screams do not save me.

19

THE DAY AFTER THE ARREST. A.M.

The next time I check the clock it's well past 3 a.m. I'm pacing around Anna's lounge while she sits on the sofa. Her knees are hugged up to her chest as she rocks back and forth, my pain etched on her face.

I've turned down a dram of whisky but she still thinks I should try getting some sleep. 'It won't change the situation Kel, but at least you can reset overnight. Everything's getting very tangled right now.'

No shit. My head's a 4D snakes and ladders board.

How could Vickers possibly have got this so, so, so wrong?

Anna's right though, wittering isn't achieving anything. Thankfully, she had the wherewithal to make me pack an overnight bag before she rescued me – so I've brought a Roxion pill.

But how can I possibly switch off when Ben is in a cell? He must be so confused and scared. I say this out loud over and over, and to Anna's credit she just keeps patiently agreeing.

Despite my world careering off a cliff, however, there remains one fact that has not changed in my mind – that man has absolutely nothing to do with the deaths in Allcreek Woods.

Ben... commit murder?! What next? The great white shark goes vegan? The Girl Guides open a brothel? The very concept is incompatible with his DNA. Ben once cried because a baby chimp *almost* died in a David Attenborough show. Almost died, not even actually died! I've studied the psychopathy test. Damn, I nearly passed the thing; Ben does not possess a single trait needed to commit cold-blooded murder. That's precisely why he's great: the yin to my yang, the Texas to my Chainsaw Massacre.

I take my pill and lie down in Anna's spare bed. It's surprised even me that the person I've turned to in my moment of critical need is her, but as officers began turfing sofa cushions over and ripping through piles of papers, I had to get out. I don't care if they find anything that incriminates me, but I couldn't stay and watch them try. So then, who to ring? Polly would be the obvious choice, but she's got so much going on herself right now, and offering comfort isn't her forte. I needed someone maternal – and yet phoning Mum was another no-go. I could just imagine her getting even more confused and highly strung than me, leaving *me* trying to calm *her* down. No, Anna is safe, secure and caring enough to deal with me at my worst.

* * *

The pill does the trick, so when the alarm interrupts my sleep less than four hours later my head initially stays glued to the pillow. But there's just enough consciousness to notice I'm not in my own bed, and with that observation, the reality of what has happened breaks back in like a Viking invader splintering my skull with an axe.

The early alarm is intentional – I need to phone Vickers and convince him to let me have a call with Ben. They probably had a first go at him last night. I bet they're playing nice, with time on their side. But they've only got 24 hours with him by law, and have to release him after that if they don't have enough to charge. As the clock ticks down the screw will tighten, attempting to break him. I need to prep Ben, reassure him, check he is doing everything the right way. But to do that I need my call before any more interrogating.

'I'm surprised it's taken you this long to call, Amari,' Vickers says, betraying a hint of fear at the volley of abuse he's expecting.

I somehow manage to stem the tide of pure fury, and instead say, 'I need my call with Ben.'

'He's allowed to call a next of kin to let them know where he is, but since you know he's at Upton police station I don't see much need for him to speak to anyone.'

'Abe, please. He won't have a clue what's going on. Has he asked for a lawyer?'

'I can't say anything about that, Kel. You know that. This isn't digging for a story is it? I can assure you we aren't going to be confirming the name of the man we've arrested for now so you're already ahead of the rest of the pack.'

I want to reach through the phone and push my thumbs into the detective's eyeballs until they burst. 'Of course I'm not ringing for a story! Are you kidding?' I want to scream. But the thought that Vickers will just hang up frightens me back into subservience. 'Sorry, Abe please. I'm not going to say anything he isn't allowed to know. You can stay on the line for the call if you want. I just really need to speak to him.'

'You can have two minutes, on my phone, with the call recorded to be passed on to the CPS if needed. He'll be brought down to the interview room in about ten minutes. I'll call back then.'

Those ten minutes fly by as I try to condense everything I want to say into a two minute monologue. I type some notes on my phone. And then it hits me that he will probably have questions of his own and won't be in any mental state for receiving multiple instructions. I re-write the list, stripping back everything except the absolute essentials.

I'm still whittling when the call comes in.

'Hello?' I put the phone on to speaker mode so I can hold it in front of me and consult my bullet points.

'Kel...'

As I hear his voice the bottom falls out of my stomach; the emotion of the last 12 hours piles into me like a battering ram. 'Oh, Ben!' I say, putting a hand up to my mouth and letting out a single, shuddering sob. But his own weeping reinforces the importance of the call. He needs my help. I cough and persevere. 'Ben, listen. We haven't got long. Have you got a lawyer with you?'

'No,' he squeaks, before gasping for another breath mid-splutter.

'OK, ask for the police station's duty solicitor. They will have offered you that last night, but you need to have them with you.'

'It'll make me look guilty.'

'No it won't, but you need someone there with your best interests in mind. Please, I promise it won't make you look bad. Just ask for the duty lawyer.'

'I still know Dad's solicitor, what about him?'

'Even better. Yes! Do that. And whatever Vickers asks you, just tell him, OK? Tell him the truth, but not until you have someone with you.'

Interrogators don't care about the truth, they care about making the person in front of them *look* guilty, to ruin their chances at trial. Ben's too honest, he'll walk into every trap they set. He needs a savvy operator on his shoulder to ward off the beasts in blue.

I carry on. 'I know you had nothing to do with it, so you've got nothing to worry about. And I'll come and pick you up from the station this evening. There's no way they'll charge you. OK?'

'OK.' He sounds like a trusting child. Not a killer, Vickers!

'I love you, Ben. It's all going to be alright.'

'I love you too,' I hear him whimper again; my heart's breaking.

'Do you need me to go home and get the solicitor's number?'

'Yes please.'

'OK, I'll do that now. Is Vickers there?'

'I'm here,' the detective asserts.

'Abe, I'll be back at the house in fifteen minutes, then I'll phone the solicitor straight away. You'll have to wait to start questioning, but it should be sorted within the hour.'

Vickers says that time is marching on so if the solicitor isn't there within forty-five minutes then Ben will have to make do with the rep on duty in the station.

'It's in Mum's old address book in the hall, Peter Stringer,' Ben says in a slightly stronger tone.

'I'll go now. Is there anything else I can—'

The phone bleeps; the call is over.

* * *

I'm as quick as my word, thanks to Anna's insistence on driving me home rather than letting me wait for a taxi. I scamper from her car to my front door and almost drown in the process. The heavens have well and truly opened.

Peter Stringer, who it turns out is an old friend of Ben's parents as well as their solicitor, drops everything and heads to Upton police station.

The house has been ransacked – all sorts of things have gone. All Ben's clothes, both our laptops, his campervan. My little Peugeot is still outside, thank goodness. I dip into a trance, tidying room after room, not because the mess bothers me, but because adrenaline is still zapping me like a cattle prod – keeping me upright. My mind accelerates round and round a circular track, incapable of building any constructive thought.

The freezer door hasn't been shut properly by whichever ham-fisted simpleton decided to search it, and now ice has edged its way over the seal, making it impossible to close. I grab a dinner knife from the array of cutlery they've left strewn across the draining board, kneel down next to the overhanging ice and start chipping away at it, except the action does nothing, so I jab harder. Still nothing. I reposition my grip so the knife handle is no longer pinched between my thumb and forefinger but is instead clasped in my fist, the blunt blade pointing at the floor. And then I bring it down on the ice with everything I have. SMASH. Again. SMASH. Again. SMASH.

The temper I'm forcing into each blow means most times the knife doesn't even hit the ice, and the shock of the steel hitting the freezer's plastic frame reverberates up my arm, making it ache. I don't care. The ache becomes a sharper pain but I take it on, raising my wrist even higher before bringing it back down with an almighty scream. The knife plunges into the ice and shatters it, forcing my palm open as the blunt tool somersaults across the floor. It's only then I notice the phone is ringing – not my mobile, the house landline. The landline that never rings.

I drag myself up using my spare arm and the table, stumble into the hall and pick it up.

'Hello?' I'm still panting.

'Where the fuck have you been, it's half one,' Martin barks.

'I'm sorry.' I'm not sorry – but that's just what you say, isn't it?

'I've tried calling your mobile like fifty times. I take it you know about the arrest? Editor wants you out talking to locals, finding out who it is.'

Do I tell him? The fact he's rabbiting on like this means the news hasn't reached London that it's Ben.

'I'll get on it.'

'I had to pull up your little boyfriend's records to get his home number. You can't just go AWOL. If you're on retainer, I have to be able to reach you,' he preaches, cold as a winter with no Christmas.

The phone is pinned between my ear and my shoulder. I raise my right hand, the one that had been holding the knife – it's juddering uncontrollably. 'I'm not sure I'm coping today,' I say, too bewildered to inject any emotion into the statement.

'Actually?!' he scoffs. 'You've got to be kidding, Kel. I'm going to look like a complete twat if you drop out after I talked you up to the managing ed'. He didn't want to get you back on board, but I pulled in every last...'

He keeps talking but I don't need to hear the words – in fact if we're going to remain civil it's probably better I don't listen to what he's saying. Wanting it to end, I eventually interrupt. 'I'll do some digging, but if there's nothing decent, I'm not just going to file dross about an anonymous arrest. Put some junior's byline on it if you want regurgitated agency copy.'

I put the phone down; the act of defiance has me feeling like myself for the first time since the arrest.

I'm OK. Ben will be out this evening. And I wasn't lying to Martin when I said I'd do some digging. There is one person in particular I am very keen to speak to about the three bodies in the woods.

20

THE DAY AFTER THE ARREST. P.M.

Todd's working all afternoon, according to Polly, which is perfect. I don't want to speak to them together. Given how he's been treating her, part of me doesn't want to be in his presence at all. But the reasons for booking in a taxi ride this wet, muggy afternoon are two-fold.

One, he has been interviewed by police so will be able to shed light on what kind of questions they are asking, what they're looking for, what scents they're picking up. But I could probably get most of that from Polly.

The second reason? All three nights the murders took place are suspected to be Thursdays – Todd's regular day off. Ben always spots him when he's doing his sets at The Irby Mill. The most direct way home for Todd from The Irby Mill is through the woods. At the very least he is someone who has been in the vicinity of the crimes on the nights they occurred, but when you factor in the bruises that have started bubbling up on Polly, the timeframe fits all too snugly. I don't intend to accuse him outright, or to leave him even feeling accused. Not yet. But having him partially distracted by the road is the perfect environment to cast some bait – maybe reel him in on a loose word or an off-guard reaction.

That said, I had to ask Polly for his number because I have never needed, wanted or tried to contact him directly before. I do not know Todd Kromkamp well enough to anticipate in advance whether he is capable of killing. But I want to follow my gut – I can imagine Dick suggesting I call it my 'killer instinct' and then laughing. Well, right now my killer instinct is a bell that rings every time I put Todd together with the deaths in Allcreek Woods.

Polly's made me promise not to confront him about anything he may or may not have been doing to her. But as far as she knows, Todd is just another local from whom I'm gleaning information about the killings. So once I've agreed to her terms and she's passed over the number, I call him.

His first reaction is to check that Polly is OK. He probably guesses I'm with her, that she's told me the truth about the black eye and that I'm about to explode at him down the phone. But I'm all sweetness and light. 'I'm reporting on these murders in the woods, and Polly said you'd both spoken to police to help with the investigation. I want to speak to as many locals as possible. Was thinking I could pay you to drive me around for a bit, so I don't waste any of your time outside work, and we can chat? Polly said that'd be cool with you.'

'Urm, OK. Where d'ya wanna go?' he asks, sounding very scouse.

'I don't mind, maybe an hour's drive? We can just go to Chester and back or something. And then drop me off in the village?'

'Am in Wes' Kirby... takin' a fella to Wallasey. Bu' could come after. I'll phone ya once am outside yours.'

The next hour drags while waiting for his call back. It's been a non-stop downpour all morning. Big, fat globs of rain pelt the kitchen window as I sit in silence, watching.

Merseyside Police announce they'll be making an official statement outside Upton police station at 5 p.m. Makes sense – Vickers hasn't spoken publicly since the arrest. I'll go to keep up appearances. If Ben's released without charge, which he will be, they won't name him. And I need to do everything possible to keep Grayson off the scent. Of course, there's always a chance loose-lipped Vickers will tell Grayson off the record that it's Ben. But if I show up, manage to keep my rage in and beg Vickers to be discreet, we might just get Ben out of the station without any unwelcome attention.

I want to do something nice for him when we get home. He'll need me – just like I've needed him so much lately. Maybe a takeaway from the Zeera Tandoori, and I could pick up some of those beers he likes from Londis, the wheat ones. The free time also has me pondering why Todd – if he is the killer – would be framing me? Or maybe it's Ben he's been framing. Ben can tell me more later based on what accusations police have thrown at him.

The fact Todd says he'll drive over without me even providing him an address gives me my first chance to test him. He never comes to the house, Polly always walks, so how will he know which property we live at? If he does make it here without an address then he must have been here before but without me knowing – why would that have been? To put a bloody rag in my glovebox, perhaps?

The call finally comes. 'Am at the end of ya drive.' That bell in my head rings.

Todd works for Grab-a-Cab. I open their app, book a journey to Chester and he accepts it, all within ten seconds.

There's a choice on the coat rack, my duffle with no hood, or my quilted parka which is far too warm for summer. I pull on the duffle and by the time I reach the taxi my hair is dripping, a sodden black monstrosity that I'll have to tame before Ben gets out later.

I bundle into the car and am immediately met with the over-whelming reek of cigarettes.

'Horrible day,' he says. The weather – the easiest and least inventive small talk.

Todd is no intellectual powerhouse. Polly's told me he dropped out of school at fifteen, was in magistrates' court at seventeen for dealing pot, then got sacked from an apprenticeship at a car garage in New Brighton for stealing tools and selling them on. He's wearing a battered old Everton baseball cap and a black Adidas tracksuit. There aren't fluffy dice hanging from the rear-view mirror but there might as well be, and he's playing house music, which he does at least turn down now I'm in the backseat diagonally behind him.

'How did you know my address?' I ask for starters.

'Phoned Pol,' he states, lighting up a Marlboro Gold and cracking the window open less than half an inch to avoid getting wet; the smoke bounces off the glass and back at us.

He's weedy. You wouldn't put him down as someone who could dominate a confrontation. But then Peter Sutcliffe was a small guy and look what he managed. I can see one of his trainers on the brake pedal when I push myself up in my seat – Nike branding, feet about the same size as Ben's size 10s. 'Ding ding' goes the invisible bell.

Slouching back down, I can't help looking at his hands as they grip the wheel too. His knuckles protrude like pebbles and I imagine the pain they could inflict if he came back from the pub with no one to punch except the woman telling him to go to bed.

We both commit to some more weather chat for a minute but the car soon falls quiet. The clock is ticking, so I begin. 'Police were round interviewing everyone in the flats then?'

'Yeah.' He keeps his eyes on the road. His accent's even difficult for me to understand – not jovial and passionate like Polly and Dick, but aggressive and excluding.

'What sort of things were they asking?'

Big puff on his cigarette, and then, 'Dunno.'

Of course he's stonewalling. It's not subtle or sophisticated, but he's buying himself time. Another toll of the bell.

'How long were they at yours?'

''Bout twennee minutes.'

'Did they ask if you'd seen anything?'

'Yeah.'

'What did you say?'

'Said I 'adn't seen nothin' or I would've gone and told 'em myself.'

He's so cagey. Most locals are fascinated by The Nailer. Every time I go into the shops or look on Twitter there's someone chatting or posting or worrying about it.

'Were you at The Mill any of the nights they wanted to know about? I know they've spoken to Ben about that,' I not so much lie as guess.

'Yeah he plays Thursdees, dun-ee? Am always there Thursdees.'

'Must be creepy walking back through the woods after, especially now we know what's gone on.'

'I never go through the woods to get home,' he states, gripping the steering wheel like it's about to fall off, eyes still glued to the traffic.

'Oh, blimey! That must take a while to get back to the flat then.'

His fists slide further round the wheel then back together several times, like he's passing a rope from one hand to the other. 'Not tha' long. Helps me sober up.'

He's lying. There's no way he walks an hour round the perimeter when there's a fifteen-minute route straight through. Even if walking into the forest at night is spooky, the Dutch courage he'd have built up after five or six hours at the bar would surely force him onwards. Ben's said before that Todd always gets really pissed and never leaves before closing time.

'So does that mean you were in the pub the night Harry Bancroft was in there? Apparently he was at The Irby Mill before he was found in Allcreek.'

'Bizzies asked me tha', don't remember.'

If this is *the* man, The Nailer, then I am going to have one hell of a story to tell after he's charged. It strikes me for the first time how courageous it will appear for me to have deliberately isolated myself with him for the sake of an undercover interrogation. It's not quite as daring as heading off to the timber yard alone the night I found Dick, but it's in the same spirit.

The seats in his car are comfortable at least. I try to pull my hair straighter, using my fingers as a comb and let the silence rest for a moment, checking for a proper hairbrush in my handbag. Stupidly, I haven't brought one.

'Good it seems to be driving that homeless mob out of the woods though. They're a nightmare,' I fish.

'Too right,' he grunts, slapping a hand on the wheel with such sudden force it makes me flinch. 'Doin' us a favour if you ask me. Put dem lot out with the bins!'

'You set up that petition trying to get rid of them a while back, didn't you?'

'Yeah,' he says, spirited for the first time in the journey. 'Council didn't wanna know. 2,000 signatures and they jus' said they couldn't do nothin'. Fuckin' joke.'

'Ding-a-ling' goes that bell.

'What made you do the petition? They broke into your car, didn't they?'

'Yeah exactly.' He doesn't elaborate. He's too macho-man to admit they beat him up too.

I'd allotted half an hour to reach Chester and the same to get back, but we're there in twenty minutes. Silly me. Taxi drivers don't believe in such nonsense as the Highway Code and speed limits – plus, Todd is most likely very keen to have me out of his cab as quickly as humanly possible. He pulls up at a rank outside Chester station.

'You'll 'ave to confirm we're 'ere, then book another journey or I'll get in trouble.'

Polly and I are set to meet at Keen Beans. I tap on the cafe as my journey destination, Todd accepts straight away and soon we're whizzing back to the Wirral.

'How are you and Pol getting on?' I enquire.

'Dunno, what's she said?' he fires back, glaring in the rear-view.

I play dumb. 'Nothing, just asking.'

'She's alright,' he goes on, trying to correct his initial incriminating tone. 'Always gettin' at me, always annoyed at stupid shit. But that's just birds innit?'

Images of Polly percolate – of her sitting alone, upset, waiting for Todd to come home. Then he bundles through the front door wanting sex or another drink or to be left alone. And she's just trying to ask where he's been or have a moment's conversation. And he's already saying she's winding him up. And she's apologising. And he's gaslighting, saying it's her fault he's mad. And she cracks, says something brave. And then...

I snap to, frustrated at letting conversation peter out. The journey is going to be over soon – especially with Lewis Hamilton in the driver's seat – and I need to leave time for my parting test.

'Weird that the third victim wasn't a homeless person,' I point out.

'Do you reckon the killer just got mixed up or maybe they aren't targeting anyone in particular?'

'Dunno,' he answers. That bell rings a little fainter. He doesn't respond with suspicion or suppressed frustration. It's more like the concept has bamboozled him. If Todd is doing this surely it's specifically against the vagrants. Harry Bancroft's death would be a huge, risky blunder on his part. He'd feel *something* about it, but he seems unfazed.

'And what about…'

'OI WATCH IT! NOBHEAD!' Todd screams, crushing his palm against his car horn as a cyclist cuts him up on a roundabout.

The outburst steals my breath. Thoughts turn to Polly again. That instant anger, aggression over nothing. I must help her escape this vile man.

But is he a killer? I still don't know.

We're on the main road into Newton when I tell him.

'They've arrested Ben.'

He turns to look at me directly for the first time and we share meaningful eye contact for longer than we should considering he's not looking where he's going.

'Wha'?' he asks.

'They took him into the station last night.'

'Ben, your Ben? Over this?'

'Yeah, sure it's only a precaution, he'll be back out tonight. But that's why I'm desperate to find out more about it. So if you do hear anything or see anything suspicious, just let me know. Please.'

More eye contact while he tries to figure out if I'm serious. My frown eventually convinces him. 'I will, I will.' He's shaking his head now and adjusts his cap, fidgeting. He's dazed, no doubt about it.

He pulls up outside his own flat since he wants to pick up a can of Coke before heading back out. I thank him, get out and wander down to Keen Beans. The conversation was odd. My initial feeling? Inconclusive. The shoes, the temper, the beef with the homeless gang, the lying about his route home. It's compelling. But it's not enough. Yet.

I'm sitting at the same table when Polly arrives with just as little fanfare as last time. The bottom edge of the bruise now burns yellow like a halo.

I don't even say hello. 'Ben's been arrested.'

She holds my gaze with her healthy eye widening as she waits for me to say more.

'They came last night, around eight. Over the murders. They should release him tonight unless they apply for extra time, but they won't. There's no way he could have anything to do with it.'

She looks shocked, her usual impervious indifference to the world nudged a millimetre off its foundations. 'Have you spoken to him?' she asks.

'Briefly, this morning. Told him to get a solicitor. I want to kill Vickers. He's going to ruin this just like Dick's case.'

'Did they say *why* they were arresting him?'

I shake my head. 'I'll find out later. Police press conference, then Ben can fill me in with details tonight.'

'That's mad,' Polly says. We're both leaning our foreheads on one hand as we stare at the floor. 'Why did you need to speak to Todd?'

'See what stuff detectives are asking local blokes. With Ben involved it's kicked me up the arse to find out anything I can, see what police are thinking.' No need to articulate my precise motivation for speaking to Todd, not when the theory is still fermenting.

'And there's absolutely no way you think Ben could—'

'Don't,' I order.

'Wait, he was arrested last night. What did *you* do?'

She's not going to like this. 'I stayed at Anna's.'

'Anna's? Why?'

Because I needed to cry and vent and have someone care for me and I knew your reaction would be exactly as it is now, detached. I can't say that though so I trot out the answer I'd prepared in advance: 'Because she has a spare bedroom. I couldn't stay in the house on my own.'

'Why not call me? I could have come over.'

'There were police everywhere. I wanted to get out. I'm sorry. It's not that I wanted to tell her first, I just... my head was in bits.'

'No, don't worry. Don't care.'

Neither of us speaks again for almost a minute, which puts a flame under the indignation I feel at her lack of sympathy. I'm going through hell and she hasn't offered one iota of support.

'Anything else to say?' I give her one last chance to show some compassion.

'Just don't get how your natural reaction could be to call her fir—'

'Are you serious?!! Ben's in...' People are looking round in the coffee shop; I lower my voice. 'Ben's at Upton station, he's probably losing his mind, they've wrecked our house, Grayson could be about to find out my boyfriend's a suspect, and all you can do is whinge about who I called first.'

'You want me to be there for you now, but it wasn't a priority, was it? When the chips are down you find out what people really—'

I could lunge for her. 'Do you really want to know why I didn't ring? Because your life is a mess and last night, I just needed some calm, someone to look after me. Somewhere with no aggro, no one else's shit. So yeah, I called Anna. And she was a good friend and gave me a hug and stayed up with me and let me rant, and didn't complain once. Yet I tell you, and I don't get even a single word of pity. I think I made the right choice, don't you?'

She stares at me and I can't work out if she's going to cry or leave.

I don't let her do either. 'You're complaining that I didn't tell you quickly enough, and yet you never *ever* talk to me about *your* problems. You've made up this BS story about your eye. I saw the bruise on your arm last week, Pol. I'm not an idiot.'

I pull on my duffle coat and leave her there in the cafe.

21

THE DAY AFTER THE ARREST. EVENING.

The beers are ready on the passenger seat. I'm not sure exactly when Ben will get released. I think technically his twenty-four hours of questioning ends at 7.45 p.m. So there might be a bit of waiting around after the 5 p.m. press conference. But whenever he emerges... the beers are ready.

There's quite a few of the national paper hacks hanging around outside the police station. I get out of my car and cross the road to join them. At least the rain's relented. And even better, no Rob Grayson yet.

Vickers will come out, give the statement then take questions. I need to push for Ben to be afforded a stealthy exit. But I'll have to make the plea once the detective's on his way back into the building, beyond the prying eyes and ears of my peers.

I recognise a couple of the reporters in the pack. It used to be a lot of the same faces at major scenes when I was down in the capital. All the chief crime correspondents. But I wasn't there long enough to build up a rapport with any of them so I keep to myself, plus I'm so nervous about Vickers accidentally giving away Ben's name I could vomit.

'Detectives set to charge The Nailer,' the talking newsstand squawks from behind me, making me wince.

Grayson – sporting new glasses, no less. 'Invested in some Jeffrey

Dahmer's, have we?' I raise my eyebrows, the closest he'll ever get to a compliment.

He winks.

I gag.

'They won't charge this guy,' I tell him, going back to his original point.

''Course they will. Chief Constable's giving the statement instead of Vickers. Means it's probably big news. Whoops, wasn't supposed to let that slip.' He rolls his eyes, pretending to be sorry for bragging about his morsel of intel.

'My cup runneth under,' I mutter back. That's bad news if it is the chief, I don't know her. I need *Vickers* if I'm going to get Ben out in secret.

'Male, twenty-nine, arrested in Irby. You must have heard *something*,' Grayson persists.

'D'you think I'd tell you if I had?' I reply.

'If they do charge him, we'll definitely get the name, knock on wood,' he drones, tapping his notepad with his knuckles.

'You missed,' I shoot back, nodding at his head.

He looks suitably scolded as I move away, putting several other reporters between us.

Wish I hadn't left my duffle coat in the car. The heavy clouds and stiff breeze are bringing my arms out in horrible, humongous goose-bumps. I don't like how confident Grayson is that Ben's been charged. He's wrong, he's bluffing. Hopefully Vickers plods out of the station, proving him wrong.

The answer comes a minute later. It's not good.

A female officer in a crisp black blazer and short blonde hair slicked to the side marches out, clipboard in hand and stops in front of us all.

'Thank you for coming,' she begins. The introduction induces a disciplined hush among the baying mob. 'I, Chief Constable Madders, am here to give an update on the deaths in Allcreek Woods. Yesterday, we arrested a twenty-nine-year-old male on suspicion of the three murders. My officers have been working around the clock to amass evidence on the case and have done a sterling job. The evidence we have includes, but is not limited to, the arrested man's height and weight fitting the build we were looking for in a suspect, sedatives found at his home that could have been used in the killings, the vicinity of his home to the crime scenes.'

This is all circumstantial. They're going to release him!

The chief constable continues. 'After exhaustive interviewing with the suspect both last night and today, we also this afternoon received the blood test results from a nail gun we found at his property. Those results came back positive for traces of all three victims' blood. It was following this breakthrough that we charged the twenty-nine-year-old male. Our investigations will continue but we...'

I stop hearing anything. That chill on my skin freezes into a numb, primal panic. I shoulder barge my way out of the crowd and run back to my car.

No! No! NO!

Ben can't be. He can't be. Everyone's going to know. Everyone's going to think it's him. He can't be. He isn't!

Hands trembling, I start the car and swing out into the road. All the reporters are still facing the detective, calling out for more details. All except Grayson, whose back is to the group. He traces my car, shocked and unblinking as I flee.

* * *

I collapse on the floor as soon as the door is locked behind me and the hall light is on. For the second time in two days, I'm howling from the exact same spot that Janice Benson has done on so many nights before. I am her and she is me. Is this what I deserve? Is this vengeance for letting her die?

I try phoning Ben's mobile. Straight to voicemail. I try Vickers. Straight to voicemail.

I can't be here any more. I want to absent myself from this world altogether. Not eternally. Not yet. Ben still needs me. But for tonight, I want nothing more than to stop existing.

Up to the bathroom, I drop to my knees and unzip my toiletries bag. Where are they? Where are my pills? Several things are missing. I check the mirrored cabinet on the wall too, but items are strewn in a mess on both shelves, the complete opposite to the neatness with which Ben always arranges everything.

And then it hits me: the police. They've taken everything that could be a sedative, to test against what they found in the victims. There are no sleeping pills left here.

Sitting in the lounge now, I scroll through my phone endlessly. Anna's seen the news and texted:

> WTF?! You OK? Want me to come round?

I can't respond.

The news breaks on every news website, I watch them all fall like dominoes. Ben's name, his age, his Facebook profile picture, all being broadcast to the world. I'm on to my ninth or tenth iteration of the story when the call from an unknown number flashes up, interrupting my death-spiral.

I pick up.

The sobs are enough to tell me it's Ben. I sit up stunned, desperate for him to say something that contradicts everything that's just happened.

'They've charged me,' he squeezes out. The tone of 'me' ascends so high it splits out of the top of my head.

I try to hold the phone steady against my ear. 'I know,' I whisper.

'There's blood on the nail gun,' he says with a fraction more composure.

'They're framing you! Whoever it is. Remember the...' I want to mention the bloody rag left in my glove box, but anyone could be listening to this. Do they record all your calls once you're charged with something? They probably do. 'What have they said?'

'Leaving me here tonight then taking me to a prison in Manchester tomorrow. Kel, you know the other night in the lounge when you said about the sleeping pills and a fugue state? Was that you... in your own way, trying to admit that...'

'No! That was completely honest as it was.' My head is plummeting deeper and deeper into an unfathomable nightmare, barely retaining enough grasp on the present to discern whether what we're saying is cryptic and innocent or damning us both forever. 'I was outside the station ready for you to come home,' I say. The words knock the cornerstone out from within me. 'Why is this happening?'

'I'm sorry,' he splutters.

'You haven't don—'

'No, I mean I'm sorry for asking. I didn't mean to y'know...'

'No, I know. I know.'

Neither of us can force out another cogent thought or a mollifying word. There's an impossible amount to say in an impossibly short time.

'I think I've got to go,' he eventually offers.

I take a deep breath so I can at least leave him with a voice that sounds strong. 'I love you.'

'I love you too.' The sound of him sniffling scrapes down the line. 'I'm not giving up Ben. I'll never *ever* believe you did this. I'm going to find out who did...'

The line bleeps three times and disconnects. I turn my phone off.

My jaw aches from screaming, my thighs throb from punching them, the skin around my eyes feels like it's been corroded away by the salt in my tears.

Ben is *not* a killer. The Nailer is still out there.

22

TWO DAYS SINCE THE ARREST. A.M.

Sleep creeps up like the tide. Paralysed on the sofa, it certainly hadn't reached me by dawn, but as the home phone rings in the hall, my bewilderment suggests I've been awoken. In no rush to approach the noise, I wait by the lounge door for the caller to give up, then unplug the line. I try checking my mobile for the time, forgetting I switched it off last night. The kitchen clock says 8.25 a.m.

I fall back on the sofa but the tide's retreated right out again, so I sit in silence, embracing the small mercy of clarity. As the day wears on, my thoughts will no doubt accelerate and get heavier until my head is filled with wrecking balls of despair. But for now, the path is clear: I need to keep digging, that's it, it's that simple. I need to keep digging, because while the police think it's Ben, they won't be out looking for who actually did this.

I can feel the first wrecking ball swinging into action though. If I was intrigued as to whether some alternative conscious within me was carrying out these murders before, having the victims' blood on our nail gun is curious in the extreme.

I remind myself again of what Ben said – I don't even know how to use a nail gun.

There's a knock at the door which I ignore, a second harder knock likewise, but the third wrenches me from behind my blanket and over to the hall. I don't open up. 'Who is it?'

'Mum!'

I twist the key and in the same second, she's through the door and throwing her arms around me. She smells lovely, like Mum always smells – honeysuckle. I forget the name of the eau de toilette every birthday and have to ask her so I can get it for her again, but it's never been so deeply comforting as it is right now. She must have heard about Ben – she hardly ever visits, and *never* hugs me like this. I need it so much.

'Smooth seas don't make good sailors, Kelli Belly,' she whispers into my ear. 'That's what your father used to say.'

I uncoil her arms from around me and usher her into the kitchen. We sit down with a cup of tea and she lets me talk. It's Mum at her best: no judgment, no dramatic gasps or shakes of head, just a stoic willingness to listen. By the time I've finished I'm feeling guilty for not turning to her when Ben was arrested, never mind Polly.

'I don't think he did it either,' she says as a declaration of support. 'And is this the same detective who couldn't find The White Widower?' she checks.

I tell her it is.

'And after last time he's still been left to run this case too?' she confirms with exaggerated astonishment. 'I wouldn't trust him to run a bath, personally.'

'Thanks Mum,' I say, aware she's trying her best to reassure me.

It's good to say things out loud, it helps organise the chaos. I don't tell her about my niggling self-suspicion, or about Todd, though he has been at the forefront of my mind all morning.

Eventually I feel brave enough to turn my phone back on. Several messages, dozens in fact: Martin, Polly, more from Anna, even my old news editor at the *Echo* has messaged. I phone Martin first and he apologises for the pressure he's put me under. I tell him I'm in no state to file today but I do want to write a piece for the paper in the next few days defending Ben. I emphasise with every adverb I can summon that Ben is 100 per cent, utterly, completely, undoubtedly, categorically, unimpeachably, absolutely, emphatically innocent. And that if Martin trusts my *nose* for serial killers like he said he did in his article, then he should stick with that instinct now.

He beats around the bush, but the long and the short of it is that the *Mirror* wants nothing to do with me. I'm too close to the case. Martin says something about 'bad optics'. I tell him this is real life, not an episode of *Succession*. But it makes no difference. For the second time in my life, I have been unceremoniously dumped by the paper. Not even a spiteful blog post from Grayson to blame for it this time.

Mum ushers me into the lounge, places another cup of tea in front of me and some toast.

'*Mirror*'s ditched me,' I state, exhausted and broken.

'You're in no fit state to be thinking about work!' Mum decides. 'It's a blessing.'

'I need to find who's doing it.'

'Maybe it'd be better to just lay low and let the police keep looking into—'

'They're wrong. Effing wrong,' I declare, remembering not to swear so Mum doesn't get side-tracked. 'If it was Dad you'd be out there trying to find out anything you could!'

She contemplates the argument, then sits, embraces me and leans my head into her chest. We rock back and forth on the sofa.

'Thank you for coming,' I say, slightly muffled. 'I'd never have asked, but it means a lot.'

'This is all very horrible Kelli. There are very few people who know what it's like to have their man called a murderer in the press. Have you seen the news today?'

'Last night, not today,' I say, taking a sip of my tea.

'He's on a lot of front pages this morning.'

Making her point for her, a knock comes at the door less than a minute later. Mum answers – it's a hack from the *Express*. She rightly guesses I have nothing to say except that Ben is innocent and she slams the door while the little pipsqueak is still drowning in a follow-up question. I pin a note over the letterbox after that:

JOURNALISTS, DO NOT KNOCK OR I WILL REPORT YOU TO THE INDEPENDENT PRESS STANDARDS ORGANISATION.

It does the trick too – no more unsolicited interruptions all day. Nothing like the threat of industry sanctions to coerce reporters into behaving themselves.

I had wanted to restart my investigating today, but when Mum goes out to check whether the coast is clear she reports back that there is a pack of hungry wolves with long lens cameras and satellite-topped vans camped at the end of the drive. The day is lost.

Mum stays though, makes me lunch, asks why all the lights are on upstairs, folds up the blanket I'd slept under on the sofa.

We're in the lounge watching a black and white film when an iPhone buzzes on the table. I lean forward thinking it's mine, but wince at the sight of Rob Grayson's name – on Mum's mobile. I do the decent thing and decline the call on her behalf.

'Kelli!' she says, the wrinkles around her mouth deepening as she purses her lips in disapproval.

'Why is he calling you?'

'I've told you... he calls me, checks up on me. He probably wants to see I'm coping after what's happened to you.'

'Yeah, but he doesn't call *me* to see if I'm coping, does he? And do you know why? Because he's not a friend, Mum. He's a cockroach.'

'Kelli, don't be so dramatic. You know he's been checking in on me. I told you. And it's not up...'

'You said he'd been round once, and I phoned him straight after to tell him to leave you alone,' I exclaim.

'Well, that's horrible. He is very good to me. I'm lonely Kelli, and if he cheers me up sometimes then why would you resent that?'

'Because he's using you, Mum – to get to me – to dig for dirt on *me*.'

'Of course. Perish the thought anyone would just want to be my friend! Anyway, we aren't always talking about you, Kelli.'

'Oh what, so you're shagging now? That would be so Grayson, unable to find one single female in his own generation, he's forced to try his hand with the boomers.'

There's a storm brewing on Mum's face, probably because I said 'shagging'. She gets up, marches back into the hall and starts to push on her shoes. 'I can't be with you when you're like this. I've come round to support you, and yet you still find a way to put me down and make me feel this big.' She raises her thumb and forefinger clamped together.

'I do want you here Mum, I just don't want Grayson anywhere near either of us.'

She opens the door, steps into the porch then turns to face me. 'I see Robert as a lovely young boy, like Danny. Not everything is about sex and violence. If you were a bit more mature, you'd see that.'

And then she's gone.

* * *

Polly and Anna both come round uninvited during the evening. I'd forgotten to reply to their messages so maybe it's my own fault. It does give Anna a chance to see Polly's bruise, which is good, as I want to talk to Anna about it but haven't wanted to break Pol's confidence. Initially the sequence of events is disastrous though: Anna arrives in her car, then less than ten minutes later Polly turns up and it looks like, once again, I've turned to Anna instead of Polly. I try to make it as clear as possible in conversation, without seeming ungrateful, that Anna showed up unannounced. As it turns out, things are relatively easy between the three of us as we chat at the kitchen table. Anna does most of the questioning, me answering. Polly sits quietly, contemplative rather than surly, and nibbles a single carrot stick as Anna and I munch through a whole garden patch worth with buckets of garlic hummus.

Thankfully Anna absents herself first, leaving me to apologise to Polly, make unequivocally clear that I hadn't invited Anna over, and that I've felt terrible about what I said in the coffee shop.

Polly, for her part, apologises too and says she *is* concerned, but often has a problem telling her face to reflect how she's feeling inside. Still no hint of an unburdening heart-to-heart about her own problems, but my relief at clearing the air discourages me from pushing any further.

For some stupid reason I've pretended to both Anna and Polly that I'm coping just fine, and that my confidence in Ben's innocence is enough to keep me sane. So when Polly offers to stay over I brush it off, telling her there is nothing to worry about.

'I really think you'd be better off with me staying,' she insists.

And then it hits me. It's so blatant and, by Polly's standards, so explicit. She wants to get away from Todd, but for a reason he can't possibly object to. This is perfect. How can I say no? My ordeal is her escape rope. I tell her she is more than welcome to stay.

Her reaction is pyrotechnic.

She announces she must go home immediately to pack an overnight bag, effervescing with excitement as if I've just surprised her with a mini-break to New York. She's high as a kite. I offer to drive her home to get the bag but she's having none of it. She's oddly garrulous as she talks me through how long she'll be gone and what she'll be bringing back, as if she's been dreaming of this moment for years.

She zips off and I'm left with a weird sense of relief. If there's one good thing to come out of all this, it's that Polly's finally agreed to spend time away from Todd. Among all those thousands of steps she insists on doing every day, this could be the most important one she ever takes.

23

TWO DAYS SINCE THE ARREST. EVENING.

What do I do while waiting for Polly to return? Not much, in all honesty. I wander around empty rooms – lights all on, obviously – trying to come to terms with Ben's house without him in it.

Despite all the rabbit food Anna and I consumed, I'm starving. The fridge is bare, nothing in the cupboards looks very enticing and the bread's got mould on. Ben always deals with the food shopping. This starved warren is unrecognisable without him.

He must be distraught all alone like that. No friendly faces. No warm bed or familiar comforts to ease the trauma even a scintilla. He was so patient and loving when I needed him most in this house, *his* house. Now he needs someone and I can't reassure him at all.

I keep expecting him to wander out of the kitchen spouting some pretentious nonsense about how 'people treat flavours as binary, when every mouthful should be a spectrum'. Another favourite was, 'Food's not a photograph Kel, it's a movie.'

I finish my plodded pilgrimage of the property and return to my nook on the sofa in the lounge. Beautiful apparitions persist for a moment, but reality soon snuffs them out. Ben doesn't come in holding a fresh sourdough loaf, or a steaming bowl of thick chicken soup, or sausages from the butchers and his special leek and cheddar mash.

And for the first time in memory, my overwhelming feeling at being stuck in this house is not fear, but intense, heart-breaking loneliness. The yearning to have him back is so painful it almost feels physical. I cross my arms, grab myself by the shoulders and squeeze, pretending he's back. Pathetic, I know. Truly tragic. I don't care.

The doorbell rings, but Ben and I are dancing a slow waltz so deep in my soul that it takes a moment to break hold. And it takes another moment to abandon a distant hope that it might be him at the door.

The visitor is, of course, Polly, still visibly buzzing, a prisoner of war suddenly freed and returning to Blighty. She bundles in with heavy bags that weigh more than she does.

'Can't believe you didn't let me drive to pick your stuff up, ya lunatic!' I tell her.

'Needed the exercise. You sleeping down here?' she asks – still panting – having already walked straight into the lounge and planted herself on the skew-whiff sofa cushions.

I nod, admitting that I find the house spooky, but saying no more than that.

'Don't blame you, the only thing creepier than this place is Mrs fucking Danvers next door.' There she is with that precision swearing I love so much. While Ben's plight is impossible to let go of, it does at least feel positive to have freed Polly from her captor. Free her first, free Ben next. That's what I need to manifest.

'So,' Polly goes on, riding the mood, 'what are we going to watch, *Pride And Prejudice* or *Dirty Dancing*?'

I guffaw and my belly aches as a second snort rolls out of me. In the cold light of day it probably isn't that funny, but *wow*, it feels good to laugh. And the fact I'd never watch either of those films and she is the only person who would dare ridicule me for it, is so disarming. Even Polly – usually the master of deadpan delivery – can't help but squeal the last couple of words in glee.

The moment's comic relief helps sandblast off some of the heavy gloom that's been clinging to me ever since Ben was charged.

After popping outside for a solo cigarette she talks me through her luggage. One rucksack of shoes and clothes, and a separate backpack with several bottles of cheap gin clinking around in it.

'Who's that for?' I shriek. We're both quite excitable and high-pitched, despite our readiness to mock anything akin to a girls-night-in.

'That's for when we want to party!' she says, as if the answer is obvious. 'Do you want some?'

She's already unscrewing the top. It's a dumpy bottle with a metallic green label on the side. I decline and she's smart enough not to insist. But when I proffer some mixer or even just ice to go with her tipple she waves a dismissive hand, unable to reply any other way since her lips are already latched to the clear glass neck. I knew she liked booze but not quite like this.

The colouration around her battered eye is more subdued now – mustard yellow – making it harder to pick out against her skin – tanned by how much time she spends out walking everywhere.

She wipes her mouth without a flinch following her big gulp. 'Helps me sleep,' she says. 'I used to like those sleeping pills, but gin's much nicer.'

It's ironic how watching a friend drink can sober me up so quickly. Some of the things she says are so tragic, but she just brushes over them, putting the 'fun' in dysfunctional.

I realise I've not told her about bursting in on Ben with a carving knife last week. Inevitably, she loves the story, seizing the opportunity to mock me as she sips away at her bottle like it's spring water.

We get comfy top-and-tailing on the sofa with the TV on. Some stupid seventies cop film where the punches don't sync up with the cartoonish 'thwack' noises, and all the male characters have their own cheesy catchphrases solely designed to make your vagina fuse shut forever. The female characters get next to no dialogue. Then the news comes on so we swap over to a documentary about the Titanic.

'Who do you think did do it? The murders...' Polly asks into the empty space; her eyes are closed and she's slurring her words. A bottle of gin, two-thirds empty, sits capless on the floor at her side of the settee.

Do I say Todd? No. Polly's here but she'll still be way too tangled up in him to hear something like that. Instead, I give her the pathetic, lazy reply of 'probably another homeless man'.

Silence descends between us again as an expert on the TV talks over ghoulish pictures of the shipwreck. Then – eyes still shut, head pinned against a cushion as if she's lost in a dream – Polly speaks again. 'If you want to help Ben you should come clean about the note on your car. Admit it was you.'

My beady eyes lock on her, adrenalin careering around my chest as I wait for her to elaborate. But she doesn't. And not long after, she starts snoring.

I stay still and staring though, failing to grasp how she could possibly have known a secret I'd planned to carry with me to the grave.

24

THREE DAYS SINCE THE ARREST.

Knowing that Pol's worked out the truth about the car note makes it impossible to sleep. Her gin-guzzling contest for one has had quite the opposite effect on her, however. The dawn sun is shining through the lounge window when I finally give up on getting any shut eye and slither off the sofa softly so as not to wake Sleeping Beauty at the other end.

How does she know about me writing the note? How long has she known? She was so drunk last night, does she even remember saying it? I won't say anything – pretend it didn't happen. Then she hopefully won't recall the conversation either.

Being up bright and early does at least enable me to phone up and book in back-to-back slots at the prison in Manchester. Ben first, then Dick. I'm painfully aware I need to speed up my own chase for the truth. But the more I can get from Ben about the police's case, the better equipped I'll be. Then bouncing the ideas around with Dick should help break the circles my mind's spinning in.

The pair won't have crossed paths in there; Dick gets one hour of free time a day, and isn't invited to share it with fellow inmates. By contrast, Ben is just another defendant refused bail – for now. Nevertheless, Manchester is the closest Category A prison, so he will share the same abode as Dick until I – or anyone else – finds something to prove his innocence.

* * *

Ben's as broken as I knew he would be when I get there. He looks like he's had about as much sleep as me too.

He tells me through all the evidence. Vickers' theory is Ben drugged Maurice and Donna using a spiked bottle of alcohol topped up with my Roxion pills, then once they were drowsy and less likely to fight back, he'd knocked them out with chloroform, then carried out the murder while they were lying unconscious on the ground. Harry Bancroft was already passed out in the woods so Ben was apparently able to skip to the final act without drugging him first.

They also think Donna woke up after it happened – unable to see or speak but not quite dead – and tried to crawl away, and that's how she ended up in the bog. The details are useful, dare I say even fascinating, but they frighten Ben. His threshold for gore is very low, and the idea of *anyone* perpetrating such pointless assassinations is alien to him.

I want to ask Ben if he's mentioned the bloody rag to police but daren't with the prison warders standing by. Or am I just afraid of planting the detail back in his head, worried he'll get so sick of his cell that he'll tell officers about it to deflect attention away from himself? I tell him that I'm meeting Dick afterwards.

'Really?' He returns. 'How can you still bother with him at a time like...'

'Someone's framing you Ben,' I state, attempting to skip past any argument and his impatient doubt of my motives. 'Dick will have more insight into the kind of mind that would do that than we would. I've got to use him.'

I've also brought in all the papers. He's the splash in the *Express* and the *Mail* for a second day running. But, as expected, he doesn't want to look at them. They're more for Dick to look at than Ben anyway.

General conversation doesn't hold for long, and I find myself willing the visit to end.

'What's the food like?' I try.

'Horrible, haven't felt full since I was arrested.'

It's hard to see him like this.

At one point he breaks down and all I can summon is the pathetic non-answer of 'it'll be OK'. He shakes his head as he wipes his drippy nose on a sleeve.

'It's not that,' he says, looking at the floor. 'Being in here, all this. I wish I was back before everything, before the crash, Mum, Dad...' He breaks down again.

It is a tad hurtful to hear your boyfriend say he wishes his life had gone in a direction that meant he'd never met you. But at the same time, I've always known that's how he feels, even if he's never said it out loud before. In a way, it just adds to the deep, agonising pity I have for him. And fuels my determination to get him out.

Then he says something truly twisted. 'Rob Grayson tried to organise to see me.'

'What? Here? Already?'

Ben nods, looking up from the floor for a moment to raise his eyebrows at me.

'He is... y'know what... of course he did,' I rationalise. 'Best thing we can do is not rise to it. You declined his request, I'm assuming?'

Another little nod.

'Right, well we just ignore him. He wants to rile you... rile *me*. We don't let him.' Smiling encouragement, I take hold of his hands again, but inside I'm apoplectic. Trying to see my boyfriend – who is going through some of the worst days of his life – behind my back, to get at me. Grayson deserves to be locked up for good. Not Ben.

We sit in silence most of the remaining time. He asks me to bring some of his old *Spider-Man* comics with me next time.

The hour ends, we both say we love each other, he pleads again for me to find The Nailer. Then he's gone.

* * *

Dick lumbers in and grins. 'Guard's just pointed out my love rival going back to his cell.'

'He's got nothing to fear from you,' I swipe back.

'So, did he do it?'

'Don't even joke.'

'What have they got on him?'

'Read for yourself,' I reply pulling out the wad of newspapers Ben turned down.

'Ooo yeah, go 'ed!' he says, snatching at the bundle but then flicking them aside with his chained-up hands. 'I'll read them later, ta. But they won't give me the inside track. What's he up against?'

'It's bad,' I say, listing the evidence. 'Blood on the nail gun, CCTV of his van parked up by the woods on the nights of the murders, my Roxion pills, right shoe size and print, right height...'

'If there aren't any witnesses, how do they know the height of the guy they're looking for?' Dick questions.

'Worked out from the stride length of the prints they found near the bodies apparently.'

'And what's his van doing by Allcreek on the nights?'

'He plays at The Irby Mill, has a few beers, sleeps it off in his van then drives home.'

Dick blows his cheeks out. 'If he didn't do it, it's a slap-up job of framing him, isn't it?'

'Mmm,' I grunt.

'OK, so what do we know,' Dick begins, like we're Mulder and Scully, about to crack this case wide open. 'Nothing taken from the victims so motive isn't avarice. But no signs of sex either.'

'Just killing for the sake of it then?' I return. 'Commit the act for the pure thrill.'

'There's got to be *some* reason though,' Dick says, dissatisfied with the simplistic explanation. 'If they wanted to dominate, feel like they had power over these people they'd take more time, keep them awake longer, stay around after. But this guy seems to disappear as soon as the deed is done. It's clinical. Like all he needs is there to be a body, and is doing it as cleanly and efficiently as possible.'

'Could be that they've got a vendetta against the homeless people?' I speculate. 'But accidentally got the wrong type of person with Harry Bancroft.'

'For a killer who's so careful, that'd be a big misstep.'

'Maybe they haven't been that careful though, the footprints, leaving one of the victims not quite dead so she could crawl away. I've got a person in mind.'

'Oh yeah?' He shuffles in his seat, intrigued.

'Yeah, tell me about your ninth victim and I'll tell you what I've got on The Nailer.'

He lets out a little snort. 'Nice try Kel. One case at a time.'

I knew he'd fob me off – was worth a try.

'Go on, who's your suspect?' he demands, tantalised.

'My mate's boyfriend. Same trainers as Ben, roughly the same height, definitely walks through the woods on the nights in question, lives by them so could disappear quickly afterwards, hates the homeless gang, violent background, got done for nicking power tools before.'

'Really?' Dick's eyes widen, amazed by the charge list I've amassed. Electricity surges at my core; heat rises in my cheeks.

'And what, he's doing it because he hates the drifters?' he adds.

'Had a run-in with them a couple of years ago.' I expect another look of approval but it doesn't follow.

Dick pushes, 'What if it's nothing to do with the tramps, what if it's about framing Ben?'

'No one hates Ben. I don't see a motive in that.'

'But if it is about the drifters, how's he gone and killed a posh young fella?'

'As I say, maybe he's not been that careful. It's pitch black out there... he's not the sharpest...'

'Maybe,' Dick ponders.

'There is one other theory I can't shake. That would, erm...'

He's quick to notice my pause. 'What?'

Praying the warders won't hear me but desperate to confess all to him, I lower my voice. 'I'm worried my sleeping pills might be making me... y'know... act in some kind of bad way.'

He's flummoxed but thoughtful enough to match my whisper. 'Do you remember doing anything?'

I shake my head. He squashes his eyebrows down and pushes his head back, a pantomime picture of perplexity. 'You don't have a single memory of it but reckon you might have carried out three identical murders without leaving a trace?'

'Maybe I have left traces, blood on Ben's dad's nail gun, the footprints could be me in Ben's shoes. I've read about killers purposefully using odd stride lengths to mislead detectives on height.'

Dick's quiet but looks sceptical.

'I found a bloody rag in the glove box of my car after the last murder.' My eyes are popping out of their sockets trying to show him how seriously he needs to take this, as I also scan the room making sure no one could possibly overhear us.

'You sure your little songbird didn't do it, you're not just covering for him?' Dick finally says.

I don't like him knowing anything about Ben, it makes me feel defensive, protective. Ben is not built for a place like this, because he is not capable of doing the crimes for which one would justifiably be incarcerated.

'He didn't do it,' I reiterate.

'Well someone's trying to set him up. Even if they are trying to kill the homeless ones, they're still willing to frame Ben so it's got to be someone who at least knows his routine. Otherwise, how would they know to do it when he has no alibi?'

'Todd knows his routine,' I tell him. 'Definitely could—'

'I know why you're worried you did it!' Dick erupts from his whisper, projecting the statement so loudly that everyone else in the room will have heard it whether they wanted to or not. What makes it worse is that I know exactly what he's about to say, and yet he goes ahead anyway, all too proud of the two dots he has just joined up. 'It's because of that—'

'Shut the fuck up!'

He smirks but it's a front; he's bruised by my coldness. I can tell because he doesn't offer a wisecrack response.

'Never mention that. Ever,' I add.

He raises his shackled hands to the ceiling in surrender and then does that infuriating sideways glance and grimace men do when a woman gets angry, as if to say, 'All right love, keep your hair on.'

There is, however, a very good reason why I need him to stop talking. In fact, it's the biggest reason I have for fearing I may be The Nailer. Something I should never have told Dick. Something I should never have done.

25

THE KILLER QUESTION.

I think Mum had a point when she suggested Dad's incarceration sparked my interest in the macabre. But until I met Dick there was no one I ever felt would understand the darkest question I had about myself. Namely, is my obsession with killing doomed to remain passive and harmless – or could I actually get away with it?

This gives rise to so many other unknowns... What would it feel like? How would I cover my tracks? When and where would it happen? And, of course, who...?

I know it's insane. Part of me wishes I didn't have this infatuation. That literally any other endeavour in the world would provoke me. But nothing ever has, not like this. It's not just that I'm curious, it's that it's holding me hostage. I can't push on in my career, I can't share it with Ben, I can't think about a family. I can't do anything, because my energy and attention is all being ploughed into this one addiction. And it won't be broken until I know... could I get away with murder?

My way of coming to peace with this handicap is that simply trying it doesn't necessarily lock me in to doing it forever. Maybe it will cure the itch once and for all. People do astonishing and dangerous things all the time simply to prove to themselves that they are capable of them. Most individuals who go bungee jumping or run over hot coals only do it the once. Then they tick it off the bucket list and move on. Maybe murder's just on my bucket list.

Besides... it'll make one hell of an addition to my CV as a crime reporter.

Urgh, I shouldn't be flippant. I'm more aware than most of the risks and the ramifications. And there is an alternative outcome that does genuinely terrify me: what if the act doesn't placate me, what if it awakens something monstrous and I can't put the demon back in the cage?

Fear of that is what has stopped me in the past.

Maybe over the last few weeks, in a fugue state from my Roxion tablets, I have overcome this fear once and for all. But I still have absolutely no recollection of being in those woods with those victims. No recollections at all. So for now, the roadblock in my mind remains.

The idea that even having such an internal quandary made me inherently evil was troubling me a lot around the time I moved to London. But there were, thankfully, a couple of details that prevented me from calling a helpline to have myself sectioned there and then. One thought I clung to was that the very fact I was conflicted over whether to act or not suggested a level of compassion and common decency that a true psychopath would not display.

The other crumb of comfort was Janice. My inertia as she lay dying has haunted me ever since, not galvanised me, not fed me, but scarred me. Surely if I had a serious bloodlust I'd have watched on with no compunction at all as Dick strangled her.

Either way, the battle for my soul still felt very real and unresolved by the time I returned to the Wirral. And it was what initially convinced me to visit Dick in prison. I had written to him, and he to me, several times during my stint in the capital. But I hadn't seen him since his sentencing. The unsuccessful spell at the *Daily Mirror* had me turning my attentions to the vague concept of a book on serial killers and my initial proposition for meeting in person was under the auspices of aggregating material for that project, especially details about the allusive Victim Number Nine. But within ten minutes of our first chat, I found myself making all sorts of admissions. The relief of unburdening to someone who wouldn't judge was so freeing. It did have a second, less wholesome consequence, however. And that was to normalise the belief that I needed to see if I had it in me to kill.

'You have to find someone you hate,' Dick had said. 'The actual victim may be incidental, but the source of anger is always linked to *something*.'

But I couldn't think of anyone I hated enough to take the risk on. As I admitted I was intrigued by the concept of taking a life, but didn't feel consumed by the requisite, cold-blooded rage, I could feel Dick losing interest. Like he was the master and I the apprentice he had now decided did not possess the talent worthy of his wisdom. And then another emotion kicked in. An agonising, maddening desire for his approval.

At the time of these early conversations with Dick, it blinded me. But I sobered up fast after the deadly deed was done and realised he hadn't been losing interest in me at all, he'd been feigning disappointment to manipulate me. It was both scary and transfixing. I had shared fewer than a dozen conversations with this man in my whole life and he already knew how to push my buttons, how to extract things from me that I couldn't even extract from myself.

So what crime did I commit? Dick suggested starting with something small. And then everything clicked into place – I knew immediately what and how. There *was* something I hated, that I could happily destroy without feeling any guilt at all – Moody Mildred's Siamese cat.

Ever since I'd moved in with Ben, that cat had been nothing but a nuisance. More than a nuisance – a damned minion of Satan. It would bring still-twitching birds into our house, it would screech and claw at our patio doors in the middle of the night as I was watching TV, it would pounce at me as I got out of my car in the dark. That animal was wicked. I had complained on many occasions to Mildred that Tyson – she literally called him Tyson – was not a happy pet and that it was up to her to control him, not for us to put up with the constant ninja attacks and bloody entrails. But Mildred, being Mildred, accused us of mistreating him and claimed he was always very well-behaved on her side of the fence.

So I had my victim. If she wasn't going to do anything about Tyson, maybe I would. And here's where the plan starts to resonate with the Allcreek Woods murders. I waited until Ben was away for a weekend – staying with his uncle on the South coast. And then I constructed my killing device, a small ball of tinned tuna squashed together with six of my sleeping pills inside. I'd waited for Mildred's bedroom light to go out and then set my trap, the tuna sitting at the back of a cat cage I'd picked up from a local pet store. It took the four-legged demon about an hour to sniff out the snack, then all I had to do was scamper on to the grass and shut the cage door before Tyson had finished chewing.

Target acquired, he spat and seethed for about two minutes then fell into the deepest, most eternal sleep he was ever likely to enjoy. I put the cage in the car and drove my victim out of Irby. It had actually been quite fun scoping out the ideal terrain to hide a furry body, like a film director location hunting. It had to be secluded so that the corpse would have plenty of time to rot. It also needed to be somewhere I would have time to dig a hole deep enough to muffle the smell – stop any hungry foxes coming along and digging him up.

Woods were the obvious choice. I could walk across the fields to Allcreek, but the idea of carrying the case as I walked seemed gross. Plus there were so many drifters loitering in there that I'd have risked being interrupted during my dig.

In the other direction there *was* a way to reach woodland in the village of Barnston undetected. After a long couple of days scrutinising my choice of spot, I was confident that even though the destination backed on to a farmer's field, and there was a 6-bar metal gate right at the corner of the woods that led into said field, no one ever crossed into the woods at that place because of the barbed wire fence separating one from the other. I could park in the entry lay-by to the gate, limber under the wire, and bury the cat there.

So I did.

In fact, it was that very patch which I fled back to initially with the bloody cloth I'd found in the car, absent-mindedly seeing it as another item that I needed to hide, and therefore coming up with the same solution. But upon arrival at the old burial site last Friday I had a change of heart. In the daylight, and with police swarming the surrounding areas in the aftermath of the two new bodies being found, I could very easily be caught digging a second hole, which would then possibly lead to the discovery of the cat too. Ultimately, I drove off again and deposited the bloody rag in a public litter bin up in Heswall – surely too random a spot for police to search on a whim.

Anyway, it took over an hour to dig a hole deep enough for the feline furbag's carcass. I'm pretty sure the cat was dead at this point – didn't want to touch him to triple-check. Anyway, if the pills hadn't extinguished the last of his nine lives, the ton of soil I scraped back over him and compacted down certainly did.

It felt satisfying. And I didn't feel guilty.

Dick wanted me to graduate to a more serious operation after that. I told him that I was done – that the episode had sated me and I didn't want to do any more experiments. But really, I only said that because I didn't want the pressure from him.

In truth, I knew that it wasn't enough. I had vanquished an animal, but it still didn't feel like I'd committed murder. Not really. Murder is bigger, darker, more dangerous. Murder is human on human, foe on foe.

So the turmoil remains. A metronome that ticks relentlessly, echoing in the background of everything I say, do and feel. It ticks with impatience. It ticks with destructive glee. It ticks with the killer question: could I get away with murder?

26

FOUR DAYS SINCE THE ARREST. A.M.

Maybe I should come clean to Polly about my suspicion of Todd. Maybe she knows deep down it's him but is too scared to say. Or maybe she'll at least have noticed something odd lately that could light the touch paper for police taking him seriously as a suspect. Vickers phoned last night to say they want to come round and speak to me. I ask him to come early to leave me as much of the day as possible free for thinking, for digging down on Todd. Should I just tell Vickers about Todd? No, not before speaking to Polly. She'd never forgive me.

It's been another night with next to no sleep on the sofa and it's becoming noticeable, not just in my pale face and the black bags tattooed under my eyes, but in my thinking. I'm worried I'll say something to Vickers that will incriminate Ben. I need a pick-me-up, but I can't get the flaming coffee machine to work. I swear if it weren't for my fatigued stupor I'd be able to figure it out, but no combination of button bashing is working.

Polly slept on the sofa opposite me again but has already got up and gone out, so she can't help either. I'm forced to spoon out two heaped dessert spoons of cheap Sainsbury's granules from the jar we keep at the back of the cupboard.

I pour the scalding water into my mug and a thick tar-like film forms on top. I give it a big stir and distractedly take a sip.

'ARGH!' I scream, slamming the drink down on the draining board. *Yeah, of course you've burnt your mouth you idiot – that's boiling water you've just slurped.*

I tilt my head under the cold water tap and leave it running, letting the stream numb my throbbing lip and the tip of my tongue. As I hold my head down to one side I can see across to Mildred's garden; there's a second car – a little black one – alongside her vintage Mercedes. I've never seen her drive the Merc but it used to be the pride-and-joy of her late husband, I'm told. Weird she would have a visitor though; Moody Mildred isn't usually one for guests. That black car better not belong to who I think it does. But before I can investigate any further, the noise of tyres crunching over gravel announces that Vickers and his own wheels have arrived.

It's the Superintendent and that DI Lauren May again; they come into the kitchen. I've shut the lounge door to avoid them seeing my makeshift, pigsty bedroom.

They ask me where I was on the night of the murders, ask me lots of questions about Ben, ask me about the nail gun, about his post-gig routine of sleeping in his van. Despite my lethargic haze, the answers are easier to articulate than I'd anticipated, given that they are all totally true. There are a few details that paint me in a worse light, like the fact the sleeping pills are mine and that Ben didn't even know they existed until after the killing started. Whether they believe me or not is hard to gauge.

It doesn't feel like they're here to sound me out as an accomplice. They just want to see if our stories match – which they obviously do.

Deep down, I still don't truly foresee Ben being found guilty at a trial. My confidence in the justice system remains and therefore this stressful, nonsensical interrogation is just a challenge to be navigated, then passed and forgotten.

Nevertheless, if my tight white vest top and lack of bra happen to distract Vickers from doing his best work too then all's the better.

I wish I could tell them about Todd. I must talk to Polly today. Bite the bullet. Risk her wrath. For Ben's sake.

DI May stays pretty quiet during the questioning, her straw-coloured hair has had a lot more TLC this morning than the last time she was here. It's been straightened since she got up; the sheen catches the light as her tresses swish – elegant and smart. It's impossible to focus on Vickers. DI May's skin is so supple, no wrinkles whatsoever. And yet she must be near my age if she's reached Inspector rank. Her eyes are alert behind those horrible thick glasses. Even the way she blinks is sexy – not in a fluttery, precocious way, but with a confidence that suits her. And her small silver earrings are beautiful, little outlines of hearts with a purple stone glinting in the middle. I must look so cheap and nasty to her in my stupid £5 booby vest.

She combs a finger under her fringe to move it out of her line of sight and asks her own first question. 'Digital forensics have been looking at the laptops. There's some quite violent pornography that's been accessed on the nights of the murders on one of them. Ben claims to know nothing about it and says he doesn't take a laptop to The Irby Mill, which would suggest...'

'It's me, I... that's my laptop. But it will only come up for two of the nights you're talking about, because, as I say, I was staying at a friend's house on that first Thursday, when you're saying Donna probably died.'

Vickers nods but doesn't make eye contact, he's too embarrassed. That makes two of us, but a pair of detectives knowing about my porn habit is far easier to accept than the fact that Ben must also now know. I think again about him sitting in his cell, already a shell of a man, stewing over his girlfriend's secret predilection for S&M movies.

'There was also a hell of a lot of data recovered from webpages accessing all sorts... suspicious death reports, homicide investigation best-practice, scientific research into corpse decay, psychological studies of serial killers, hundreds of posts on gory chatrooms...' DI May adds.

'I'm guessing you'll claim all that too,' Vickers states, happy to answer for me. 'Par for the course with crime reporters,' he explains to DI May, who very much doesn't need it explaining to her.

They don't stay long after that. DI May is first out of the door. But as Vickers reaches the porch steps, he turns back to me and puts a tender hand on my shoulder. 'I was reading about victims with brain damage. Temporal lobe trauma affects impulse, frontal lobe damage can reduce compassion. Put them together and you have the makings of a killer. I know Ben fractured his skull in that car crash – maybe what he's done isn't his fault, in a way...'

'Ben's not brain damaged, he's innocent...' I have to force the words past my teeth, such is the fury I'm struggling to keep down. '... Abberline!'

The door is slammed shut with his eyes still stuck on me. I've never used his nickname before, I always thought it was unfair and mean. But an enemy of Ben's is an enemy of mine.

That car is still outside Mildred's house when I return to the kitchen. It's bugging me. I do know someone with a little black one like that. Would he dare speak to Mildred? Of course he would.

I stand there for a couple of minutes, spying on my neighbour's driveway. A muffled thud and tiny shudder reverberate through the walls. I know that noise – it's Mildred shutting her front door. And then I see him – Rob Grayson – marching away from the house, notepad in hand.

Outside and up to the fence before he even reaches his car, I ask the obvious question: 'What the fuck?'

'I don't trust suspect's girlfriend, claims scared neighbour.' Talking in headlines, classic Grayson.

'What, my mum not old enough for you?'

'Normal protocol to knock on doors in the area after someone's charged with murder, Kel.'

'And what about tapping up Ben?' I seethe.

'If a suspect wants to talk to me, I won't say no.'

'Except he doesn't want to talk to you.'

'Not yet,' Grayson shrugs, like he's Nostradamus.

'Please Rob, he's not guilty!'

'That's where we agree.' He smiles, forcing out half a chuckle. He lets his gaze fall on to my braless chest with all the subtlety of an airhorn. I want to lambast him for it but can't think of anything to say, exhaustion weighing so heavy.

Instead, the gawping goblin butts back in. 'As Mildred said, it's not *him* she's worried about, it's you.'

I re-emerge from the mire. 'Yeah, and it's also wildly defamatory. Seriously, can't we call a truce?'

'I'll call a truce when you tell me what happened with Dick Monroe in the timber yard. Plus, Mildred tells me that not long after you moved in here, her cat went missing.'

I look at the front of the old hag's decrepit house and all the 'Missing' posters for Tyson she still has Blu-Tacked to the inside of the windows.

Grayson uses the break in eye-contact as an excuse to move towards me. Then he lowers his voice and adds, 'She also saw you bleaching the inside of your car a few days ago, then throwing everything into a black bin liner. So I'll call a truce Kelli, when you give me an innocent answer for all that.'

I don't look into his eyes, I look at his chin – red and blotchy behind dark prickly stubble with dead skin dried to it. 'You're sick!' I snarl. 'And when I find out who really did this, I'll be reminding the *Echo* who you were busy harassing, rather than taking this case seriously.'

I march away, not wanting him to have the final word, but he can't help hollering one last headline: 'The Nailer frames her own boyfriend.'

Utterly passive, I walk back up the steps and shut the front door softly to disabuse him of any notion that he has gotten to me.

27

FOUR DAYS SINCE THE ARREST. P.M.

The clash with Rob brings a burst of energy that propels me forwards. First port of call will be the homeless guys. They may have tiptoed back to their usual bolthole near Vino'clock again now a suspect is in custody. If anyone has spotted Todd, or anyone else, lurking around the woods it will be them.

The strategy is to befriend the homeless group. Don't buy them drinks in return for information. Come bearing gifts in the first place, a boozy schmooze: find out their names, commiserate about the unfair hand they've been dealt in life. I'm confident I can eke *something* useful out of them. This crazy summer of terror in Allcreek Woods has always been about the homeless victims – it's just that the press doesn't attach the same value to their lives as to someone with a house and a job.

Was killing Harry Bancroft a deliberate ploy from the killer to garner some mainstream publicity, or just a case of mistaken identity? Does the killer despise vagrants or are they just easier targets, the same way so many murderers have targeted them? Burke and Hare, The Stoneman, Alexander Pichushkin, Arthur Gatter and a thousand other twisted minds through history. The concept is not new. Gatter and Pichushkin especially showed very similar traits to The Nailer.

All these variables and questions need to be fed back in and tested

against the Todd theory. Overturning the police's case feels like trying
to skewer a dragon with a toothpick right now. But I *will* slay the beast. I
must.

I make another coffee with the cheap granules – successfully
adding some cold water this time, so I can gulp it down – then drive
over to the woods.

Jay is alone in Vino, sitting behind the counter fiddling on his
phone.

'Jay, the usual suspects. Have they come back or are they still in
hiding?'

'Nah course der back. My drinks are cheapes'.' He talks like Todd,
accent as thick as the silt at the bottom of the Mersey.

Off the shelves behind his counter I point to a clear liquid that
doesn't even bother to attach itself to the respectable families of gin,
vodka or rum, and instead simply claims to be 'white spirit'. I'm not
sure whether it's meant to be a pun but with a 54% alcohol content and
only costing £13-a-litre the name is probably apt. I request three bottles
and Jay bags them up.

'So who are the homeless guys? The ones who've come back. Two
guys and a girl, isn't it?' I ask, passing over £40 in cash and waving away
the £1 in change because I'm a modern-day saint.

'Usually more than tha', but the three 'ere every day are Shaz Atkinson, Neil Drum and Lee Inkly.'

My blood runs cold. 'Lee Inkly? *The* Lee Inkly?'

'Google 'im', Jay says, not interested in small talk as he settles back
on his stool and gets his phone out again.

It can't be, can it? I do Google him. It is! How did I not recognise
him last time I bought them booze? Probably because he's aged about
ninety years in less than two decades. Alcohol really can ravage a man.

He's a paedophile, that's the reason he's been in the news. There are
court stories galore as I scroll on my phone. Conviction after conviction. Spent more than half his life in prison for molesting primary
school kids, according to one old *Echo* report.

My throat thickens making it hard to swallow as I find the piece I'm
looking for though. An archived article from my dad's trial. Lee Inkly

was close friends with the guy Dad killed. They lived in the same hovel. Lee made up some nonsense testimony to try to get my dad done for murder. Lied. Said it was unprovoked – that Dad attacked that vile man for no reason.

Lee wasn't even there when it happened! I despise that piece of useless vermin. If I tell Mum he's still hanging around Irby she'll probably come straight over and extinguish him herself. I contemplate leaving, giving up on the hunt for evidence.

No. Ben *needs* me to keep digging. These drifters may hold the key. I keep putting one foot in front of another, forcing myself into the woods. For Ben, and only Ben.

The search is short. I follow the sound of voices along the edge of the trees down to the south-easterly corner of the forest. The recent rain has left it muddy, making my footprints far clearer than they have been on other recent ventures into Allcreek. I find them sitting around a circle of white ash which looks like it may have been keeping them warm the previous night. There have been three murders in these woods in less than a month, and yet they've still flocked back to Allcreek time after time for Vino's cheap liquor – now that's customer loyalty!

There's six of them in the circle of trust today, all suddenly silent as I introduce myself. The stench of stale piss makes it hard to speak without gagging. I explain who I am, not assuming any of them will remember from the last time I spoke to them outside the offie, but Inkly does.

'More booze for more answers, is it?' he asks as if he's too clever for my games. His eyes haven't left the bag at my side though, so if this is a game, I know who's winning.

'If you want,' I say, doing incredibly well to sound innocent and generous. He looks like he's lived five lifetimes since the trial, skin haggard as a truck tyre and thin silver hair that all seems ready to fall out the next time he sneezes.

The lies he told about Dad haven't aged a day though. The longer I look at him the more his eyes do feel familiar: hollow, unashamed, remorseless. Am I really going to smile and give this man a gift?

Thoughts of Ben win out again and I pass over the bottles.

'Cheapest shit in Vino,' Lee Inkly mumbles as he unscrews the top and swigs. He winces, takes another princely gulp then passes the fire-water on to a timid henchman. 'Our tongues still work y'know? This stuff's fucking foul.'

'You're fucking foul,' I think. Outwardly I apologise, obsequious to the last. I need a line from them. Something – anything – on Todd.

I recognise Shaz and Neil too and also hand a bottle to each of them, making sure to say their names and make eye contact as I do so.

Shaz is on an up-turned bucket with her hands awkwardly placed towards the back of her hips. All the men are malnourished, with vomit-stained tracksuits clinging to shoulders as lean as coat hangers. But she's a bit younger, not as sallow, there's some firmness to her cheeks. She's actually really pretty. I suddenly want to whisk her away from all this, put her in my car, drive her somewhere safe, tell her she can even stay with me if she needs to. What horrors must befall any woman to wind up with this lot?

The Mother Teresa instinct only lasts a second, however.

No distractions; I'm here for Ben. Back in the zone. 'Thought I'd come back and speak to you again,' I say to deeply suspicious glares. 'Two of those who've died were mates of yours, and you are in and around Allcreek a lot; there might be something you've seen that other people in the village didn't, and that police never bothered to ask you.'

'We'd have told the bizzies if we'd seen anything,' Neil asserts, as if I'm a moron for trying to treat them like human beings.

'So there's nothing out of the ordinary, no one been lurking in the woods since? Killers often like to go back to their crime scenes after-wards to relive what they've done so maybe...'

'You trying to say one of us did it?' Inkly spits.

'No, no, not at all. Just that if someone else is here a suspicious amount of the time you'd be the best people to spot them.'

'It's someone who knows their way around the woods, trust me,' Neil declares, slurring.

'Why'd you say that?' another of the group asks my question for me.

'Coz we don't ever hear them!' he explains. 'They must get close enough to us over ere' to get one of us on our own, but we never hear 'em and they sneak away again in the pitch black without a torch or nuffin.'

'How d'you know they ain't got a torch?' the other retorts again, aggressive and belittling.

'Have you ever seen a torch round 'ere at night?' Neil asks. 'Trust me, they are doing all this and sneaking away without leaving the path and without making any noise or using any light. You don't do that if you don't know your way around.'

'You probably just didn't notice coz you're always pissed,' says the sceptical one, before launching into a throaty, sonorous bleat of laughter that fails to catch on.

'How has the killer got two of you on your own if you always sit together?' I probe.

'Sometimes we go for a wander. Go for a piss,' says talkative Neil.

'But none of you have ever heard or seen anyone suspicious?'

None of them answer.

The rate they're drinking my bottles of bribery, I can well imagine why they haven't seen this silent assassin yards from their camp – they're all sozzled by sundown every day.

I try a different line of attack. 'Some people are saying it could be Todd Kromkamp. You heard of him?'

A few blank stares and head shakes around the group.

'I think he had a run-in with you a couple of years ago. Thought one of you were breaking into his car. Chased you. Then got beaten up.'

'Oh him?! Weedy fella. Lives above Newton shops?' Neil remembers. 'We did him good and proper.'

'Who's "we"?' I check.

'Was it me, you and Maurice?' Neil calls over to Inkly.

Inkly nods, taking another slurp of the rocket fuel.

'Maurice Williams was one of the ones who attacked Todd?'

'We didn't attack him!' Inkly cries. 'He ran after us! We sorted him out. That's it.'

'Surely that's a good motive for him to...'

'I don't like all these questions,' Inkly decides. The others shake their heads in agreement and he tells me to leave.

I try to think of a counter question to keep them talking but the revelation is too big to compute in one go, scuttling me under the waves of exhaustion and possibility.

It takes Inkly getting to his feet to shake me back to life. 'I've told you! GO!' he shouts, hobbling in my direction with a deranged look in his eye.

Apologising, I scarper back to the road and that fresh, fresh air.

Maurice beat up Todd. Maurice beat up Todd. I repeat it over and over in my head. That's massive. That's massive!

On top of all that it's still sinking in that I've seen Lee Inkly again after all these years. But I must speak to Polly about Todd. She *must* know something.

28

FOUR DAYS SINCE THE ARREST. EVENING.

Ben uses one of the prison phones to ring late in the afternoon and I'm able to give him some much-needed words of love and assurance. Not a lot for him to report of course. I choose to keep my fledgling theory to myself for now. But there's an excited bounce in my voice as I comfort him and that infectious joy in turn leaves him sounding brighter by the time we sign off. It feels good to have helped him, or to feel like my mood could positively affect his. I think I've very much taken for granted his affectionate words and tiny acts of kindness since we've been together. That tenderness I need so badly, given my own insatiable penchant for the unhinged. His wholesome influence could be the biggest factor keeping me out of a padded cell. It's high time I pull my weight in this relationship.

Polly was out walking before Vickers and DI May arrived this morning. It looks like she may have popped back in when I was out, as there are supplies in the fridge now. She's been here five minutes and she's already adult-ing better than me. Polly... the responsible one in this friendship. Where did that come from? It's like a beggar whipping out a chip-and-pin machine – I'm not sure whether to be shocked or impressed.

After Ben's call I sit at home for the rest of the afternoon, pensive, nervous and impatient for her to return. Finally, she does. I ask her to come and sit on the sofa. She can tell something's up, but sits anyway. I'm ready with my line.

'Pol, I think Todd's The Nailer.'

'No,' she says without missing a beat.

I give her my litany of evidence.

She shakes her head over and over.

'You must have seen something, suspected something,' I tell her. 'I'm not blaming you or anything, but if you've got *anything* we can use it. Get Todd. Free Ben.'

'I'm sorry,' she whispers, suddenly fragile and scared. 'I can't.'

'Can't what? Can't remember or can't tell me?'

'Kel, don't do this. Don't go to the police saying it's Todd.'

'But if you've got evidence, we can make sure he's locked up. You'll be safe from...'

'And what if the police don't believe you? He'll know I said something.' She's shaking now, staring at the ground in blind terror. 'He'll come for me. He'll...'

She bursts into tears.

'Come on! We can do it together,' I plead.

'No! No!' she sobs. 'If you try to say it was Todd, I'll give him an alibi, I'll testify for him. I'm not doing it! I'm not doing it!'

'OK, OK,' I row back, regretting being so gung ho.

'I just can't, Kel.'

'OK Pol!' I say as I hug her close. 'I'm sorry, I'm sorry.'

'Please don't go to the police,' she splutters.

'But you do think it could be him?' I urge.

'I'm not saying, I'm not saying,' she repeats. 'I can't.'

I'm torn by her predicament and Ben's. Of course she's intimidated by Todd. But Ben cannot go to prison for this. I need time to think. How do I get through to her? Get her to open up? Will she ever open up? She must have something damning. You don't react like this if the idea of Todd being The Nailer is completely new to you. She's petrified, not shocked.

I rock her back and forth. 'I'm sorry,' I tell her again, stroking her shoulder. 'Look, go grab a shower, take a breather, then we'll have a chilled evening, yeah? No more Nailer talk tonight. Promise.'

She takes the advice. I stay on the sofa with all sorts of thoughts swirling. The more I contemplate, the bleaker I feel that Polly will ever give Todd up, or at least any time soon. It's Thursday night. Another body being found in the morning would do Ben's case the world of good. But am I really praying for another murder? Maybe if it was Inkly it would be OK. Ben freed, Dad avenged. But *any* body would at least prove to Vickers that Ben is innocent.

Desperation and resignation swamp me. Polly is even more brittle than I'd anticipated. How do I break Todd's hold over her? She comes back in and can sense I'm overwrought.

'I know what you need!' she chirps, looking like she's forgotten all about the conversation that had her convulsing less than an hour ago. Just like her to blank out her feelings rather than face them. She skips out of the lounge and comes back in waggling a fresh bottle of gin. 'Go on, please. Please! Just for tonight!'

A second's hesitation, then I snatch at the bottle, spin off the top and cock my head back. I abhor the taste. Well, it doesn't 'taste', it just burns. But the flourish is flamboyant enough to make Polly do a star jump and then leap on me in excitement.

'So what do we do now?' I ask, passing the gin back to her.

'Drinking games!' she exclaims, displaying the sort of enthusiasm she wouldn't have dared show a week ago. Todd's influence on her must have been absolutely crushing.

'Dare me to do something and if I do it, you take a swig, and if I fail, I'll take a swig,' she suggests.

My initial sip is still warm on my tongue. I pull off Ben's old Glastonbury hoodie that I've been cocooned in and cross my legs to face Polly on the sofa.

'Urm, alright. I dare you to... urm... I dare you to text Anna saying she should leave Henry.'

Polly grins, shakes her head and brushes the curve of her blonde hair out of her bruised eye, which is looking a lot healthier this evening.

'There's no way,' she says, taking a gulp from the bottle. 'My turn! I dare you to run and hide, and I'll come and find you.'

Wait silently among the shadows in this haunted house? No thanks. I take another small sip of the spirit.

The game keeps us entertained for quite a while. I manage to avoid most opportunities to drink but an unsteady sway starts to build behind my eyes all the same. Polly is making me laugh though, distracting me from any sickly sensation as her dares become more and more outrageous.

She dares me to shout 'Mildred's a mad old witch' out of the lounge window – a task I am most happy to fulfil.

We're still laughing our heads off as I stumble back to my place opposite her on the sofa, a little closer now.

'Your turn!' she giggles.

I don't say anything but gaze at her. The air around us is suddenly heavy, forcing us together.

'What?' she breathes.

My heart's crashing against my chest. 'I dare you to kiss me.'

29

FIVE DAYS SINCE THE ARREST. A.M.

It's light outside when I wake up, still on the sofa with Polly. I inhale Ben's smell on his thick hoodie that I'm back wearing. I will get him freed. That's what I need to remember through all of this. I am going to get him out.

Making a disappointing coffee with the granules, I huddle up on a seat at the kitchen table as early morning sun floods in. What's that phrase for when weather reflects mood? Pathetic fallacy! That's how this feels. A crisp clear morning where I know exactly what I have to do. What happened last night was wrong, I definitely can't tell Ben. But it was at least part of a plan – a plan of necessity. Polly's head is in the sand, she won't let herself accept what Todd's done. But the idea of losing *me* might just be enough to change that. And what better way to tighten her dependence than a kiss? It's emotional super glue. Now I need her to be stuck to me more than Todd. That's the gamble my gin-emboldened mind came up with last night, anyway. Because if this doesn't work, I'll be in custody by lunchtime.

Suppose I could have slipped my hand into her shorts to seal the deal. No. Leave them wanting more, that's the old adage; whether you're talking about an aging rock band as they stagger off stage or a desperate crime reporter trying to emotionally influence her best mate: leave them wanting more.

What the kiss will do to our friendship longer term, I don't know. Polly may despise me forever for toying with her. But as scared as she is of Todd, she cannot put that fear before justice and Ben. I will not let her.

Friday morning and no news flashes up of a fresh body being found either; the last hope that could have side-stepped all that is to come.

It's almost 9 a.m. when she eventually stirs and wanders into the kitchen. She opens the fridge and pulls out a bunch of grapes.

She looks far more awake than I feel. 'Last night was fun,' she can't help but say, green eyes glowing as they land on me.

'Pol, what we did... it can't happen again. I'm still with Ben.'

The glow turns to a glare, as if I've just poured all her gin away. Her strop is immediate – as I'd expected. She storms off up to the spare room where she's been keeping her bags. I follow her up and see her stuffing multiple long-sleeved tops into one of her rucksacks.

'What are you doing?' I demand provocatively, which only fuels her nuclear reaction.

'You want me to move back in with Todd, fine!'

'I never said that. I don't want that at all. But we're friends, Pol. Ben is still going to come home.'

'Is he though?' she stares up at me, a hatred in her eyes I don't recognise. 'Is he actually going to be let off? Because...'

'He didn't do it, so I still believe he won't be—'

'What if he did though Kel?! Partners never want to believe the worst. I've been living with an animal for years and haven't wanted to accept that he...'

'Yeah, Todd is an animal. That's why we both know it's him doing all this, not Ben, right?' My first stab at getting a straight answer misses wildly.

'Oh no, you could never make a bad call on a boy,' she fumes. 'Not the famous Kelli Amari, whereas if Polly's being messed about it's probably coz she's too thin or too weak or too stupid to stop it. That's Polly's fault, isn't it?' she yells, sitting on her bed and flapping her arms like a grounded teenager. At least I can take some pride in regaining my title as the mature one in the relationship, I think to myself. I plonk down too and try to put an arm round her. She shrugs it off.

'Pol, I need to tell you something. I have never been surer of anything in my life than the fact that Ben is innocent.'

No stir or recognition for what I'm saying.

'It's up to me to get him out.'

She'll look when I say this next thing. That's a certainty.

'If you won't let me go to police about Todd, I'll have to tell them it was me.'

A blink and her eyes are now fixed where they should be – on mine – but it's unnerving. Her head still hasn't moved, forcing her to stare at me out of the corners of her flinty eyes. No trace of a reaction beyond that.

'I've gone round every last potential suspect and every piece of evidence. I think it's Todd, but if you're going to defend him then the next best suspect is me. Police will buy it.'

'What if they think it's you *and* Ben?' she asks, lips moving and leer still angling out of the side of her head. She's a ventriloquist's dummy, engaged but soulless.

'They're looking for a lone killer. I'll make sure it's me.'

Silence expands until it's smothering us both. I've only one line left to deliver. Getting off the bed, I turn, lean on the doorframe and say, 'Please don't tell anyone about this conversation.'

I'm halfway down the stairs when the dummy comes to life.

'You're not serious,' she checks from the landing.

The urge to simply reply 'deadly' is strong but the conversation doesn't warrant it. 'Completely serious.'

'They'll know you're lying,' she implores.

'We're about to find out.' I've reached the kitchen now and Polly is racing after me, a petrified child who's lost sight of her parent.

'Don't say that! You're not thinking straight.'

'It's those pills you put me on to, Pol. The Roxion tablets. I've been looking up the side effects. The triazolam in them, it can cause sleepwalking.' Mouth dry, arms shaking, I can hardly get the question out. 'What if I have been doing it in some sort of daze?'

'No. Don't think like that. You couldn't.'

'There are loads of cases of people being found innocent by juries on evidence like that. It could be a fugue state, "dissociative amnesia" they call it. What if that's—'

'Kelli stop it!' She's on her knees at my feet now, scratching at my calves underneath my jogging bottoms as she clings to me.

'I'd claim it was the pills. I could get off, maybe. Or at least get manslaughter.'

'But no one suspects you. There has to be another way!' A snot bubble pops on her nostril as I stare down both barrels; her eyes are bright pink as if burned by the wind as the tears form a constant stream down each side of her face.

I'm engulfed by pity for putting her through this but she needs to realise the cost of what she's doing. 'Close to the woods, no alibi, obsession with killers, weapon nearby. It all fits Pol. I still don't think I did it, but I'm one million per cent sure Ben didn't. I can't let him take the blame. I have things I've done, reasons I deserve this. But Ben? No.'

She's hyperventilating. 'Please, don't do anything. Let's talk about it.'

'If you know something about Todd, tell me. If not, this is it.'

She gawps, mouth moving but no words forming.

'That's it then,' I say, my stomach lurching as I contemplate actually doing this. Please break Polly. Sober up! Before it's too late for both of us! 'I'll tell them about the note I left on the car. I found a bloody rag in the glovebox after one of the deaths too. Did you know that?' I say, my own voice wobbling.

She is back on her feet trying to fasten us together, both arms locked around me. I let her keep her grip on my blouse for now and tell her again that there is no other way.

'Don't. Please! I can't live without you Kel. I can't lose you. I CAN'T!'

Her head's squashed into my shoulder so I push a palm up each side of her jaw, letting the fingers split around her ears, then pull her head back so we're staring at each other, our noses an inch apart.

'Ben is not going to jail,' I state.

Flinging off her weightless arms, I take out my phone. My fingers quiver as I unlock the screen and find Vickers' number.

One ring and he answers.

'No, no. DON'T!' Polly begs.

I speak loudly and clearly. 'Hi Abe, it's Kelli.'

'NO! NO! STOP IT!'

I put my hand over the mobile's microphone. 'This has to end, Pol. I'm just going to tell him.'

'NO!' She snatches the phone, hangs up and slams the handset into the floor like a firecracker.

'What the...?'

'YOU CAN'T TELL HIM YOU DID IT!' she screams.

'WHY?!'

'BECAUSE IT WAS ME!'

30

THE DAY OF THE CONFESSION. A.M.

Slumped on the kitchen floor, I stare at the ground, too numb to function. Polly has been talking and talking and talking for what feels like hours. I haven't heard a word.

Polly.

Polly is The Nailer.

It's too much.

Polly is The Nailer. The words keep knocking at my head, waiting to come in. But I can't let them. It's not possible.

How didn't I see it? How has she got away with it? How, what, why? A million questions and yet no room for any. I am blank, bewildered and broken.

I move to the lounge for escape. But she follows me, still gabbling. I shut my eyes and try to block it out.

Am I in danger? Is she going to kill me?

No, the whole point of this was so she could have me to herself, that's what I think she keeps saying a thousand different ways, trying to justify everything she's done.

I can't take any more.

'Shut up!' I order.

She does, eyes desperate for the kind of acceptance she will never receive from me again.

'I need to think,' I mutter. Understatement of the millennium.

* * *

Polly goes out for a walk, leaving me to piece my shattered mind back together. What does this mean for Ben? Do I go to police? Tell them she confessed? Would they believe it? Is there enough proof to get Ben off? I'm not sure there is. I could just be the heartbroken girlfriend trying to pin the blame on literally anyone else rather than my man.

The gravity of what she's done, and why, begins to permeate. I think about asking her to go to police herself and confess if she really does care about me so much, but I know she won't. Commit murder? Yes. But a lifetime in prison? No. For her, that would defeat the point of doing all this in the first place. It's starting to sink in just what lengths she has gone to in a bid to meld her life to mine. The profound desperation of it makes me dizzy.

What Todd can't have realised as he was beating her black and blue was that he was forging a monster. And she was willing to do absolutely anything to get what she wanted.

On the surface the obvious solution – as much as framing someone for murder can be an 'obvious solution' – would have been to pin the killings on Todd. He gets arrested. Simples.

But she didn't just need to be rid of Todd. She needed to remove Ben too. Because this has always been about Polly needing me, and needing all of me. There is no sharing in Polly-land. She is a parasite, always has been. Todd's new-found taste for violence accelerated the need for a new host – I was the target. What's terrifying to the point of horror is to think how deranged and mentally unwell she must be to assume this was the best course of action.

I return to my original conundrum. I need hours, days, aeons to think. Just go to the police. Just go to the police! They will arrest her. They'll find a clue – the shoes, the spiked booze, the chloroform, *something* that will prove I'm not lying. It's a certainty.

And yet I know I'm not going to do that. Deep down, I know more as each minute passes. There's another solution. One I can't unsee. One my whole life's been leading to.

Can I do this? The potential is intoxicating. I'm all twitchy. Maybe I should wait, mull it over longer, sleep on it.

But I won't sleep. Not now the idea's seeded.

Polly comes back in from her walk sometime in the early evening. She chooses to go straight to the kitchen rather than joining me in the lounge.

I reach the kitchen door in time to see her spinning the lid off a fresh bottle of gin and taking a prodigious gulp. She glances up at me as if I'm about to cook her with a flamethrower.

'If I turn you in there's no guarantee they'll believe me,' I say.

'Thank you! Oh, thank you! That's...'

I interrupt. 'So you're going to frame Todd.'

'OK, yes. Yes! I was thinking on my walk, if it's between you and him, I choose you every time. No more protecting him. I'll go to the police now. I can tell them he...'

'No,' I shake my head.

Retaining my grip over her as I get these next few words out is essential. Grenades are erupting in my chest because I think she's going to submit. I clench my jaw, hold her gaze, then speak slowly. 'You don't go to the police.'

She frowns, not understanding what I'm telling her.

I answer her silent question with authority. 'You frame Todd with one more body.'

31

DAY OF THE CONFESSION. EVENING.

The next two hours are so unique I can draw no parallel in my whole life. We sit at the table, discussing how to frame Todd for an additional murder.

'How have you not been caught?' I begin.

She's been clever. More observant and exacting than I thought her capable. Rubber gloves. Waiting until one of the homeless lot had wandered off from the group. Bags over her shoes that she only removed when in position to kill. Using Todd's trainers, multiple layers of socks and a lengthened stride pattern – apparently she got that tip from me. She lays a lot of her anti-detection techniques at my door – thoughts I've absent-mindedly shared down the years regarding how to hypothetically leave a crime scene untraced. It begins to make sense as to why it's been so hard to shake the idea that I carried out the murders myself. All the tools were my own.

Donna and Maurice were just the unlucky stooges who left themselves isolated when Polly was lurking. She'd pretend to be upset, a damsel in distress, and produce the Roxion-spiked gin, offering to share it with her new-found pal. They'd agree and take a swig while sitting to comfort her. When it was apparent they were getting dozy she'd stand up, move behind them and pin a chloroform-soaked cloth over their mouth. They'd slump and she'd pull something even more lethal out of her backpack – Ben's dad's nail gun. It was a weapon she would pick up and return to our shed on every occasion.

And to avoid suspicion at home, she'd even wait until Todd had stumbled back from the pub, pour him one last strong JD and Coke, topped with three Roxion tablets of his own, and wait for his heavy head to hit the pillow before leaving the flat.

'I noticed months ago you don't lock the shed. It's surprising how many gardens you can mooch around during the night if you do enough walking,' she says.

Harry Bancroft was slightly different. She found him already passed out in the woods after too many drinks at The Irby Mill.

'How do I know you're not saying all this just to stop me phoning the police again?' I ask. 'I know Todd lied to them, pretended he hadn't walked through the woods on his way home on those nights. How do I know you're not covering for him even?'

'Todd couldn't do this,' she says, her eyes begging for a titbit of praise. 'My plan did leave room for if police decided it wasn't Ben though,' she adds. 'Keeping to Thursday nights, I knew Ben would be at the pub... and Todd too. So if any DNA or tracks or whatever did lead back to our flat, I'd still be the least likely suspect. That's why I bought Todd the same trainers Ben has. If it wasn't one, it was the other.'

'You put that bloody rag in my car.'

'Stops blood spraying on you if you hold a cloth around the nozzle bit as you shoot. There are so many capillaries in the head, it comes out like a fine mist if you aren't careful. I wanted to put the rag in Ben's van but it was locked. And anyway, no one would ever believe the famous Kelli Amari could leave something so incriminating in such an obvious place. Was hoping the police would find it and assume Ben put it there. What did you do with it?'

'Put it in a bin outside the Barclays Bank in Heswall. Near the post office.'

'Shame, that would have been damning for sure.'

Rage is bubbling at the back of my throat; explosive fury ready to spew out and burn her face off. Her apathy for Ben is grotesque. I stare at her, hoping my gaze will crush her to death and save me the chore. 'What does Todd know?'

'Nothing, obviously. Wanker.'

'I still don't believe it's you.'

'You want more proof?' she asks.

I nod.

She can barely get the words out fast enough. 'There's a detail I'm pretty sure you don't even know.'

She pauses for effect and I fall for it.

'What?' I bark.

'There was a fourth nail in Maurice and Harry. Two in the eyes, one in the throat, *one* in the side of the head. I did only three to the lady.'

'Donna.'

'Yeah, Donna.' She throws the name away, as if it's a waitress that's got her order wrong at Wagamama's rather than a woman whose life she's ended. 'I did just the eyes and throat to her thinking that would be enough. She wasn't moving when I left, but she must have crawled away afterwards. I only planned to do it the once, pin that on Ben and that would be it. But then the body wasn't found and I was worried she'd survived or something. So I had to do it again. Made sure to do four nails with the next one – Maurice. I looked it up, there's some blood vessel on the side of the head.' She taps her temple just in front of her ear.

'Middle meningeal artery,' I inform.

'That's it. Apparently it helps people bleed out quicker. Anyway, I did the second one but police still didn't arrest Ben. So I started going back into the woods at night, trying to see if I could find that first body, thought I might be able to report it anonymously the next day or something. But that's when I stumbled across Harry what's-his-face, passed out on the path. Didn't take too long to get over to yours, get the nail gun, do it, then get the gun back to the shed.'

There's a peculiar lack of appreciation for what it means to have taken a human life. She might as well be reading the T&Cs on a bank statement.

It's very different from Dick's quiet but passionate frame of mind when discussing his victims. He may not care about the women he throttled, but it is always very clear how profoundly important those memories are to him. Polly, on the other hand, speaks with chilling indifference; she really does not seem to have derived any discernible emotion at all from what she has done – either positive or negative. All that seems to matter is whether I am impressed or not.

I'd always considered her as ticking several of the sociopathic boxes, but only in an innocuous, quirky way. Now, as she talks me through everything she has done, I can see with crystal clarity that she has not been harmless all these years, she has been dormant.

We move on to the project at hand – framing Todd for an additional murder, with the signature fourth nail to telegraph that this is the original killer, no copycat.

It's accepted as read that I will take no part in the act itself, and The Nailer assures me that she will give me plenty of notice in advance of the plan being 'executed' – her word, not mine – so I can organise my alibi.

We speak details as well. Thoughts of how I'd frame someone for murder have crossed my mind a lot in the past, I've just never had reason to put them into practice.

Not all deceptive manoeuvres work in any one case obviously, circumstances rule out most otherwise brilliant ideas. That's OK though, all we need are three or four crumbs of evidence, almost too subtle to be found, but not quite.

One little trick I've devised will link Todd's DNA to the crime scene. All Polly needs to do is dig out his woolly gloves – she confirms he does own a pair – and wear them on top of her own rubber ones when she carries out the killing. The rubber ones will protect her from contaminating the gloves with her own DNA. Once the woolly pair are conveniently found by police there will only be traces of Todd's skin on the inside of them, and the victim's blood on the outside. Simple yet compelling evidence.

We also agree that Todd's claim that he never walks home through the woods is manna from heaven; officers will be able to refute this very easily by checking CCTV cameras around the perimeter of the woods.

So we have my 'gloves' con, we have him lying to detectives in his own words. Polly also suggests she could phone police the morning after the killing, to ensure evidence remains pristine and is collected immediately. A call saying she suspects her boyfriend of being The Nailer may throw some suspicion her way also, but given the very clear examples of brutality he has inflicted on her, it won't take them long to put things together.

The plot is forming with frenetic pace. We bounce off each other, sparring and brainstorming, no idea too mad or too obvious. Anything goes.

'One very important thing,' I tell her.

'What?'

'The victim. It needs to be Lee Inkly.'

'Who? It's not that easy to just...'

I describe him to her and precisely why he must be the target. 'It's got to be him, I don't want any more innocent people dying. But Inkly's vermin. It has to be him.'

She says nothing.

'I mean it, Pol. The only way I can be OK with this is if it's someone who doesn't deserve to live. After what he tried to do to Dad. It has to be. You owe me that.'

Holding my guilt card until now pays dividends. 'OK,' she says. 'I'd do anything for you, Kel.'

Anything? She isn't going to go to police and confess, is she? But whether she gets caught in the act or successfully pins this next one on Todd, either way will exonerate Ben for sure. That's enough. And anyway, all this scheming has got me feeling more alive than I've felt in years.

Polly tells me we must do it on Todd's night off – next Thursday – as always. I point out that Ben's nail gun is locked up in a police evidence room. Three flicks on her phone and she's found one on Freecycle in Chester. She suggests tricking Todd into picking it up himself during a taxi shift.

'He'll know you've got the nail gun then though?' I say.

'So what? He's not going to go to the police over that, is he?'

'But after he's been caught, when they ask where he got it, he'll say he picked it up because *you* wanted it.'

'Once he works out it's me who dobbed him in, he'll start pinning everything on me either way. I'll tell police I knew nothing about it. Then they just need to believe me over him. And if the other evidence sticks then he'll just look like a pathetic wanker trying to blame his girl-friend to save himself. Plus, better for him to be seen picking it up – rather than either of us accidentally being spotted buying or stealing one.'

I mull over the idea. It's neat and I wish I'd thought of it. 'And he definitely won't go to the police beforehand?'

'No, I'll make up some daft story about us needing to put up some shelves or something. He won't suspect a thing.'

'And by the time he puts two and two together he'll be in custody.' I reiterate her point, trying hard to avoid complimenting her.

'Exactly. It will mean me having to go home and sleep there for a few days, so I can make the booking on *his* laptop. I'll just tell him you're feeling a lot better so there's no need for me to stay any more.'

'You're sure he won't hurt you?'

She shrugs and I decide I don't care enough to object any more.

* * *

She goes up to bed soon after – in the spare room for the first time. I stay up, eager to conjure another clue we can use to incriminate Todd. We still need something more.

A shadow looms in Polly's absence, however – exactly how deep does her psychological damage go? It's still grating that I didn't spot it earlier, but then the genius of the psychopath is in absorbing the ordinary behaviours of others to convince the world that they themselves are also ordinary, rather than a tangled yarn of mirroring, fakery and self-service.

I re-familiarise myself with the 'Psychopathy Checklist' – those twenty traits deemed pertinent to a clinical diagnosis. One point if the characteristic partially applies, two points if it strongly applies – for a maximum score of 40. Bundy scored 39. Dick Monroe got 36.

Flicking through the test, I calculate that The Nailer probably has a score nearer to 30. So not quite as impressive, but clinically significant, nonetheless.

Features from the list that resonate with Polly's character include her 'parasitic lifestyle', 'proneness to boredom', 'pathological lying', 'manipulation', 'irresponsibility', 'lack of realistic/long term goals' and 'impulsivity'. It probably explains why I've always been fascinated by her far more than the basic, normalness of, say, Anna. That same compulsion which draws me to seek out twisted, ugly tales in the wider world sees me looking for complex, broken characters in daily life: Dick Monroe, Polly. Does that make me one of them, or just an admirer? I'm still not sure.

And yet the biggest epiphany of this whole desolate mess in Allcreek Woods has been regarding Ben. He's taught me something new and profound about myself. For, as much as I gravitate towards the macabre and revel in the obscene, my reliance on him has soared without him here. There's something deep that I'm rooted to, something palpable – a trust, a maternal protection, a love that offsets all my flaws. I need him, and nothing is more important than that. Without him, all that's left is the darkness.

So how do we ensure Todd gets caught? What's the clincher? Come on, Kelli. This is your moment. What have you got? I stare at Polly's pack of cigarettes, open on the table. Should I have one, go to the garden, change of scene, clear my mind? Maybe it'll dislodge some inspiration.

No, it's too dark. It'll just freak me out. I do kind of want a cigarette though.

Wait.

My body locks.

I have it.

A masterly clue to frame Todd.

It's perfect!

And the idea is, well, elementary.

32

DAY AFTER THE CONFESSION.

Elementary indeed. It's a line from Sherlock Holmes that triggers the idea:

> I flatter myself that I can distinguish at a glance the ash of any known brand, either of cigar or of tobacco.

A few powdery flakes of ash. That's the final flourish. Smoke one of Todd's Marlboro Golds at the scene leaving a small but conspicuous dusting on Inkly's clothes. Take along a separate one of Todd's butts from the ash tray at their flat to discard close to the body. Forensics will analyse it and ascertain that the cigarette butt and the ash on the body are from the same brand of cigarettes. A further test for saliva on the butt will produce one DNA match – to Todd.

Add this to my trick with the gloves, his lack of alibi, identification by the freecycler who passes on the nail gun, his girlfriend's injuries, and the fact he lied to the police about his route home on the nights of the previous killings; and the case is solid. Deceit, DNA, witness testimony, history of violence. Open and shut.

As for me. I just need a cast-iron alibi, which will involve going to stay at Mum's and suggesting a nice long video call with Dan and his family out in Australia late at night. I phone her to suggest it.

'That's not like you to organise a big family catch-up,' my mum correctly points out when I ring with the innocent suggestion.

'Make the most of it, might not happen again. I think just with Ben not here, I'm feeling a bit like I've taken you all for granted. I want to make an effort.'

'Oh, Kelli Belly, that's so nice. Shall we have a Chinese beforehand too?'

Strictly I don't need to be there until 11 p.m. for an alibi, but if there's one thing I'm as obsessed with as serial killers, it's prawn crackers.

'Only if we get extra lemon chicken,' I tease. 'You always eat that first!'

'I've got a doctor's appointment on the Thursday, it says here on my calendar, but that's at 4 p.m. so should be home by 6 p.m.'

'Doctor's? Everything OK?'

'Oh yes, nothing to worry about.'

* * *

The difficulty faced as I sit commiserating with Ben during visiting time at Strangeways is making sure I'm not too chipper. Obviously, I can't let on what's about to happen five days from now.

He's down, of course, and prickly as a hedgehog.

'Saturday 16 July. Hit me with a fact,' I suggest.

'NASA launched Apollo 11. Will Ferrell's birthday.' He makes the statement without any of the pride or joy with which it is usually delivered and doesn't bother to look at me as he says it. His curls of fair hair, usually in tight coils hanging over his forehead, are greasy and limp. And a nervous tick of pushing his palm back over his head is beginning to leave a cow's lick in the hairline. His shoulders are more hunched than last time too. If I wasn't so confident of his imminent release, I'd be heartbroken for him, and for us. The shy, sweet candle of his soul is going out.

The hour crawls by and it takes all my self-control not to whisper the masterplan to him, to lift his suffocating gloom.

'Keep fighting, my love,' I tell him instead when we hug.

I've got an hour booked in with Dick too so stay seated after Ben leaves. What do I tell Dick?

My discomfort at the two men in my life being in such close proximity, and having to see both in the one trip, is frazzling. No time to decompress from one or ease into the world of the other. Both so different, and feeding such different parts of me, parts that seem more confusing and contradictory when they are smashed together back-to-back.

Dick trudges in; he's not in a good mood either. I can tell. No physical contact, no yellow grin. He slumps into his chair, the guards chain his hands down and he waits for me to break the silence.

'Hey!' I overcompensate.

'I'm not sure I like playing second fiddle to the Little Chef.' He finally makes eye contact, his coldness makes my stomach squirm.

'Don't call him names. He's my boyfriend, what do you want me to do?'

'I'm just telling you.'

'I'm here with *you* now,' I say. 'Let's make the most of it.'

He doesn't reply.

'Maybe it's time you told me about Number Nine.'

'Not feeling it today.'

'Of course you aren't,' I snort. 'You never are. I'm losing hope you'll ever spill. If there is even anything to spill.'

'Is there a question there?' he mumbles.

'Was Number Nine your first victim, last victim, or one in the middle?'

'Would you still come and see me if you knew it all?' He asks without looking up.

'Yes,' I reply, assertive and instant.

'When you say last victim, d'you mean Janice Benson, the one you stood in silence and watched me do?'

Panic is all-encompassing. I pray with every last fibre of my being that no one is listening as my head snaps round, checking the whole visitors' room. 'What is wrong with you?'

He shrugs and bites the inside of his cheek, staring at his dirty fingernails.

'I don't have to be here.'

'No that's right. Lucky me!' he shouts. A warder paces over and puts a remindful hand on his shoulder, making him twitch in anger.

I usher them away, reassuring that we're fine.

Grasping Dick's warm, clamped hands, I wait for him to look up. 'Listen to me. We get each other, don't we?'

He doesn't speak but neither does he look away or stop holding my hands.

I go on, voice low and soft. 'If you want to know just how much effect you've had on me, just keep an eye on the news on Friday morning. And know that if it wasn't for you, I wouldn't have been able to pull it off.'

He's calmer after that.

'Friday morning,' I remind him later as I leave. 'Don't forget.'

33

SIX DAYS SINCE THE CONFESSION.

This week has been the longest of my whole life. The countdown to Thursday evening is agonising. And yet maybe necessary. After finding out Polly was The Nailer, the plot to frame Todd came together so quickly, so naturally. It's been important to have several days to poke and prod at the beats of the plan, to hone every aspect. But my goodness, have those seconds ticked by slowly.

Polly moved back in with Todd and successfully convinced him to pick up the nail gun. We have met up a couple of times and run over every detail of the night. How to place the clues, how to avoid leaving traces of herself. But given her care in not being caught until now, I have full confidence. Not that I'd tell her. Polly is still clearly desperate for my approval, desperate to rekindle the old 'us'. But I can never forgive what she tried to do to Ben. Her willingness to turn on Todd is as motivated by self-preservation as it is out of love for me. I know her secret; she needs me on-side, whatever the cost.

I've tried to keep busy, seem natural. A lunch date with Anna, calls with Ben in prison, daily messages to Vickers reiterating that Ben is innocent. The press furore around The Nailer has died away with no new bodies for two weeks. It will re-ignite when the new body's found, that's for sure. And Ben will be freed. That's all that matters. Inkly will be dead, Ben will be out. Two birds, one Polly-shaped stone.

Finally, all those sluggish, reticent seconds run out, and I arrive at Thursday night. The reckoning.

I get to Mum's at 7 p.m. and we order the Chinese straight away – not a sliver of restraint between us.

'So... how's things?' I ask as we gorge.

'Oh, you know, good days and bad days. It's so lovely to see you, Kelli. I can't remember the last time the three of us all chatted together at the same time!'

We aren't due to Zoom Danny and his family until 11 p.m. – 8 a.m. Melbourne time. As well as catching up we've promised to co-watch a Disney film with his kids over the link too, which should keep us online until at least 1 a.m.

I've told Polly not to contact me, whether she's able to complete the task or not, and ideally the first I'll hear of it will be after the body is found, or even after Todd is arrested. While this is the only way to ensure a rock-solid, unsullied alibi, it does make all these hours alone with Mum a tad tedious. She's definitely developing an old-person talent for repeating herself.

'You people can never leave those things alone,' she tuts at one point as I check my phone for the millionth time, even though I know Polly won't be in touch.

'*You people?*' I scoff back.

'Young people. I can barely make a call on mine, much preferred proper ones where you tapped the number in and away you go.'

'You just need to get more familiar, then you can get Dan and the kids to send you pictures on WhatsApp. You could watch old videos or black and white films on your iPad too if you ever used it.'

'I'd rather watch them on the television,' she says, her nose physically turning up in disdain for the technology. 'That screen's too small.'

Belt and braces – I've also taken another precaution. Rather than leave my Peugeot on Mum's drive, I've paid a morally illegal £24 overnight fee to park right at the other end of her road underneath a

Co-op supermarket security camera, just to make sure the authorities can see that the vehicle stays put all night.

Eleven o'clock ticks up and Danny messages me. 'Miracle... we're all in position if you are.'

Mum's iPad – sent to her by Dan for the sole purpose of these long-distance video chats – sits on the glass coffee table in front of us as I begin the call. Her hands initially wringing with excitement, Mum's arms fly open as two sunny little faces appear on the screen: Lily's seven, Kingsley's four.

'Hello Granny, hello Auntie Kelli,' the pair say in that annoyingly adorable, slightly drawn-out assembly-style way.

'Hello, hello my darlings!' Mum bellows as if she's actually trying to make her voice carry halfway round the world.

'Quieter!' I whisper.

Sitting behind them on a chunky grey sofa is my sister-in-law Carla – a beautiful woman who came over to Liverpool for university, met my brother, graduated, then packed him up in her suitcase and headed back to Oz. We have little in common but she's nice enough and I could spend all day just watching the swish of her red hair, which never disappoints.

Dan wanders into shot, coffee in one hand and texting with the other, giving me another spasm of angst at the phone sitting heavy in my jeans pocket, searing my thigh with its silence.

'Nice of you to join us,' I quip at him.

'I thought we were going to get Ben on the call... live stream from Strangeways for the kids,' he shoots back, a dumb grin disappearing behind his mug as he sips. He's always had a mean streak reserved for me. He doesn't put Mum down, he doesn't put Carla down, but I'll always be his little sister: good for throwing into a nettle bush to retrieve his football, a decent moving target for his plastic bow and arrow, but never quite his equal.

Carla slaps his leg and glares at him.

'I'll make sure you're next on his list,' I say before Mum cuts us both off; family dynamics die hard.

The conversation is gentle after that. Lily and Kingsley both have to relay every single detail of their sports and music clubs, what their weekend plans are with mummy and daddy, what they both want for their birthdays – which are months off. It's winter in Australia so technically this is term time, but Dan and Carla home-school the kids. If you ask me, it's a terrible idea and must be so smothering. But it does at least mean that this Thursday evening – their Friday morning – they can build in some time to chat with Granny and Auntie Kelli.

I stare at Carla, who is happy to watch her children bear the brunt of Granny's Stasi-esque interrogation. How does she always look so immaculate? It's 8 a.m. there; she's had to feed and dress both children, probably without help from her husband, and on top of that she had to give birth to the little cherubs not so long ago. Yet she looks divine.

Meanwhile, sitting in the dim glow of Mum's lounge with a single lamp on, I must look abysmal. We probably appear more like sisters than mother and daughter, given Mum's big smile and my resting ogre face.

Kingsley's desperate to watch *Snow White and the Seven Dwarfs* so we put the video on at our end – Mum's kept all our old VHS tapes and a million other knick-knacks from yesteryear. We press play at the same time as them and mute our sound. The audio doesn't quite sync up but it will do.

Mum doesn't make it through, inevitably, but keeps the snoring down so it doesn't disturb the rest of us as we watch – the children too engrossed to notice Granny sleeping.

It's almost 1 a.m. when I give her a nudge. 'It's about to finish.'

Her eyes blink wide and she composes herself in time for the credits. 'Wasn't that great!' she beams. But she's soon apologising and admitting it's time for her to go to bed.

Peeling away, she kisses me on the cheek and tells me not to stay up too late. Carla sweeps the children off too, leaving Danny and me to catch-up. He's a graphic designer, something I know diddly squat about. So my questions about how work's going are limited to, 'How's work going?'

Thankfully he's fascinated by the deaths in Allcreek Woods which keep us talking for some time.

'Ben's not a murderer. No way,' he says after a while. He's not saying it to comfort me, he's saying it because he thinks he's omniscient, but I thank him all the same.

'He won't get found guilty,' I reply, trying to sound hopeful rather than certain.

'It's not made it on to any news sites here but reading the online stuff from home they all think he's guilty. Didn't you try to get the *Mirror* to...'

'I was writing about the case until Ben was arrested, then they ditched me.'

'Shit,' he commiserates.

'You coming over at Christmas?'

'Yeah.'

'Cool.' I need to keep us chatting, keep the alibi breathing. But what's there to say?

He changes subject. 'You got anything lined up for Monday? You do know that's—'

'Yeah, I know it's Monday.' He's talking about the date on which Dad did what he did, killed who he killed.

Dan's got sticky-out ears, a black beard like Dad's and his nose is the same shape as mine; all these features are leaning closer to the screen now, as if he's finally giving the conversation his full attention. 'You know, it's eighteen years this time? Can't believe it.'

'Yeah.' I wonder if he knows how ridiculous it is to suggest I wouldn't know that it's eighteen years.

'Told Mum we'll Zoom her, she said you haven't mentioned it at all.'

I haven't got the spare headspace for this topic. He may want to talk it out, unburden himself – all his thoughts, all his feelings – but I've got enough going on without opening up that old wound. It's alright for him, he ran off to start a new life. He has the luxury of getting to think about Dad on one allotted day a year, and tell himself he's a good son for remembering. Meanwhile I'm still here, driving past Dad's favourite chip shop in Irby, his favourite pub in Prenton, the park we used to go to in Bebington. It's my every day, not just my 25 July. So I don't want to hear about how Dan's worked through all the anger and shame, how counselling has made him a better husband and father. Find your way to heal, I'll find mine.

'That'll be nice to Zoom her,' I say. 'When was the last time you popped round?'

His shoulders slump in faux-disappointment at me for snapping. 'Good to talk Kel, I gotta go.'

* * *

A night as tumultuous as this one is tailor-made for being chemically coerced to sleep. The fact Vickers took *all* my sedatives when he arrested Ben is one of the many, many things I will never forgive him for.

Where is Polly right now? Has she done it? Is it over? What if she's caught in the act? What if Inkly fights back? What if she can't find him? What if Todd smells a rat?

It must take a special kind of person to suppress all those fears and unknowns deep enough to carry out such a unique and intricate plan. To a layman, and most of the media, drugging someone then firing nails into their head sounds like a ham-fisted approach to life-taking. But given that The Nailer has not left a single trace of her own for the police to follow, her handiwork has been astounding.

Comprehending the sheer scale of our accomplishment – if this works and Ben's freed – is enough to make sleeping impossible. I lie there, trying to fathom the magnitude of my palpable contribution to this. But also, the exquisite distance I have put between myself and suspicion.

I stare at the ceiling, waiting for dawn. Maybe with it will finally come the answer to my question.

34

THE DAY OF THE 4TH BODY. A.M.

It's 9.18 a.m. when an alert flashes up on my phone from the BBC news app:

THE NAILER STRIKES AGAIN: FOURTH BODY FOUND IN ALLCREEK WOODS ON THE WIRRAL

Despite not getting a wink of sleep, I hadn't dared Google for updates on the murders any earlier as this would look incriminating if my phone was ever taken into evidence. But now the headline has come up naturally I click on the link. It isn't very enlightening: Body found just after 6 a.m.... No arrests yet... A number to call police with information... More to follow.

I head into Mum's lounge and turn on Sky News, hoping they might have scooped a few more details, namely that Todd – or at least 'an unnamed man' – has been detained.

And while Sky News is reporting an extra detail than the BBC, it is not a positive one in the slightest.

Polly hasn't killed Inkly. She's killed Shaz – the woman among that group in the woods. The only woman.

Sky News hasn't named the victim, but a reporter at the scene has been briefed that it is a homeless female in her mid-30s. The journalist adds that police have strong evidence to suspect the crime is the work of the same person who committed the other murders in Allcreek Woods.

Grief expands inside me until there's not even room for relief that Ben will probably be home by this evening. That vulnerable woman, her lonely eyes and thin downwards-turned lips, is all I can picture. Have I contributed to this? Is Shaz going to haunt me like Janice?

No. I told Polly to find Inkly. Inkly. I stated it *had* to be Inkly. The paedophile, not the vulnerable woman. Anger flushes out guilt.

I sit watching as the news anchor states the same limited script again and again based on the few facts they have about this fourth murder. By 10 a.m. Mum is up too.

'Kelli, please turn that horrible stuff off.'

'Have you seen though, Mum! Another victim! Ben will be released!' I try to sound surprised.

She leans over and kisses me on the cheek. 'That is wonderful Kelli. Wonderful!' She says the words but stays standing, still gazing at me.

I shoot her a perplexed look. 'Do... you... want a seat?'

She doesn't move.

My stomach flips over. 'Mum... what?'

Her eyes are brimming with tears.

'Mum?' I squeak, starting to panic.

She's shaking as she lowers herself down next to me. The smell of her honeysuckle perfume is strong and sickly as I give her elbows a squeeze. 'What is it, Mum?'

'I'm so sorry. I should have told you. I meant to tell you both last night. But then the kids were so happy. And now you've got all this going on,' she whimpers, motioning at the TV.

'What, tell me what?!'

She leans back enough to make eye contact.

'The doctor's yesterday. They...' she takes a deep, wobbly breath in, then a long, steady exhale. 'They've confirmed it. Alzheimer's, early onset.'

'No.'

She nods, unable to look at me any longer.

We hold each other for a very long time, not speaking. Too shocked. Too heartbroken.

Not now. That's what I keep thinking. Not now. Life was about to get back to normal. Ben's coming home, the killing is going to stop. This was the next chapter. The future was so bright. And now this shadow is going to hang over it all. Impossible to remove or ignore.

'I don't know what to say,' I mumble. I just want to hug and comfort her. She looks so small and sad.

'Don't say anything,' she says, her arm gripping around me. 'And hey, the sooner it's over, the sooner I'll be back with your father. I miss him so much,' she says with a stoic smile.

I try to reply with 'me too' but the words are too painful.

We stay holding each other as she talks me through the science. An initial PET scan. Toxic beta-amyloid plaques detected in the brain. No prediction how quickly it will progress. Incurable.

'It's been affecting my memory for quite a while I think. I've noticed it's harder to keep lots of things in my head at once. At first I thought it was just old age, but it was getting a bit embarrassing, so I went to Dr Armstrong, he referred me and then, well...'

The word 'incurable' has my mind in a choke hold, leaving no room for emotion yet.

It's clear she's relieved at telling someone. Her thoughts are all over the place. Memories of Dad, fears for the future, worries over telling Dan and a dozen other friends. Remembering Ben's just been exonerated. Wondering if she can still book a trip to Australia. Hoping that certain drugs will slow the symptoms. Trying to stay positive.

She talks, I listen.

I feel *so* guilty that I made fun and got frustrated at her mental lapses of late. It all makes sense now. How can I ever take back the callous reactions? I can't.

It's gone midday when my mobile rings.

Vickers.

'Take it, take it,' Mum insists, passing the vibrating phone over to me.

'Courtesy call,' he announces in that thick Yorkshire drawl. 'We've arrested another bloke. Ben's being released at 3 p.m.'

I tell him I understand and put down the phone.

After so many days of clock-watching – seeing each new second as a fresh injustice for Ben – now, at his moment of triumph I am not in any state to have him home. I can't leave Mum like this. I'm still in shock, stuck between mourning and denial.

Mum has a very different view. 'He's your man!' she implores. 'What I'd give to be able to go and pick your father up. You've missed him so much, Kelli Belly. Please, please, please don't let me get in the way. I'd hate that. I've told you everything, that was the biggest thing. I'm fine.'

'You're honestly OK? No! I can't...'

'I have good days and bad days, but I think today's a good one. Now go!'

35

THE DAY OF THE FOURTH BODY. P.M.

Leaving Mum straight after hearing such life-redefining news is wrong. I have no intention of going. I tell her as much. But she's adamant. Almost like *she* needs me to do it as much as I do. Then I picture the prize waiting for me at the other end of all this. Ben.

Frog-marched all the way to my car outside the Co-op by Mum, she literally unlocks the car door and shoves me into the driving seat. I tell her I love her, promise to visit at the weekend and start the engine.

First stop: home. The eternal optimist, I'd already planned what I'd wear if Ben were released. Yellow bodycon dress with blue orchids – bit tight but I force it on and check the bedroom mirror. Yep, still got it. Game on.

Something else stews as I come to terms with what's already been a bruising epic of a day. Ben and Mum. That's it. That's all that matters. Invest in Ben. Cherish Mum. The profound grief I feel at her diagnosis laser-focuses my priorities. But *that* future comes with one six-foot-five-inch, psychopathic stumbling block.

There's just enough time to see Dick before Ben's release – if the warders permit it. They've scuppered attempts at last-minute trips in the past.

I get out my phone – roughly a gazillion missed calls from Anna.

She must have heard the news about the fourth body. I feel bad but I haven't got the headspace to answer right now.

I call the prison. I'm coming to pick up Ben Farrer, any chance I could squeeze in a chat with Dick Monroe first? Stars are aligning; they agree.

* * *

Sitting in the oh-so-familiar visitors' room, part of me is glad I'll never have to come here again. Lifeless, soulless, hopeless – and that's just the receptionist.

Dick plods in, his usual self, however – giving the space some much-needed zest. Enough energy to power the whole room.

'I know you said to look out this morning, I didn't expect you to come straight here,' he breathes, touchingly understated. 'And that's quite the outfit too.' He doesn't even try to maintain eye contact, taking me all in.

'Don't know what you mean,' I pull off a befuddled tone. My face, of course, doesn't reflect the confusion in my voice.

Dick re-finds my eyes; the deepest, warmest gaze he's ever wrapped me in.

Neither of us speak, neither of us blink. Remember this, Kelli, embrace it, one last time.

Aware he's not going to get a direct answer, he nods and gives one of those huge, toothy grins.

'Turns out they hadn't caught The Nailer after all,' I say, raising my eyebrows.

'I saw,' he replies. We're both playing the game. This sort of telepathic connection is so rare, so valuable. Can I really end this?

A ripple of reality stabs me. Ben and Mum, that's all that matters. I'm not here to flirt, I'm not here to wallow, I'm here to act.

'So, Number Nine,' I state. 'Now or never.'

The change of topic is objectionable, I can see it in his hardening eyes. He has more questions, wants to revel in what's been happening these last few weeks in Allcreek. But I've got a very tight grip on all that;

I've never been more in charge. You want to hear about the woods – tell me about Victim Nine.

I watch the whole conversation play out across his face, the shift in dominance, the realisation he may finally have to give me what I want. He wrings his hands in their shackles, those hands I'm going to miss so very, very much.

'Long pause there,' I say as he continues not to reply.

'You'll stop coming to see me,' he murmurs, the most vulnerable I've ever seen him.

'That's happening either way,' I jump back in. 'Today is the end. Ben's coming out. I've already got enough material to write two books about you. This is it. So prove it, Dick; if I really mean anything to you – tell me. Victim Number Nine.'

He's silent again, agitated in the extreme at being flipped over. His thumbs scrape at each other manically, trying to scratch their way out of the room.

In truth, I don't like the shift in dynamic. It distorts the usual mixture of awe and infamy I have plugged into every other time I've visited Dick.

But it also feels right.

I take in his rugged, lined complexion. Still no answer from the human monolith. I answer for him. 'You're never going to tell me, are you?'

He glances at me. The White Widower. World famous. A true legend of the sport. But here he is, struck dumb by *me*.

I nod. 'I get it.'

'Kel, don't do this,' he pleads. He's quiet, ardent, real.

'You get me in a way no one ever has,' I confide. Mustn't cry, can't let the war paint run before I've seen Ben. I push the emotion back down. 'The things we've shared... I won't forget. But I need to leave this behind.'

'Leave *this* behind?' he repeats.

'This... you, Allcreek, everything.' I explain, drinking in every last atom of him.

Pleased with how composed and clean the message cuts across, I grasp his chained hands a final time, look him so deep in his eyes it could spear his soul, then plant a single kiss on his cheek.

* * *

Desperate to extricate myself, I stalk out of the room and onto the courtyard outside the prison.

Error.

In the last hour word has got round that Ben Farrer is going to be released imminently. Reporters, photographers, TV cameras, all lined up to shout and holler at him as I attempt to smuggle him back to Irby.

Worst of all? Rob Grayson is among the rabble.

No headline shouted at me thankfully; he's shier with the baying crowd of other journalists around.

Annoyingly, however, this is the exit at which Ben will be released at 3 p.m. I try going back through the entrance and asking to wait inside. The same stern receptionist explains that won't be possible, I wander back out to my former colleagues.

'Got an alibi for last night, Kel?' Grayson mutters into my ear from behind, carcinogenic personality worn very much on his sleeve.

'Stop creeping up on girls from behind, Rob, you'll get a reputation.' I say the words loud. A couple of other hacks around us hear and titter at my very funny line.

'You looking forward to having your landlord back?' he asks, bizarrely interested now he knows others are listening.

'What?' I mock with a laugh. 'Never you mind! You looking for fresh content for your little blog or something?'

'What you on about?' he blurts back.

'My love life's got nothing to do with you, OK? Just coz you're not getting any...'

'I do fine, thanks,' he lies. The panicked, blunt pathetic-ness of the defence only underlines how false it is.

'Please,' I start, rolling back my shoulders for our growing audience. 'Asking ChatGPT to talk dirty to you does *not* count as a girlfriend.'

The crowd laughs, Grayson nudges away and I'm left to contemplate whether I've just pulled off the greatest conversational coup in the history of time and space.

A couple of the reporters catch me up on what news the police have put out ahead of Ben's release.

Suspect arrested. Thirty-three-years old. Not named yet.

It's definitely Todd.

Better yet, he is apparently the only person they are pursuing. The last victim's full name is Sharon Atkinson; Ben Farrer is no longer a suspect in the investigation.

'How can they know it's the same murderer and not a copycat?' I ask.

'There's a tell-tale sign apparently, police won't say what though,' a short, petite woman from *The Daily Telegraph* says.

Polly's magical fourth nail has done the trick.

'Any early guesses at...' my next question is cut off as the exit to the prison swings open. And there he is.

I can't help it. I charge at him and envelop him in a monster hug before he's even reached the seven small steps down to ground level. I hear photographers' cameras click click click as I cling to him. But who cares!

Everything since Ben's arrest has been so impossibly hard, so unpredictably harsh and frightening, the feeling of his soft lips resting on my neck as we sway from side to side triggers a wave of utter euphoria.

'22 July – John Dillinger was shot; Prince George was born,' he says gently, pleased with himself for playing our reunion so cool.

Mascara and eyeliner are definitely running now, not ideal in front of so many snappers. It doesn't matter. Ben's smile broadens to match mine and he wipes a small tear of his own away.

'I kept imagining this moment, trying to think of nothing else in case that would help force it into happening,' his eyes move up to take in the crowd behind us. They're shouting all kinds of questions.

'Let's go!' I urge, leading him to the car.

I want to bask in this joyous moment, acting like there's nothing else to care about except getting home and treating him like a king. But

Mum's news slowly encroaches on that dream during the drive home to the point that I don't think I can bury it until tomorrow.

I tell him as the car comes to rest on our driveway. Predictably, his protective instincts kick in and despite having spent so long away from home, he insists on making *me* a late lunch and fixing *me* a beautiful cappuccino from the coffee machine.

'You're too good for me,' I tell him when he greets me with the drink and some fresh kisses. 'I realised that while you were away. You're too good for me. So I'm never letting you speak to any other women ever again. That way, you won't leave.' I pull the dead-pan expression off perfectly but he sees straight through it.

'I don't want to talk to anyone else,' he says. 'Anyway, I've had a few ideas for making sure you never leave *me*. I'm going to chain you to the bed.'

Ben talking dirty catches me off guard, but it's all the more exciting for the surprise – as is the fact that he then chases me up to the bedroom.

* * *

The next few days are blissful. We spend so much more time *together* rather than floating around the house at random, occasionally colliding like we used to do. He's teaching me to cook complicated, delicious things, and we go out for long, pointless walks, just to see how far we can get away from the house before one of us throws in the towel and we meander back home.

We have the kind of stupid chats you don't ever get round to unless you've run out of all normal conversation but retain the urge to keep talking: Worst nightmare you've ever had; sexiest superhero; the word you'd most love to scream in a library.

His time in jail has forced us to look hard at the relationship, and rather than seeing the cracks, we saw a future. He waits on me hand-and-foot and has finally set up security cameras all the way around the house to make me feel safer at night, despite his belief that The Nailer is behind bars.

Mildred next door has a fall in her garden, so Ben takes her to hospital, but that is literally the only time we're apart.

Sleep doesn't come easily, however. Guilt shuddering in my subconscious. I haven't seen Polly since she did it, but she haunts me. Time hasn't helped. Anger grows as the days pass. I'd hoped it might fade now I've got Ben back. But it's the opposite. Honestly, how did I not see it? There were clues, signs, tips that it was her. Like the note on my car – the only person who could have known for sure that it wasn't written by the killer would have been the killer themself. It feels so obvious now, and yet I was so blind. That and a million other details niggle and gnaw at night. I've ordered some more Roxion pills but they're yet to arrive.

And worst of all... why Shaz? Why not Inkly? I told her – it had to be Inkly. It *had* to be. And now another innocent woman has died with me an accomplice. I message her. We need to meet. I need closure. I've left Dick behind, maybe it's time to move on from Polly too. But only once I've got answers.

36

TEN DAYS AFTER SHAZ'S DEATH.

I need to keep level-headed. Any screaming could be heard by neighbours and reported as suspicious behaviour to police. What on earth would I have to scream at Polly about when she's supposedly just been through such an emotional mincing machine? Todd might be in custody, but we aren't out of the woods yet... I imagine Dick sniggering at such a poorly chosen metaphor.

I knock at her flat and am suddenly apprehensive that she's going to tear open the door and attack me. My mistrust over what she is capable of has quickly grown over the days we've been out of contact. It's the longest we have gone without at least texting in months. I wonder if the distance has been harder for her than me. Footsteps approach the door; I clench my fists at my sides in anticipation of something horrible.

But she opens up and shows off her big front teeth in a grin. 'Hey, come in.' She looks the same, she sounds the same. I feel stupid. Of course she's exactly the same. She's been through this several times, and I never noticed anything before, so why would this time be different? If anything, she's oddly animated. It's me that feels the burden, me that's going through it for the first time.

There is one difference: she makes me hand over my phone on arrival and leaves it in her bedroom to ensure I'm not recording her.

Smart move. It's indicative of her attention to detail; nothing left to chance – or trust.

I shuffle into the lounge and circle round without taking a seat.

'You can relax, you know,' she says.

'Sorry.'

I've never liked her flat. She and Todd have a thing for leather: leather sofas, leather lamp shades, leather picture frames. It reminds me too much of Ed Gein.

Gein was a 1950s Wisconsin farmer who lost the plot after his mother died. He'd dig up corpses or kill old women then use their skin for all sorts – chair covers, waste paper baskets, face masks. Police even found bowls made from the women's skulls when they searched his house. He inspired some of the 20th century's most iconic horror flicks: *Psycho*, *The Texas Chainsaw Massacre*, Buffalo Bill in *The Silence of the Lambs*. Quite the legacy.

I force myself onto the brown leather sofa and try not to think about Mr Gein.

'Tea or coffee? Or gin. Remember what happened last time you had some gin?' she smirks.

She wants to play happy families, nestle up together, carry on like nothing's changed. Those days are gone. 'What happened to Inkly?'

'I told you I might not be able to get him,' she says. Zero contrition.

'She did *not* deserve it,' my voice is shaky but hushed. My eyes begin to prickle with the first sign of tears but the dam doesn't break.

She is making no such effort to lower her tone as she gesticulates wildly and acts offended. 'Kel, it's all done. Todd's down, Ben's out. You got what you wanted. D'you think it's easy to just do it? It took ages to even get *her* alone.'

How do you live with yourself? That's what I want to ask. But the answer is that she lives just fine. It makes no difference to her if it's Shaz, Inkly or the king who dies. As long as she gets the outcome she wants, it's mission accomplished.

'Even if *you* don't care, *I* have to live with the fact she's dead. That's why I told you it had to be Inkly. I can't just forget about her. Inkly is evil, he's a paedo, he lied about Dad. Mum had to listen to his lies in court, then read about it for weeks in the news afterwards. He was the *only* one who deserved it.' It's taking all my energy, but I'm still just about managing to keep my tone steady and quiet.

'For all we know, Shaz was a kiddy-fiddling machine too,' Polly laughs. 'You don't wind up drinking in the woods with a load of hobos for no reason.'

'You're fucking vile,' I hiss.

It's in this moment I realise I've been protecting the fuse to the wrong stick of dynamite in this room.

Polly explodes. 'I DID IT FOR YOU! IT'S ALL BEEN FOR YOU! ALL I WANT IS FOR—'

I leap up and slap a palm over her mouth. The force sends us thudding on to the floor with me on top.

'Shut up,' I whisper. 'Your neighbours!'

I remove my hand and she stares up at me, startled. Her pupils dilate and I lose myself in them, gazing at her long enough to notice the gin-warmed breath patting against my lips.

'It was you, wasn't it?' she eventually says. Those wide eyes full of yearning and pain.

'What was me?'

'It was you your dad found being abused, not Dan.'

My mind blanks. Next thing, I'm on my feet with her bony arm around my back. She's saying things but I don't really hear. I'm telling her no one else knows and just keep saying it. 'No one knows. No one knows.'

Then her voice rolls closer and I begin to make sense of the words she's saying... 'It's not your fault.'

* * *

The next hour is a blur as Polly tries to comfort me like we're still friends. I wonder what it means, if it means anything, that another person knows. More immediately, I'm forced to confront the anguish and hatred that's been buried so deep for so many years I'd begun to hope it might be gone for good. Silent, not crying, barely blinking, I realise the dark, cold cave of unresolved hurt I'm now trapped in has only grown since I was last here. The agony of permanent, involuntary separation as raw now as it was all those years ago when we got the call to say Dad had collapsed and died in his cell.

I've always told people Danny was the victim, it's simpler that way. There'd been reporting restrictions on revealing the identity of the child involved during the case, so only the jury knew it was me. I could pretend it was Dan, and no one dared ask him to check. Even in school with the girls, I thought I'd hidden it so well no one would ever find out.

I'm thinking about Dad so intensely it physically aches my brain, trying to summon him back into being through sheer force of will. He doesn't come back.

How does Polly do that? She reads through me in a way no one else can, except maybe Dick. It may have taken her years to work this secret out, but she still did it in the end. It's unnerving in the extreme.

She is also wrong. It *is* my fault.

If I, aged thirteen, hadn't agreed to a lift with a stranger just to spite my brother on the walk home from school, then none of it would have happened. Dan wouldn't have had to run home and describe the predator to my parents, Dad wouldn't have realised he knew the man and raced over to the address, he wouldn't have kicked down the door, found me being pinned to a sofa, screaming and helpless. He wouldn't have killed the man and gone to prison for manslaughter. And he wouldn't have died from the shock and the shame of the court case and being separated from his family.

It is all my fault.

She keeps asking questions as I sit stunned on her horrible sofa. I don't want to talk about it. I've never wanted to talk about it. And Polly now is the very last person I would bare my soul to.

'I want you to tell me what happened to Shaz. We need to get our story straight,' I state eventually, ignoring all her quizzing. 'Todd's not going to confess so there'll obviously be a trial which we could both have to testify at. We need to be on the same page. And that's it.'

'Kel, we need to talk about your dad, I'm here for you,' she says, trying to hold my hand, which I yank away from her.

'I'll never forgive you for what you've done to Ben. What you did for me, to get him out again, is the one thing keeping me civil,' I say.

'You never used to care about him. You used to say he was dead dull.'

'No. *You* used to say that,' I clarify. 'And some innocence is exactly what I need right now.' I pause. 'Not that I have to justify anything to you.'

She glares, hurt by my frostiness, but I give as good as I get – staring straight back into those cold eyes, wondering if they still yearn for me or if they are beginning to nurture feelings far less tender.

'Tell me about Thursday,' I suggest with genuine intrigue, the thrill of such a tantalising conversation not lost on me. I also soften my tone, just temporarily, in case that will coax out a more thorough, juicy retelling of the story.

She lights a Silk Cut without offering me one, sucks in, lets the smoke come rolling out over her chapped lower lip, and begins...

She entered the woods with the intention of isolating Lee Inkly, so she says. But after more than an hour of waiting, none of the men had left their places by the fire – if they needed to piss, they'd just turn around and let the stream trickle back through their legs and into the circle apparently. Sounds delightful. Maurice, she tells me now, had been an anomaly, already so pissed that he'd wandered away from the group to 'find somewhere to sleep'.

Women have more modesty – that's why Donna was caught first.

And so it was this time, Shaz got up to go and find a private place to relieve herself, and that's when she walked past Polly, sitting on a tree stump, crying quietly. In that sinister, detached way of hers, Pol explains that it was vital to make the victim think they'd found *you*, how this lowered their guard. Then the pair had chatted. Polly pretended to swig her gin, then offered the spiked bottle to her new friend. You'd think maybe Shaz would have smelled a rat given she knew about the other bodies; but then Polly seems so completely vulnerable herself, she is her own perfect disguise. Polly gave the sleeping pills a couple of minutes to work, then softly retrieved the chloroform-laced cloth from her bag. You have to be assertive at this point, she states. She was up behind Shaz in a flash, pinning the rag against her mouth as the victim tried and failed to stand up. Within two seconds Shaz was unconscious.

Polly then hauled out the nail gun, rolled Shaz on to her back, administered the four shots, then left. Job's a good'un.

The heavy stench of tobacco in the flat can be distracting. But what she is saying is so formidable it makes it easy to concentrate amidst the smoke.

She goes through the unique circumstances of this final murder too. The cigarette. The separate cigarette butt. Todd's woolly gloves and marigolds. The planting of the gun and gloves in the car boot.

Where did she hide the marigolds? They were disposed of in a public bin several-miles walk away from the flat very early the next morning – copying the trick I'd used to get rid of that bloody rag. She then returned to Newton, by which time the body had been found, and she called the police on Todd.

It's the second time she's talked me through her MO, but there is so much more detail this time, she's so much more generous with her knowledge, egged on by some positive reinforcement.

Police have already interviewed Polly twice since Todd's arrest and appear satisfied with her testimony. If I am called to the witness stand it will more likely be as a secondary observer who can give insight into her and Todd's relationship, and if that is the case I can point to the bruises and the fact Polly came to stay with me because she was scared of him.

I get up to leave, content that we are both shrewd enough not to let this web we've spun collapse in the coming months.

'You don't think anyone will suspect me, do you?' she poses, genuine paranoia in her voice.

I shake my head.

'Just worried about what stupid people online might say with their conspiracy theories, like that idiot blogger giving you a hard time when you were in London.'

I pace into her bedroom to retrieve my phone.

'When can we hang out again?' she asks.

I pocket the mobile and turn to her at the front door. 'I think it's best we don't see each other for a while.'

Her eyes harden but I don't wait for a response. I need some fresh air. I need to think. Something isn't right.

It isn't until I'm alone in my car that it hits me. How does she know about those blog posts that ruined my time in London? I made a point of never telling anyone.

It changes everything.

37

EIGHT WEEKS AFTER SHAZ'S DEATH.

Over the next few weeks I see Mum dozens of times. I pop in for an hour or so three times a week, with a phone call to cover the weekends.

Her decline is gradual but noticeable. Sometimes she doesn't remember I was coming, sometimes she stares off into nothing for minutes at a time, sometimes she talks as if she's got a shift at work the next day, even though Asda have terminated her contract now.

But on the whole she knows what's what, understands the dementia has put a number on the days she has left, and that Dad's waiting for her whenever that number comes up.

Today we catch-up about her latest doctor's appointment, then talk about Dad – a hobby I'm enjoying more and more, acutely aware that I need to extract as many anecdotes and facts as possible before those memories leave with Mum forever.

'How's that poor lady next door to you getting on?' Mum asks, an encouraging reminder that her memory is still quite well intact.

'Mildred? Still in hospital,' I tell her from my usual chair in the kitchen. 'Ben went to see her and said she could talk but was bed-bound. It was a stroke they think now, not just a fall. She'll be moved to a nursing home soon I think. She's been his neighbour his whole life!'

'Dr Armstrong says I'll probably have to go into a home towards the end. Hopefully I'll get my own room.'

'Everyone gets their own room at a care home Mum,' I chuckle.

'Do they? Oh... good. And how's Polly? Must be in shock still after everything that happened.'

'Yeah I think so,' I say. The turn in conversation is my prompt to leave.

There's one last thing to do before I depart, however.

Getting up, I wander into the hall, shouting back over my shoulder that I'll come over some time in the afternoon again tomorrow. As always, Mum's phone is left redundant on the mantelpiece. I call her number from my phone, answer on her handset, then scurry into the lounge and slip the device under the smaller of the two sofas, out of sight. My hands are shaking as I return to the hall, just in time to meet Mum coming out of the kitchen.

'Tomorrow afternoon sounds lovely.' She kisses me on the cheek and smiles. Her eyes are pale; I find it hard to look into them for too long.

She waves me off from the door and I get back into the car, light from the lamppost opposite painting a shadow over my lap as I slip my phone back out of my pocket – the call to Mum's phone is still connected. The relief is immense; my heart's thudding so strongly it's making my neck twitch. I start the engine, flick the main beams on, give Mum a final wave and set off down the dark road towards home.

It took weeks for Lee Inkly to crawl back to Allcreek Woods after the fourth murder. I've been waiting. But he's back now.

38

THE FIFTH BODY.

After Inkly's body is found, it takes police less than 15 minutes to have Polly in handcuffs. At least that's what Vickers says in his press conference. She admits to the first four murders. Then claims it was Todd. Then claims she doesn't know who committed any of them. Then confesses to all five, but refuses to give any details or offer a motive.

She gets mauled in the newspapers for her silence as much as for the actual killings.

Vickers, despite his posturing, gets similar treatment and is buried under gardening leave less than a week later. The press have labelled his mishandling of the case as a historic low for British policing.

Officers come to search our house, given the property's past links to the case, but find nothing.

The murder charges are dropped against Todd but he's still bailed on several counts of actual bodily harm against Polly. Police theorize she was trapped in an abusive relationship and took her latent anger out on the defenceless down-and-outs in her back yard – originally setting up her best friend's partner to keep suspicion away from her door, but then framing her own boyfriend when the urge to kill seized her again after Ben's arrest.

As for the fifth victim, she hadn't even bothered to implicate anyone else this time, suggesting a further deterioration in her state-of-mind and grasp on reality.

The barrister she was designated has already called for Polly to be sectioned, but a callous judge refused and sent her to HMP New Hall – former residence of one Rosemary Pauline West.

The jail is twice as far away as Strangeways and I only make the journey once. The building isn't half as imposing or grand, but once I'm given my obligatory pat down and shown into the meeting room with its white florescent tube lights bleaching the colour out of everything, things become far more familiar. A whiff of detergent prickles the air.

Polly comes in a minute later and the first thing I notice is her hair: shaved short but still thick, it suits her. The warder clips her handcuffs into a horseshoe of stainless steel jutting out of the top of the table then wanders away.

There's no immediate acknowledgement from Polly and I haven't worked on an opening gambit, so for a moment we both stare – her out of the window, me at her. The skin shrink-wrapped to her jawline looks more taut than ever.

'You're going to be in my book Pol,' I say eventually. 'You and Dick. It'll be about covering both cases.' I hadn't planned to start with this, but it's important I say it early. If she finds out from anyone else or suspects I am trying to butter her up before telling her, she could take offence and blurt out something unsatisfactory.

'Just us two?' she says in a weak croak, still yet to make eye contact.

'Just you two.'

She raises her eyebrows and head in a synchronised nod.

'How have you found it being...'

'How did you get Inkly?' Now there's eye contact, narrowed pupils perforating my own like crossbow arrows.

'Same as you, that was the point,' I say.

'No but how did you get *Inkly*?'

I pause and a smile twitches at the sides of my mouth which I have to pin down. 'I shouted his name out to make him come looking for me, then just played the damsel in distress all the same.'

My instinct is right – Polly erupts with a bark of laughter before letting her head loll down in front of her. 'There's me doing everything to stay quiet, when I should have just been a town fucking cryer.' I've missed that controlled swearing. But my reciprocal laughter riles her.

Her face goes blank again. 'And your alibi?'

'Left my phone at home on a call with Mum's until long after I got back from the woods at like 2 a.m. She's such an unreliable witness at this point that even her saying she didn't remember the call wouldn't matter. Police checked the phone records, checked the location of my phone throughout the call and it all tallied. I'm not sure they even bothered asking Mum to corroborate it.' My voice is barely reaching her but she's taking in every word, guzzling it down.

'Solicitor said they haven't found the weapon either.'

I want to tell her everything. I want to impress her. But I need to draw the line. Give away too many details and she'll sound convincing when she changes her story again. Best to stick to things that can't be proven or disproven.

'What weapon?' I tap the side of my nose and shake my head at her.

She stares out of the window again. 'Why are you here?'

'I thought you deserved an explanation.' There's not even a twinge of recognition at my answer. I maintain a whisper, scouring the room for eavesdroppers. 'You should know why I did it.'

'I did everything you asked, apart from Inkly,' she says at a frighteningly blasé volume.

'You were the person writing those blog posts about me when I was in London, weren't you?'

She says nothing.

'I always thought it was Grayson,' I say. 'Bitter about me getting the big break.'

She scratches her arm and looks off into nowhere again.

'But it was you. You never wanted me to go, wanted us to move in together. Was that my punishment? If you can't stop me pursuing a career, you can ruin it from afar.'

'So what? You hated it down there.'

'But it made me see, Pol. The manipulation. Those innocent people you killed like it was nothing. I'd thought it was because you were obsessed with me, because you had this weird infatuation with me. But if you were willing to wreck *my* career even before that, it shows you never thought about me at all. All you have ever done is think about yourself. You couldn't do that to me if you actually cared about me. And if you are *that* self-centred, then I'm not special. So what happens when you get bored with me? What lengths will you go to in getting rid of me once the parasite decides it's time for another host?

'And then I started thinking about how your grandad died – that fall, just before I went to London. Was that the same thing? You trying to force me to come running? And the more I dwell on it, the more I think you didn't find him dead at the bottom of the stairs, you said goodbye to him from the top of them. That's what those blog posts tell me.' Speaking for so long in a punchy whisper leaves me feeling light-headed.

She ignores my accusation. 'Don't be stupid, Kel. If all you wanted was to dob me in then you could have called the police. You wanted to see if you had it in you. You've always wanted to see.'

'I needed to guarantee they'd think it was you. What if I'd told police, and they still decided it was Todd... or Ben... or me?' I scan the room again. 'We did a fucking good job framing Todd. There needed to be another body to make it...'

'Y'know, I've been wondering a lot since I've been in here,' she interrupts, passionless, '...wondering about what makes people do things, and I've got a theory.' She tugs the sleeves of her prison overalls back down to the wrists as best she can in her handcuffs and leans forward on her elbows. 'It's like there's a little black box recording everything you ever say, everything you ever do, everything you ever think. And *all* your experiences stay stored on that black box. And you tell yourself you can change, and that the past doesn't matter. But the old you never goes away, not really. Then you find yourself contemplating the unimaginable, and that's when you realise you should have been more careful about what you committed to that little black box, because all the bad decisions, all the dark thoughts, they're still there, and they're stronger than you are. You're desperate to destroy that black box because of what it's making you do, but it's indestructible, leaving just one other option – and that's to destroy absolutely everything else and everyone else around you.'

'That's your little loophole is it?' I mock. 'That's your clever way of excusing everything you've—'

'I wasn't talking about me, Kel...' She leans in closer and I jolt backwards in my seat, frightened and exposed. 'You can come here and blame me, hoping it'll help you sleep better. But we both know there's a monster inside you too. And what you've done will never, ever, ever go away.'

The words tighten around my neck. Failing to cover the silence with a sneering rebuke, I elect for a different kind of retort, and get up to leave.

'Kel...' Her voice sounds fuller now – much more like real Polly. She pauses, staring up at me, then asks. 'Us on the sofa. Was that real?'

I look into those eyes, eyes I know I'll never see again – and for the very first time they remind me of my own.

'That was real, Pol.'

One last lie; one which will hopefully buy a lifetime of silence.

39

123 DAYS SINCE THE FIRST BODY WAS FOUND.

Halloween feels too frivolous a date to release a TV series centring on some of the most depraved human beings in the history of mankind. But that's the gimmick Netflix has chosen to publicise the forthcoming programmes. And it appears to have worked.

A week in advance, articles start popping up online with titbits from the different episodes.

Shocking twist to Glasgow Hacker murders in new documentary

Holly Little's mother speaks for first time about discovering her daughter's body

The Nailer's BFF reveals friendship with second serial killer

The articles prove popular. The Nailer one receives more than 10,000 shares on MailOnline alone. I can imagine Dick seething that some clickbait being used to hype-up a programme all about him, doesn't even mention his crimes or name in the headline.

I, on the other hand, am inundated with texts from people who didn't bother to get in touch when Ben was taken into custody but deem it appropriate to slither out of the woodwork now.

The whole series drops on the evening of 31 October and Anna talks me into holding a get-together for a 'premiere'.

It's going to be me, Ben, Anna and Mum. Anna's boyfriend Henry cancels at the last minute, 'work emergency' apparently. Let him lie all he likes, I only invited him out of politeness in the first place. None of the actual attendees have any appetite for grisly documentaries, but they want to support me all the same, which is very nice.

I tell Ben specifically that he doesn't have to watch, given the trauma he's been through and that the documentary will most likely touch upon the murders in Allcreek. But he is sure he wants to be there.

He also takes it upon himself to cook all the food for the evening. Given Anna's a vegetarian, he bakes a lentil moussaka with homemade garlic bread, then makes little pots of chocolate mousse for pudding. The smells wafting through the house during the afternoon are irresistible and I lick every last clump off the mixing bowl after the desserts are safely stored, out of reach, in the fridge.

Anna's offered to pick Mum up and drive them both over which is very helpful.

'I am *so* excited!' Anna gushes upon their arrival. 'I've bought Champers!'

'What for?'

'Because you've earned it! You're on Netflix! It's so nice to celebrate. We're all so proud of you.'

Mum follows her in, arms laden with a lemon meringue pie she's made – unrequested – for the occasion.

'Hello Kelli Belly,' she says, putting the pudding down and giving me a long, happy hug which I make sure to savour.

'This all feels far too fancy for fifteen seconds of fame,' I blush.

I pluck four flutes out of the cupboard and pour us all a glass while the ladies crowd around Ben at the cooker, distracted by his menu for the evening.

Anna then insists on a selfie with me and our drinks. She's wearing silver glittery eye shadow like she's attending a Love Island reunion party. She posts the photo on Instagram with the hashtag #NetflixFamous.

We've been getting on better than ever without Polly around pulling me in the opposite direction. Anna just wants to be stable, wants Henry to propose, wants to build a comfortable life. Really, the set-up Ben and I have isn't too dissimilar. I even found myself looking up the pros and cons of different juicers on John Lewis's website the other night, before I caught myself and shamefully deleted the results from my search history.

Ben dishes out the moussaka and we eat in the kitchen. I look around the table, heart filled to the brim at the friends, family and future rolling out ahead of me. There's a peace I've not felt in years, probably ever since Dad was arrested. Just uncomplicated, effortless harmony. I'm only sad it took Mum's diagnosis to bring the two of us closer together again.

Meal polished off, including double helpings of dessert – Ben's chocolate pots and Mum's lemon meringue pie – we retire to the lounge for the 'cinematic experience of the year' as Anna puts it. Mum sits next to me, and I can feel her flinching and tensing with infantile innocence whenever something scary is said or shown on screen.

It's quite surreal to see the case I know so well being given the 'true crime doc' treatment. I've watched bazillions of these kinds of shows, but to be an actual player in one doesn't sink in quickly. They do use a lot of my interview with Annabelle Ludgate, I notice. Much more than Grayson's snippets.

I wonder if Dick will find a way to watch it. Inmates smuggle smart-phones into the prison all the time, he's told me in the past. I can imagine him pulling strings to make sure he's got a phone and Netflix account ready for his big moment.

The hour speeds by, the producers have missed masses out. My book is going to be so much more thorough: the gold standard when it comes to learning about both The White Widower and The Nailer – definitely.

The programme's music starts to build with slow-motion pictures of Dick getting into a prison van, surely this is the end.

But Annabelle Ludgate is still talking; panic tears through me as I realise what is about to happen.

'My question to you is, if I could guarantee you wouldn't get caught, that you could pull off the perfect murder and no one would ever trace it back to you... would you do it?'

The score reaches a crescendo then cuts out. The camera cuts to me in the hotel room, a slight smile on my face. 'I guess rule number one of committing the perfect murder would be convincing everyone you weren't contemplating murder at all.'

The credits roll in silence.

The pressure of knowing three pairs of eyes are all fighting not to look at me becomes crushing. Who am I fooling? I'll never be a normal person, not after what I've done!

Clocking how uncomfortable I am, no one can think of anything to say afterwards. Anna and Mum make their excuses to leave.

Ben, with a wink, then suggests we head up to bed. Phew! At least he can't be too disturbed by my performance.

I decline. I want to stay up. I need to watch it again, see if the ending still feels as embarrassing on a second viewing.

He kisses me goodnight and I get comfy on the sofa, under my blanket. Late night, alone in the lounge, true crime on the TV – it's like the old days.

I do watch the documentary a second time and feel slightly better. It's not just me hinting at how to get away with murder. It's a general warning about how others get away with it. At least there's enough of that essence for me to defend it.

It's 1 a.m. when I contemplate a third viewing. The initial self-consciousness is abating, replaced by pride and excitement. I did a damn good job in front of the cameras!

The home phone blares from the hall. No one ever calls the home phone. It makes me jump, but in the same second I'm on my feet and speeding into the hall, even forgetting to switch the light on as I go, such is my haste to stop the shrill echoing up through the house and waking Ben up.

'Hello?' I say into the darkness.

'Nice work, Kel.'

My mind shatters, my heart jolts in fear. I know that voice. I know it so, so well.

'How did you get my number?'

'Ben Farrer's records are still on the system at Strangeways. Amazing what a warder can find if you ask nicely. I saw the documentary,' Dick says.

I don't speak. I don't want to stutter and sound afraid. We're going to have to change our number. That's my first thought. Maybe I should just put the phone back down. I wish I'd turned the light on, this is the very worst spot in the house to stand in the dark.

'You looked great, you sounded great. Made me miss you,' he says, tender and coveting.

'Dick, I'm sorry. I meant it when I said we can't see each other any more.'

'I was just wondering...' he pauses, knowing I'm still there, '...maybe it's time I tell you about Number Nine.'

40

NUMBER NINE.

I haven't told Ben I'm visiting Dick. He was so relieved when I explained I'd broken off ties with The White Widower, I think he'd fear I was slipping back into bad habits. That is not what this is. Dick has one chance to tell me about Victim Number Nine. If he doesn't do it today, I'll never fall for the ploy again.

Ben may also worry that there's something about Dick that I'm still attracted to. Also not so. I am actually full of nerves at having to face Dick again. I'm here for answers, but the rendezvous serves no social, sentimental or sexual purpose – for me at least.

If I do get a name and location for Number Nine, it'll be a huge selling point for my book. That's the only reason I am here. But whether he's wasting my time or not, this truly will be the final time I see Dick Monroe.

The jail's changed subtly in my three-month absence. Well, the corridor outside the visitor room has, anyway. There's a futuristic new vending machine with a huge touchscreen on the front that you press to see the options on offer. There's also a second-hand, emaciated sofa outside the room that looks about as comfortable as gout.

Thankfully I'm on time so no waiting around. Body checks done, ID checked, I take a deep breath and turn the corner into the room.

And there he is. Another change, he's not chained to the table. He rises properly to welcome me. It's only the second time I have stood in his presence at his full height – the other time was straight after he'd killed Janice Benson. It's easy to forget just what a mighty specimen he is.

'Kel,' he beams, arms outstretched as he embraces me. His blue overalls smell fragrant with a faint musk of tobacco smoke. 'I knew you'd come,' he says, still grinning as he takes his seat again.

There are definitely more guards in the room than usual, almost as many warders as visitors. Maybe that's the pay off – Dick can be unshackled, but there are more hands on deck if he were to decide to try anything silly.

'Good to see you,' I say without any conviction.

'How you been?' he asks with enough gusto for both of us.

'Fine.' The response has become second nature and I inject it with enough confidence to sound believable.

His eyes stay on me, intrigue sticking to his face like dried plaster. 'Lee Inkly, hey? Wasn't expecting that.'

I give him some real eye contact. 'Yeah, but they've got the killer now – a woman.'

'So it was your mate, was it?' He says. '*Polly?*'

'She's no friend.'

He raises his eyebrows in a playful pause. 'Let's not be judgey Kel.'

He wants me to smirk back, have one of our silent conversations, all eyes and body language.

'Victim Number Nine,' I say, shooting him an impatient eyebrow raise of my own.

'That's why you're here,' he admits, slouching back in his chair in a way he never could before when he was cuffed down. He moves his hands behind his head and holds my gaze for a long time.

'Do you want me to be honest?'

'Yes,' I say flatly.

'Then I ask the same of you.'

'I'm always honest,' I state.

Still slouching back in his seat, he gives his watermelon of a head a little shake. 'No Kel, because I asked you how you are, and you said you were fine. I'm looking at you now. You're not fine.'

'I literally have no idea what you mean.'

His expression morphs and it sends a shiver down my spine – it isn't the vacant stare of someone not taking in what you are saying, it's the tortured look of someone who knows you're lying to them.

I keep talking, hoping I'm mistaken. 'I've been busy. They want me to turn the final chapters of your book in by January 1 so they can proof it and send it out for some cover quotes. Oh, I don't think I told you, I've got a publisher. Book will be about you and Polly.' Still he's unmoved. 'They think it'll sell very well, especially locally.'

He pulls his seat right in, leans forward and squeezes my hands. 'What is it, Kelli?'

'What's what?'

Much to my own dread, I can feel a hot flush sweeping under my eyes and tears forming without permission.

'Kelli, whatever it is. You might not have anyone else you can talk to, but that's why we have each other. You can tell me anything.'

'You need to tell me about your ninth victim,' I insist, but the high-pitched warble and the way I snatch my hands back off him say so much more than the words. How do I placate him without telling him? How do I answer without answering? I'm breathing heavy now as a thick, clammy sweat spreads across my neck.

'Kelli, I can see it. Something's wrong.'

I shake my head.

'You wanted me to know something, that's why you told me to look out for the news that Friday morning. Part of you wants to tell me. Let me help. I will not leave today without giving a full explanation about Victim Number Nine, I *promise*. But I hate seeing you so... not yourself.'

I've dreamt about it, about telling *someone*, explaining it all so they can really listen and really understand; I've fantasised about the relief it could bring and the burden it could lift. But now as I look up at the one person who knows me well enough to ask, I feel too ashamed to mutter a single word.

'No one knows you the way I do, Kel, and you are not being honest, I can tell you...'

'You want to know what happened?' I hiss, eyes wide and locked on him now as I too lean in to make sure no one else overhears. 'It *was* Polly. She was The Nailer. But she'd framed Ben, and then Todd. And for what? For me! She told me every last detail of how she did it, so what was I to do? Wait for her to kill me too? Wait for her to get jealous of Ben and kill him? I did what I had to do. I killed that paedophile because he fucking deserved it.'

Dick opens his mouth but I don't let him speak. '*Polly's* the virus. I got rid of the virus. Me! That's what I did. And if keeping that to myself is the price I have to pay for making sure the serial killer went to prison and the right people went free, then I'd do it again.'

'How did you have an alibi?' he asks, fascinated.

The procedural question allows me to regain some composure. 'Set a call going to Mum's phone and left my one at home while I went to the woods. She's got dementia so Vickers just took my word after they'd checked phone and GPS records.'

He wants to know everything. How I haven't been caught, how I pulled it off.

I tell him I bought the chloroform from the same dodgy site in America that I get my Roxion pills from. I tell him I spent three weeks scouting out a hardware shop that was far enough away, with lax enough security, to purloin a nail gun without paying so there's no evidence I own one. I tell him how I had to pretend to Ben that I was on the phone to Mum that night until he went up to bed. I tell him how I then clambered across on to Mildred's first floor balcony and left through her back garden rather than our own to avoid Ben's new surveillance equipment. And I tell him that the murder weapon, the clothes I wore, the chloroform and the spiked bottle of gin are all hidden next door in Mildred's empty house while she's still in hospital and we have her spare key.

It's satisfying to brag about how well I've outsmarted everyone. Dick is contemplative, taking it all in, making suitably impressed expressions as I explain how well plotted my plan was.

'Just because I'd do it again doesn't mean I'm OK though,' I gulp, letting go of his hand to wipe the tears off my cheeks. 'Getting found out terrifies me constantly. The idea of Ben knowing, I can't get past it. It's like there's a tornado and I have to stand perfectly still at the very middle or everything will be destroyed. But it's closing in tighter and tighter and I can't breathe. Every time I hear a police car, every time someone mentions the woods, every time my phone rings – it's crushing me to death.

'And Janice comes at night, louder than ever. I should have stopped you.' There's a steady stream of silent tears running down my cheeks as I concentrate on not letting the emotion break out into sobs that could garner unwanted attention from the rest of the room. '...watching you do it. I just froze. Maybe I even wanted to watch. The fact I'm not sure in myself if I was scared or fascinated is something I think about every day.'

I'm panting as I finish, but there is no response.

'Say something!' I command under my breath, our noses four inches apart. He doesn't speak but shuffles back a bit to crack his knuckles as he looks down at the table.

I go on, desperate for anything but silence. 'Polly said something when I saw her. She said nothing we do ever really leaves us. Maybe it was watching Dad drown that man and watching Janice die that turned me into what I am now. But I am determined to change. And I will.'

He's still looking away. Was that more than he bargained for, a bit too emotional, a bit too deep?

I move back to a more comfortable position and puff out my cheeks, wiping my fingers under my eyes to brush away the tears.

'So,' I say at a more normal volume, 'Was that honest enough?' I let out a half-laugh, desperate for a moment's levity.

'Oh, Kelli,' Dick says in commiseration. 'That really was honest enough. Thank you.'

I offer a small but genuine smile in return. 'Here we go,' I declare, picking up my pen and waving it for a second. 'Number Nine, then. That's all that's left.'

'The thing is, I am going to go into all of that today. Just not with you.'

I look up to check he's joking but his eyes have changed, that grim darkness has descended, the one that falls whenever he's talking about his victims.

He lifts his arms up and begins to undo the top button of his overalls.

'Your old pal Rob Grayson's been trying to come and see me for a long time, but I never gave him the time of day.'

First button undone, he begins to undo the second one, those thick dextrous fingers don't fumble.

'But then you decided to leave me behind and tried to flaunt the fact you were getting away with murder.'

Second button undone, on to the third.

'So I got back in touch with Grayson, and we made a little deal.'

Third undone, on to the fourth, hair sprouting out as the two sides of the top begin to fall open.

'I wanted to record you admitting what you did. I told him that if he could help me with that, I'd tell *him* what happened to Victim Number Nine.'

Fourth button undone, he pulls back the open shirt to reveal a skinny, white wire taped to his chest.

Grayson is recording this. He's played me. He knows everything.

The eye of the storm swallows me. I can feel my heart being torn to shreds as humiliation and panic explode from the inside out. I will myself to die.

Dick lets go of his shirt, lunges forward and snatches my hands so tightly between both of his that the pain breaks through my shock. His look is icy cold and terrifying now. 'You don't get to leave me behind Kelli.'

ACKNOWLEDGEMENTS

First, I would like to thank God, who is with me everywhere I go. Next, Hannah, for accepting me as I am, loving me and effortlessly being the most beautiful person I've ever met. I can't wait to read literally anything except this book to our baby girl at bedtime. Dad, your excitement, advice and belief in my writing hits deeper than I'll ever be able to convey. I'm so lucky to have you and Paula as champions. Mum, thank you for embracing my writing despite it temporarily leaving you fearing for my state of mind. Your devotion, love and support are fundamental to me as a person.

Next come the heroes who read my unpublished manuscripts for years, toiling on my behalf when there was nothing in it for them. That level of loyalty deserves naming and shaming. So Phil, Mike, Nick, Jo, Spizz, Carrie, Alex, Charlotte and Nibbles... thank you so so much. Such labour's of love are very powerful.

There were also friends and family who went out of their way to encourage me and give me heartfelt support, especially Baskers, Josh, Fothers, Tom T and Nat. I love you all!

To my agent, Euan Thorneycroft, thank you for taking the chance, investing in me and for your uncanny ability to improve my work in subtle but profound ways.

I am so grateful to Francesca Best and Boldwood for taking me on. I've been made to feel so welcome and at home by the whole publishing team from the day I joined.

Liverpool FC – thank you for winning the title in lockdown; blink-182 – thank you for counselling me through my teens, twenties and now thirties; Peep Show – thank you for revealing my own sense of humour to me; my fellow PoW imbibers – thank you for all the beer.

Last but the opposite of least, thank you to YOU if you have read this book. The idea that any sane-thinking person would pick up something I have written is hard to get my head around. Your backing is very special and humbling.

Time to make another coffee, then let's crack on with the next one...

ABOUT THE AUTHOR

Tam Barnett is a journalist, living in London. His debut with Boldwood was How To Get Away With Murder, a darkly comic thriller set in the Wirral.

Sign up to Tam Barnett's mailing list for news, competitions and updates on future books.

Follow Tam on social media here:

f facebook.com/TamBarnettBooks

X x.com/TamBarnettBooks

📷 instagram.com/tambarnettbooks

♪ tiktok.com/@TamBarnettBooks

THE
Murder
LIST

THE MURDER LIST IS A NEWSLETTER DEDICATED TO SPINE-CHILLING FICTION AND GRIPPING PAGE-TURNERS!

SIGN UP TO MAKE SURE YOU'RE ON OUR HIT LIST FOR EXCLUSIVE DEALS, AUTHOR CONTENT, AND COMPETITIONS.

SIGN UP TO OUR NEWSLETTER

BIT.LY/THEMURDERLISTNEWS

Boldwood

Boldwood Books is an award-winning fiction publishing company seeking out the best stories from around the world.

Find out more at www.boldwoodbooks.com

Join our reader community for brilliant books, competitions and offers!

Follow us
@BoldwoodBooks
@TheBoldBookClub

Sign up to our weekly
deals newsletter

https://bit.ly/BoldwoodBNewsletter

www.ingramcontent.com/pod-product-compliance
Ingram Content Group UK Ltd.
Pitfield, Milton Keynes, MK11 3LW, UK
UKHW020155300125
4318UKWH00002BA/41